THE HIDDEN HAND

BY THE SAME AUTHOR

The Liz Carlyle series

At Risk
Secret Asset
Illegal Action
Dead Line
Present Danger
Rip Tide
The Geneva Trap
Close Call
Breaking Cover
The Moscow Sleepers

The Manon Tyler series

The Devil's Bargain

Non-fiction

Open Secret: The Autobiography of the Former Director-General of MI5

Stella RIMINGTON
THE HIDDEN HAND

BLOOMSBURY PUBLISHING
LONDON · OXFORD · NEW YORK · NEW DELHI · SYDNEY

BLOOMSBURY PUBLISHING
Bloomsbury Publishing Plc
50 Bedford Square, London, WC1B 3DP, UK
29 Earlsfort Terrace, Dublin 2, Ireland

BLOOMSBURY, BLOOMSBURY PUBLISHING and the Diana logo are
trademarks of Bloomsbury Publishing Plc

First published in Great Britain 2025

Copyright © Stella Rimington, 2025

Stella Rimington is identified as the author of this work in accordance with
the Copyright, Designs and Patents Act 1988

This is a work of fiction. Names and characters are the product of the author's
imagination and any resemblance to actual persons, living or dead, is entirely coincidental

All rights reserved. No part of this publication may be reproduced or transmitted
in any form or by any means, electronic or mechanical, including photocopying,
recording, or any information storage or retrieval system, without prior
permission in writing from the publishers

A catalogue record for this book is available from the British Library

ISBN: HB: 978-1-5266-5273-7; TPB: 978-1-5266-5272-0;
EBOOK: 978-1-5266-5274-4; EPDF: 978-1-5266-5276-8

2 4 6 8 10 9 7 5 3 1

Typeset by Integra Software Services Pvt. Ltd.
Printed and bound in Australia by Griffin Press

To find out more about our authors and books visit www.bloomsbury.com
and sign up for our newsletters

To John, without whose help when my eyesight worsened, this book might never have been finished

I

At three in the afternoon the Boston Public Garden was not crowded, and the bench nearest the Charles Street entrance was unoccupied. It was a good time to meet, Li Min thought as she sat down, holding a copy of the *Boston Globe*. It was after the lunch hour, when the benches would have been filled with office workers eating their sandwiches, yet too early for the parents and children coming to feed the ducks straight after school.

Lost in her thoughts, she only noticed the man when he was seated beside her on the bench. He liked to arrive stealthily, as if from nowhere, but she knew he would have made the journey north from the Embassy in Washington D.C. to see her – and possibly others like her? Li Min wondered.

As always, he was dressed very formally, in black suit, white shirt and shiny city shoes. His face was expressionless as he turned to acknowledge her with a curt nod. She knew nothing about this man save that he represented her government and that he must be obeyed. Even his full name was a mystery to her; she knew him by one syllable only: *Deng*.

'I have brought my report,' she said to pre-empt his habit of asking for it as an opener. She picked up the newspaper beside her on the bench, feeling the folder inside as she did so. But for once Deng did not reach eagerly for the paper. He took it almost casually, saying, 'Thank you. I will examine it later. But now I have something else to discuss with you. A change in your situation.'

Li Min tried to hide her shock. She was a doctoral student in computer science at Harvard, specialising in Artificial Intelligence, and she could not think of a better place than this to do her work. After university in Beijing, she had spent two years doing a Master's at Cal Tech, where she had improved her English and her technical know-how. Here at Harvard she had begun to specialise, discovering an aptitude for developing video and audio simulations of individuals which were entirely AI-created but seemed so real that they would fool all but the most expert. They were known as deepfakes.

It was at Harvard that these meetings had begun. With the funding for her studies supplied by her government, Li Min had always known there would be a price to be paid. Until now her contact with officialdom had consisted of regular meetings with Deng at which he asked for reports on her work. But today seemed different.

'You have been granted a great honour. Oxford University has established, with the approval and cooperation of our government, an Institute of International and Cultural Affairs.' He said this mouthful as though he had learned the title by heart. He probably had, thought Li Min cynically.

Deng went on: 'The Institute is part of one of the ancient colleges, St Felix's. It has its own Director and trustees, but ultimately it answers to the Governing Body of the college. These teachers, known as Fellows, hire the Director – and can fire him.'

He spoke with an authority derived from twenty minutes spent reading St Felix's website and its entry in Wikipedia. But Li Min was not to know that.

He continued: 'You will find in the Institute a large group of postgraduate students and some senior visitors. The students work in many different fields and come from all over the world, though naturally since much of the funding is Chinese, so are many of the visiting students. The intention is for these groups to mingle and get to know each other.'

'How interesting,' Li Min said, without meaning it.

'I am glad you think so because you have been selected to join the Institute. You will continue your work on Artificial Intelligence – I am told by my superiors in Beijing that it is most promising – but you will do it as a student at Oxford, not Harvard, and your new address will be St Felix's College. My understanding is that the two universities are equally prestigious.'

Li Min resisted the desire to argue; on the one occasion she had tried, and that had been over something minor (her attendance at a particular lecture which Deng had requested), he had slapped her down brutally, even threatening to discontinue the Chinese government's underwriting of her course. It seemed wiser now to find out more about what she was being asked to do. *Asked*? Told more like it. So she said mildly, 'When am I meant to start at Oxford?' Surely they would have to give her another semester at Harvard to complete her dissertation.

'The new term begins in three weeks. After their Easter holiday.'

'What?' She could not help herself.

Deng ignored her protest. 'Mrs Lu, my assistant, will help you pack up your belongings. Do not worry. If anything gets left behind, we will send it on to you.'

'But three weeks is not enough time for me to do everything I need – to see my advisers and explain to the university that I am leaving.'

'Who said anything about three weeks? Your flight to London leaves Sunday evening, and you will be on it.'

2

'My goodness,' said Louise Donovan, 'I don't know what you've been doing since I last saw you, and I'm sure you are not going to tell me. But whatever it is, it suits you.'

'I might say the same about you,' replied Manon Tyler, smiling. 'You look years younger.'

They had first met when Manon had visited England on a university exchange course and had been hosted by Louise. That had been seven years ago, but since then they had kept in touch, and seen each other occasionally. Manon had gone on to do graduate work in politics, but soon found the academic life was not for her – too devoid of action, too dry and abstract. She had applied to and been accepted by the CIA, and had worked at its Headquarters in Langley, Virginia for three years before being sent to London. They'd had plenty of time to further their friendship then since Louise was already living there, working for a political party. She had become involved with a man who had turned out to be a Russian spy. Following the trauma of that case, Louise had come to Harvard to study for a degree at the Kennedy School of Government.

Having accidentally been caught up in that investigation, Manon had discovered she had a taste for fieldwork and action; her superiors had seen this, too, and also noted her ability to keep a cool head in difficult situations. Manon had accordingly been sent on the CIA training course for field officers. She now had a period of leave before her first posting and had come to Boston to visit Louise before going on to spend a few days at her parents' holiday cottage in New Hampshire. They were sitting in the living room of Louise's flat, a pleasant two-bedroom apartment on a leafy street about a mile from Harvard Square.

They chatted on, catching up with each other's news. Louise was enjoying her course, though it was both intensive and hard work, and she said she had little time for social life.

'What about you?' she asked Manon. 'Is there a man in your life?'

'No. There was a super-cute guy in my training programme but it didn't happen. He screwed up an exercise and got chucked out. I lost touch with him. And you?'

'No luck. Everyone around here's so young they see me more as a mother hen than as a girlfriend. There is someone I wanted to mention to you, though. It's a young woman called Li Min. She's a Chinese graduate student. I met her at a party last week – and this is where the mother hen bit comes in. I don't know exactly what she does, but I know it's to do with AI and these deepfakes everyone is talking about. I tried to read about them but had to give up; it all got way too technical for me. But anyway, Li Min talked cheerfully about her life here and how much she loved Harvard, and then suddenly she became very upset, almost in tears.'

'Why?'

'That's what I wondered. She told me that she's leaving Harvard even though she's only halfway through her degree. Transferring to Oxford, she said.'

'Why is she doing that? I know Oxford is wonderful but so is Harvard.'

'She knows that, but it's not her choice. Her government is making her move. They pay her fees, so she has to do what she's told. It's a pity because somebody told me that she is doing very well here. They say she's super-bright.'

Manon said, 'Does she know why they want her to move?'

'I tried asking, but she was quite cagey about it. I think they're moving her on because of her research; from what she did say, Oxford is in the vanguard of her particular field. I also had the distinct impression that she's being sent to find out about the research already being done there. She called it a "fact-finding expedition" – but I think she was being sarcastic.'

'I bet she was.' Manon thought it sounded more like a polite way of saying 'to steal secrets for Beijing'.

Louise laughed. 'That's more your line than mine, so I thought maybe you'd be interested in meeting her. She calmed down with me eventually, but a mutual friend says she's still terribly troubled. Would you mind if I invited her round, perhaps for breakfast tomorrow?'

'OK,' said Manon slowly, wondering what Louise might have said to the girl about her house-guest's job. No, she decided, Louise had more sense than to make that kind of mistake.

'Shall I ask her for ten-thirty?'

'Yes,' said Manon. 'That's fine.' She found she was looking forward to finding out more about this whole business.

Louise had gone out and bought croissants and the Sunday papers, and Manon had read more than her fill of the gargantuan Sunday *New York Times* when the buzzer rang in the apartment.

'That'll be Li Min,' Louise said. 'I'll sit with you for a minute and then go to my bedroom so you can talk in private.'

But when she came back a moment later, she was still alone. She held an envelope in her hand and looked puzzled.

'What's the matter?' asked Manon.

'That was a friend of Li Min's. She said Li Min had asked her to drop off a note for me.' She opened the envelope.

'Maybe she's ill.'

'I don't think so,' said Louise as she scanned the note, and then read aloud: '"*Dear Louise, It was a great pleasure to talk to you. I am sorry not to be able to join you and your friend this morning, but circumstances make that impossible for me. My apologies. With very good wishes, Li Min.*"'

'I guess she got cold feet,' said Manon. 'You know, was worried the Chinese authorities would find out she was complaining.'

'I see she's included her address in Oxford. It's St Felix's College. It's almost as if she's asking us to get in touch, but I won't be going to England anytime soon.'

'I don't suppose I will either,' added Manon, but more wistfully.

3

'YOU'RE LOOKING WELL,' SAID Ben Fleishman. He was wearing one of his collection of sweaters, each featuring a different animal (today's had two squirrels chasing a walnut), and his jacket was hanging from the back of his chair. He was a roly-poly bear of a man, with a ready smile. Behind his thick-lensed glasses, he had warm and friendly eyes that missed nothing.

'Have a seat,' he said, pointing to a chair opposite his desk.

As she sat down Manon took in the smart new quarters of her former boss. He had moved to the central office building of the Langley, Virginia headquarters of the CIA. He had been promoted since she'd seen him last, almost nine months before, and now occupied a large corner room high up in the main building, with a view of the inner courtyard.

Ben had encouraged Manon to switch to the agency's operational side, and she suspected his recommendation had been at least partly responsible for her acceptance into the training programme. She had promised to come see him when she finished the course, for if she had anything approaching a mentor in the agency, it was Ben.

'This is quite the palace,' she said half-admiringly, half-teasing. Fleishman gave a self-deprecating smile. He'd always been appealingly modest, letting his juniors take credit even when behind the scenes he had saved the day. He was known within the agency for his affable astuteness and his refusal to play politics.

'I had to move,' he said, scratching the bald dome of his head, 'because my new duties include fielding courtesy calls from visiting firemen. So the powers that be decided I had to have enough room to host several people at a time in reasonable comfort.' He shrugged. 'At least it frees up the conference room for everybody else,' he added. 'But anyway, here you are. It's been a while, Manon. You look great. Not everyone survives the course, and most look absolutely drained when it's finished.'

'It was quite challenging,' Manon admitted.

It had lasted six months – the minimum time allotted to training recruits for the Operational side of the CIA. The range of topics and activities had been extensive: everything from defensive driving to using the latest cyberspace encryption techniques. There had been plenty of written exercises and nightly homework; physical fitness had also been part of the regimen. Each day several hours were spent outside. Manon had always considered herself athletic – a keen skier and a good swimmer – but the past six months had set a higher bar than she was used to.

'At least you had the advantage of some real experience. I gather your time in the UK got quite exciting towards the end.'

'Yes,' she said. It was true she had had a little operational experience under her belt before the course. Unlike the other candidates she wasn't new to the CIA; in a few months she would mark her fourth anniversary in the agency.

'What was your favourite part of the programme?' asked Fleishman.

Manon didn't hesitate. 'The Farm,' she said simply.

Fleishman looked surprised. 'Really? Why was that?'

She thought for a moment. 'The Farm' was the nickname for the training facility set in a Virginia military base, 150 miles south-east of Langley. It was used by the CIA almost exclusively to train new members of its Clandestine Service Division. The site combined some of the normal buildings of an army base (though there were more meeting rooms than one might expect of a military setting), a 'town square', a mock-Main Street (storefronts and all) and a replica of a city block where they practised everything from freeing hostages to hiding themselves from pursuers.

Manon said, 'What I liked best of all was the work we did on asset handling. You know – gaining assets' confidence, getting the best out of them while reassuring them. That sort of thing.'

Fleishman nodded at her reply. 'I'm not surprised. That's because you're a people person, Manon. That showed in how you handled your asset over in the UK. That was good work; for a beginner, it was remarkable. People like you when they meet you, and most of the time you seem to like them. That's not something that can be taught. Most operatives are loners, which helps when you're working on your own out in the field. But to recruit a source you need empathy, and the sensitivity to know when to push and when not to. Loners aren't very good at that. You are.'

Manon shuffled her feet slightly; she was never comfortable with outright praise. It was true, however, that the whole business in the UK had given her an injection of confidence that had carried over into her induction into the CIA's operational side. In particular, she now trusted her instincts – even if this sometimes meant bending the rules.

To change the subject, she said, 'By the way, Ben, there's something I'd like to mention. It's someone I heard about at Harvard two weeks ago. A young Chinese woman who is a student there. Was a student, I should say.'

'Tell me about her,' said Fleishman, interest piqued.

Manon tried to keep her account of what Louise had learned about Li Min brief and to the point. 'I don't even have the name of the Chinese Embassy official who seems to have kept tabs on her, but the point is that he demanded that she leave Harvard and move to Oxford, with no notice at all.'

Fleishman said, 'I have a pretty good idea who that is, or else it's one of his minions. Whoever it is, they're probably from China's Ministry of State Security. It used to be their main intelligence agency, was part of the Chinese military, but the MSS has grown tremendously and is especially active overseas.' He turned his head and looked out of the window, thinking hard. 'This isn't the first report of this kind we've had. In fact, there's been a spate of them. Chinese students usually, though sometimes they are hi-tech employees. They get moved around by their government, often out of the blue, and sometimes they are not happy about it. Enough to complain to friends, and one way or another it gets back to us.'

'I see. Just like Li Min. So what do you think is going on?'

'If I had to guess, I'd say it was part of a campaign. Not espionage exactly – more like theft. These students are stealing intellectual property and shipping it home. They transfer from one institution to another if it's thought there are better pickings elsewhere, or if they have picked somewhere clean.'

'Well, she was careful about what she told my friend Louise. But I'm pretty sure she's unhappy about her situation.'

'Hmm. Would it be difficult for you to see Li Min? Maybe find out a bit more – like the name of this man at the Embassy? Could your friend Louise help you to do that?'

'Normally I'd say yes, but Li Min's already left for Oxford. She's now attached to one of the colleges there – St Felix's.'

Fleishman nodded and sat thinking for a moment. Then he said, 'In that case, I might give Dave Saunders a call over in London.'

Manon stood up. 'I must run. I'm viewing an apartment in Georgetown. Have you heard that my next assignment is here in Langley?'

He saw her disappointment. 'Cheer up,' he said. 'I know you might have preferred a foreign posting, but remember, Manon, this where the real decisions are taken. This is the heart of the business.'

He paused for a moment, thinking, and then added slowly, 'But things can always change. Don't sign anything on this apartment you are seeing, just for the moment.'

'I won't. It's just a first viewing.' Why was Ben telling her to go slow with this? Did he have something in mind for her, something elsewhere? Don't get your hopes up, Manon thought, but she couldn't stop them from rising.

4

Charles Abbot was a Londoner born and bred though he had spent much of his working life in various embassies abroad. His father had been a GP with a practice in a working-class part of the East End. Charles had met his wife Gillian at Cambridge where they were both studying modern history. They had married young, but to their sadness had no children. When he had joined the Foreign Office, she had accompanied him on all his postings abroad, enjoying the life of a diplomat's wife. He had been expecting that the apex of his career would be a minor ambassadorship. So when a friend had drawn his attention to the advertisement for the Oxford post, he had hesitated, but Gillian had persuaded him to apply. Perhaps his diffidence had helped him with what mattered most – the interview before a board of academics who seemed keen to recruit someone from the outside world. She had been pleased when he had been offered the post at St Felix's College and the Directorship of the Institute, and they had shared their delight in the charming grace-and-favour house on St Giles' that came with the job. Her sudden death had been an appalling shock.

Now alone, Abbot realised he had mixed feelings about Oxford, finding the place more urban, busier than Cambridge. Oxford was more bustling, yet also more Gothic, even gloomy.

A few months after Gillian's death he had moved from the pretty house in St Giles', finding that without the warmth of her presence the place seemed cold and unwelcoming. He had found a flat further from the centre in a quiet part of the town, which seemed to suit him better.

He liked his new position as Director of the Institute of International and Cultural Affairs, discovering after years of frankly middling status in the Foreign Office that he was now enjoying being in charge. However he found the formalities of High Table dining irritating, and preferred to eat at home except when someone he found interesting was being entertained or when he needed to impress potential donors to the Institute. During his years posted abroad he'd attended enough formal dinners to satisfy anyone for a lifetime. On occasion he invited former colleagues, ambassadors or experts in various countries, to give talks at the Institute, but though it was technically part of the college and Abbot had become one of its Fellows on taking up his position, he did not regularly meet the others except when he dined in or attended meetings of the Fellowship – St Felix's Governing Body. The Fellow he saw most of was his predecessor, Professor Cole, whom Abbot found cold, superior and unfriendly.

Still grieving deeply for his wife, he found work was the best antidote, and most days his routine was unvaried – he walked from his flat through the Parks and then, just off the Broad, straight into the world of the Institute. Then one evening, as he was collecting mail from his pigeonhole, he noticed an envelope marked PRIVATE, addressed simply to 'The Director'. He took the mail back to his room, and sitting down with a glass of wine, opened the letter first.

'*Dear Professor Doctor Abbot,*' it began, which puzzled him, for he was neither. It must be a mistake, he thought, and read on.

> *I write to alert you to a pattern of sabotage and theft which is being perpetrated within the Institute of your beloved university. I myself have been watched and surveilled by a fellow student, Mr Chew, who for no reason I discovered in my private room at the Elm examining my belongings. I discover too that Mr Chew has been in the laboratory in Parks Road where I have been researching.*
>
> *I am not the only victim of such intrusion, and besides, there are many all too willing to help him gather information, which is then sent back to the government of the People's Republic of China. It is the price exacted by the authorities for paying our study fees and living expenses. Do not blame the others, but also do be aware.*
>
> *I have been conscious of this activity for some time and have gathered further evidence than my own experiences. You will understand my earlier hesitation to approach you, but I am willing now to disclose the evidence I have collected – though only in confidence and in private. I will be in my room (#37) all afternoon tomorrow at the Elm and trust you will be able to join me there.*
>
> *Yours in confidence*
> *Jia Hao*

Who the hell was Jia Hao? Abbot called up the database of resident students and scholars. There he was: Jia Hao. A native of Hong Kong, interestingly enough, which meant that young as he was (twenty-six according to the file), he would have spent his youthful, possibly formative years in a then-democratic enclave, which for a time had retained many of its former allegiances and traditions. And more interesting still, he was an orphan, raised by Catholic nuns in a children's home funded by the Catholic Church. Which explained why the English in his note was so formal. Yet he must have been trusted by the Communists to be allowed here as a government-funded research student.

Abbot saw from the file notes that Jia Hao was a historian of science, and in fact had been doing a PhD at Princeton before coming to Oxford to complete it. This struck Abbot as a strange move, since in the field of History of Science, Oxford was no further advanced than Princeton. But the subject was certainly broad enough to have given him an excuse to spend time in the labs where actual research, much of it highly advanced, was being conducted.

The question was whether this was a case of an aggrieved person spouting paranoid accusations, or someone genuinely frightened, threatened, yet willing to spill the beans on what sounded like a foreign government's espionage. Abbot wondered for a moment whether there was anyone or anybody from whom he could seek advice. Professor Cole was the obvious candidate, though Abbot had learned not to expect much help from that quarter. The man resented his arrival; there was an unconcealed frostiness in his manner and he had made none of the offers of help usually proffered to a successor.

5

Professor Arthur Cole sat in his room at St Felix's lovingly stroking a Ming vase. It was part of a collection of Chinese ceramics he had built up over the many years he had lived in Hong Kong and taught at the University of Hong Kong. Those years had been largely friendless, but he was not a man who needed friends or made them easily. He had contented himself with collecting Chinese pottery and porcelain, including some fragments dating back as far as the Tang dynasty. He had pursued his interest on the Chinese mainland, travelling as widely as the authorities had allowed and visiting any number of cities, towns, and even some of the smallest villages, in search of rare items. He had been lucky, gradually amassing a remarkable collection containing some very valuable items.

The guides on his travels had all been employed by the Chinese government, which had insisted that he be accompanied wherever he went. This had not been a problem for Cole; it had in fact been a positive advantage; since although the guides were a mixed lot of old and young, male and female, he had found with them the chance for real personal exchange. As for his standing with their government, he knew that the best relationships are hard-won. It had taken time, but gradually the People's Republic of China had seemed to realise that his admiration for their country and its art was sincere and deep.

After several years they had shown their trust in him by giving him free rein to travel where he wanted, not always accompanied. On occasion an official would visit him in Hong Kong and ask him about his research and his students. When the offer had come from Oxford of a lectureship in his subject, combined with a fellowship at St Felix's College, he had mentioned it casually to a government minister while he was visiting Beijing, and to his bemusement an official came back to him the next day urging him to accept. The PRC hoped that he would continue his visits to China, but also that while in Oxford he might perform small services for them and help increase the number of Chinese students studying there.

This he was more than happy to do, especially as the Chinese government placed no restriction on him taking his collection back with him to England. To Arthur Cole's way of thinking, the China of the post-war world had been remarkably well governed, not that one would know that from commentators in the West. In his opinion, any country that had created items of such beauty and significance as he now owned was worthy of respect. No one starved in China anymore; something that the spoiled generation of baby boomers and their progeny of Generations X and Y could never understand. When he thought of the struggle so many Chinese students had endured to get to Oxford, he could only react with scorn and distaste to the spoiled Western students of higher education.

Over the following years he had done more for the Chinese authorities than he had ever expected. This had given him the confidence to float to them his pet scheme of an institute within the college where Chinese students conducting postgraduate research could meet socially with those from other countries. It would act as a place for cultural and intellectual exchange between Chinese and European students.

The Chinese government had been immediately receptive, offering financial backing, and St Felix's had welcomed the idea, seeing it as a new source of funds and a prestigious venture. True, there had been initial resistance to his proposal from three or four xenophobic Fellows, but Cole had manoeuvred round them quite adroitly. Few knew the extent of the Chinese subventions, or how cleverly they had been disguised by routing them through a Scandinavian foundation. The university at large thought the chief funding had come from a Norwegian philanthropist, made rich by his country's oil boom and happy to pay for an educational establishment in another country, provided its brief was international.

Cole had fought hard to become Director of the Institute. Given his crucial role in its founding it might have been an automatic appointment, but he was not a popular figure in college; even he would admit that. Still, he had eventually got the job, and had enjoyed five glorious years at the helm. He'd hoped he would be allowed to serve a second term, but the malcontents had kicked up, and under the pretext that it had never been conceived of as more than a one-term post, removed him.

Scandalously, his successor was not even an academic. Just a Foreign Office stooge who might have seen much of the world, but pretty much its most unimportant parts – Africa, South America, God knows where else. He hadn't made Ambassador, this man, his last posting some dreary job in Whitehall. Standards must have slipped there; Abbot didn't even wear a tie most days. With his determined friendliness and open-necked shirts, he would have been anathema to Arthur Cole whatever he did. But for him to have taken Cole's rightful place – he who had originated the Institute – seemed unspeakably unfair. Cole still had considerable influence, of course, and without letting on enjoyed cordial relations with the Chinese, but he had a smaller room in college these days, and fewer privileges to dispense officially. Though his years at St Felix's and his role in establishing the Institute meant his views could not be casually ignored.

He looked at his watch. Fifteen minutes until his next appointment, so he thought momentarily of going to the Lodge to check his post. No point; these days ninety per cent of his communications came via email, a development he had acceded to, though he drew the line at texting. No, he decided, he would stay put and wait for his next visitor happily enough, since he had a new print to look at that he had hung on his wall that morning: a white swan beautifully depicted against a background of marsh and mountain. He had found it in the recent catalogue of a Hong Kong dealer, and its arrival two days before had been the highlight of his week.

He got up from the wingback chair and sat down at his desk, a teak beauty from a southern province, picking up the file on the student he was about to see. Opening it, he looked again at the original letter from the Cultural Attaché at the Chinese Embassy in London, which he had received six weeks before. He had met his predecessor, a man roughly Cole's age named Mr Lau, on many occasions and they had got on well. But Lau had been promoted, it seemed, though he remained at the Embassy in London. His replacement was a young man, not much past thirty, who had learned his English – fluent if slightly bureaucratic – during three years at Stanford Business School, which he liked to talk about at irritating length.

My dear Professor Cole,

I write to you on behalf of a student of computer science named Li Min, who for various reasons is eager to transfer her studies to this country, and to Oxford in particular. She is a talented researcher in the field of Artificial Intelligence, engaged in investigating the impact new technologies will have on the humanities – surely a growing field of study at this stage.

Given the potential importance of her work to my government, it seems best to place her in the Institute, where we can be sure she will be well looked after. Her academic record is outstanding and, I believe, easily good enough to justify her admission to both the Institute and St Felix's. I ask therefore for your help in facilitating her entry.

That much Cole had done, willingly, indeed eagerly. He did not need an interpreter to help him read between the lines of the missive. If this woman would be useful to the People's Republic, then very well, he would help her. What harm could it possibly do?

He was feeling content about this and enjoying the silence of his room when the quiet satisfaction of the moment was suddenly disturbed by a noise at his door. Was that a knock? His visitor was not due for another ten minutes. Another knock came, and with a sigh he said loudly, 'Come in.'

A man entered the room. He was casually dressed in a jacket and open-necked shirt. Still no tie, Arthur Cole noted in disapproval.

'May I have a word?' asked Charles Abbot, the new Director of the Institute. 'I have a possible problem – with a student. I thought I should speak to you first.'

Cole was startled. Recovering, he said, 'Of course. I have to see someone in a few minutes. Is that enough time or would you like to come back later?' Later, he hoped, since once deferred the man might not come back at all.

'It won't take long.'

And it didn't. The upshot, as far as Cole could tell, was that the new Director was concerned that one of the students at the Institute was snooping around the rooms of some of his fellows, almost as if he were spying on them. It didn't sound very serious to Cole; more a case of too much curiosity than anything malign. But Abbot seemed to think it could be something much more sinister; part of some larger attempt to keep tabs on the student body at the Institute. The snooper was a Chinese student, he said, implying that this was why he'd come to Cole.

'Have you asked this person what he was doing?'

'Not yet.'

'I see.' There was no point getting angry, Cole told himself. Instead, he said, 'You're very fortunate to have come to me.'

'Oh, good,' said Abbot.

The man looked relieved, but Cole ignored this and said, 'Because anyone else would report you.'

To Cole's satisfaction, Abbot seemed taken aback. 'Report me? For what?'

'Racist assumptions. Unconscious racism, I'm sure, but people are pretty literal in their interpretation of these matters these days. I am however happy to overlook it – just this once, mind you.'

'There's nothing racist about what I'm saying.' Abbot was visibly outraged by the accusation. 'The student happens to be Chinese, but he could be Icelandic for all I care. I'm worried about the other students' rights to privacy, not their nationalities.'

'So you say, but what evidence have you that the student was doing anything but a bit of harmless snooping? From which you've jumped to conclusions I can only label highly speculative – and that's being charitable.'

'But—' Abbot started to protest.

Cole cut him short, raising his hand to indicate that Abbot should be quiet. 'Say no more and I will do my best to overlook this unfortunate exchange. I shan't mention it to anyone else and would strongly advise you to do the same. Now, forgive me –' he looked ostentatiously at his watch '– I have a student to see. A new arrival. She also is Chinese and, coincidentally, is herself coming to join the Institute. Her name is Min. Li Min. I do hope you're not going to tell me she's a spy too.'

6

Abbot would know better in future than to ask anything of Arthur Cole, that was now clear. It had been a mistake to consult him, if an understandable one since the man knew China inside out and knew St Felix's Chinese students too – indeed, was responsible for most of them being there. So now Abbot did what he realised he should have done to begin with – he went to see Jia Hao.

No one seemed to know why the Elm was called that, since the trees surrounding it were all ancient oaks. The original building, which still stood, was an enormous red-brick Victorian family edifice, built on a rise between Cumnor and Boars Hill, south-west of Oxford, and so about a six-mile drive from St Felix's.

Behind the Victorian mansion ran two wings, extensions built in the fifties judging by their ugliness, Abbot guessed. Each held a surprising number of tiny study/bedrooms. At their far end, connecting the two wings and making the space in between a quadrangle of sorts, was a brand-new building, in black steel and glass, that was handsome if incongruous.

On arriving in Oxford, Abbot had at first been puzzled by the Elm and its curiously mixed architecture. It was useful in providing rooms for some of the Institute's students and housed virtually all the Chinese ones.

Why would so many Chinese students want to live in the middle of the countryside rather than in Oxford, with its restaurants and cafés and cinemas and pubs, all the recreational venues of student life?

Abbot parked outside the mansion, got out and walked through the front door. Inside, corridors ran to right and left towards the new wings. In front of him was the administrative office with its door standing open. Having no wish to advertise his presence, but with no idea where Jia Hao's room was, Abbot paused. As he hesitated, the building's manager, Nina Pierpont, emerged.

They had only met once, on his brief initial tour of the Elm, when she had struck him as competent and professional, if perhaps a touch humourless. She could not have been much more than forty but he had noticed on that occasion that she dressed like an older woman. Clearly that had not been a one-off; today she was wearing a brown jacket and skirt, her blouse the palest possible blue – almost as though she were making a deliberate attempt to look colourless and plain. She wore no make-up or jewellery, and her shoes were dull grey flats.

'Can I help you?' she called out sharply, as if he were a suspicious person who needed to be challenged.

'Oh, hello,' Abbot said.

Recognising him, she flushed slightly. 'Forgive me, Mr Abbot. I didn't realise it was you. Can I help with anything?'

He didn't really want anyone to know he was seeing Jia Hao, so shook his head. 'Thanks, no. I'll manage.'

He could see she was curious but ignored her and went towards some swing doors leading to one wing. As they closed behind him, he resisted the impulse to look back, but he was sure Pierpont was still watching.

He got lucky: he was in the right wing. Jia Hao's room was on the second floor. He knocked, wondering if they should talk in here or retire to the café on the ground floor of the new building. When no one answered, he knocked again, but no sound came from within. He tried the door handle, not really ready to enter uninvited, but thinking that if it were unlocked, it meant Jia Hao was somewhere nearby. But when the handle turned easily in his hand, he gave the door the smallest encouragement and it swung inwards and open.

Looking in, he was taken aback to find that the room was empty. Not just unoccupied but stripped bare: bedding, clothes, personal effects – there was nothing there or in the tiny bathroom. He knew that at the end of term, students were required to empty their rooms completely, in readiness for the business conferences held at the Elm during the vacation weeks. But term had just started. So where was Jia Hao? Or had Abbot got the room number wrong?

He stepped back out into the corridor as a student came along, a Westerner. He didn't seem to recognise Abbot, who stopped him, saying, 'Excuse me. I'm looking for Jia Hao. Do you know where his room is?'

The boy stared at him. 'That's it there,' he said, pointing at the door Abbot had just come out of. 'But they say he's gone home.'

'Home?'

'Hong Kong, I think. I'm not sure. I didn't see him leave. One of the others told me.'

'Right,' said Abbot, nodding, inwardly disturbed by this news.

On his way out he stopped at the office and, finding Nina Pierpont back behind her desk, said cheerfully from the doorway, 'I was looking for a student named Jia Hao. But I gather he's left us.'

'Yes.'

'He seemed to think someone had been in his room, going through his things.'

'I know,' she said with a loud sigh.

'I thought I'd better come see what he was on about.'

'I'm not a psychiatrist, but if you ask me, Mr Jia was a clear case of paranoia. He kept complaining so we even changed the locks on his door for him.'

'He mentioned a Mr Chew,' said Abbot a little reluctantly, since he didn't like bandying accusations about, especially second-hand.

Pierpont was shaking her head. '*Cherchez la femme*,' she said, then seeing Abbot's puzzlement explained, 'They were both interested in the same young woman. I'm afraid it's a pretty clear case of jealousy raising its ugly head. As I understand it, in the competition for the girl's... hand,' she said, smiling wryly, 'Mr Chew was the winner. He's a great big chap, our Mr Chew, not like little Mr Jia. And Mr Jia hated him, probably for that reason.'

'Ah, I see. Well, anyway, do you know where Jia Hao has gone?'

Pierpont looked suddenly a little flustered. 'He's flown home – to Hong Kong. I don't know for how long.'

'Was this expected? I mean, term's barely started.'

'Well, I certainly didn't know about it until he came by this morning and returned the room key. He said there was a family emergency. I didn't think I could question it.'

'No, of course not. I suppose we'll hear more eventually.'

Pierpont said nothing, even when he waited a bit. So at length he said, 'Please let me know if you hear from him, or anyone else does.'

'All right,' she said, but the request seemed to have gone down badly.

Why? wondered Abbot, as he walked slowly towards his car. He sat in it for a while, wondering what he should do next. Since there was nothing useful to be done at the Elm, he decided to go up to the old barn perched on top of a low hill a few hundred yards away. It belonged to the Institute, but Abbot realised he had never inspected the building. So he turned his car and drove up a rough farm track to the front of the barn. He parked and got out, thinking he would have a quick look inside before getting back to Oxford.

Just then a man came out of the open door, dressed in olive workwear, shirt and trousers. He was tall with a farmer's build: forearms the size of lamb shanks and a pot belly formed by too many hours spent behind the wheel of a farm vehicle.

'Good morning,' Abbot said politely. 'I'm Charles Abbot and I wonder if I might take a quick look inside this building.'

'Oh, no,' said the other man, sounding defiant, 'you can't come inside here. The Council's been out and they say the building isn't safe. Concrete's substandard. Beams could give way any time now.'

Abbot was taken aback. He wondered if the man was always this rude. He said a little crossly, 'What is your job here, and what's your name?'

'Who's asking?' the man demanded.

'The Director of the Institute.' In case there were still any grounds for misunderstanding, he added, 'That's me.'

It was the other man's turn to look surprised. 'I'm Gillroy,' he said grudgingly, though not quite as gruffly. 'I do the maintenance around here.'

'OK, Mr Gillroy. I'm just going to take a look round.'

'Be careful then. I tell you, this place needs a lot of repair work. It's half falling down, but no one wants to spend any money putting it right.' All the same, he followed Abbot into the building.

Abbot took a few steps inside and peered around. On the barn's floor there were a few spades, various other tools propped up against a wall and several bales of hay. A ladder in one corner led up to a hayloft, but he could see that there was nothing up there.

'So you don't keep any animals?' he said to Gillroy.

'No,' came his reply. 'The animals you see belong to the farmer in the next field. He keeps his hay here, but to tell you the truth, there isn't much need for this place. I just store stuff here.'

Abbot nodded. He walked out of the barn and Gillroy followed him. 'You've got a pretty good view,' Abbot remarked. Then, after a pause, 'I wonder whether you saw any strangers at the Elm yesterday evening or this morning? Like a car you hadn't seen before… that kind of thing.'

'No. Just the shuttle bus going off to Oxford, same as usual. I knock off at five in the evening, so I didn't see anything last night because I wasn't here.'

'OK,' said Abbot. He added, 'Great Land Rover you've got here. How old is it?' he asked, stroking the side of the parked vehicle. 'Must go back to the nineties at least, yes? Or more? You keep it very well,' he said, looking inside and seeing nothing remarkable except that the backs of the rear seats were down, making a large space in the rear. 'What do you use it for?'

'Oh, just moving the hay bales when I help out the farmer,' said Gillroy dismissively, beginning to walk away.

'Well, thanks,' said Abbot. 'I'll see if there is anything I can do about the state of the barn.'

'Good on yer,' said the man, not looking back over his shoulder.

I wouldn't trust him further than I could throw him, thought Abbot as he walked back to the car. 'Why do we seem to employ such uncommunicative characters?' he wondered as he drove away.

7

When he got back to Oxford, Abbot wondered what to do next. Was it pure coincidence that Jia Hao's warning letter had almost immediately been followed by his hasty departure? It seemed improbable. And Cole had reacted so strongly – and weirdly – when told about the letter.

If there was anything in the young man's accusations, Abbot really needed the input of someone who knew about security threats, could judge whether this was likely to be something serious or whether it could be safely ignored. He knew no one at Oxford who could advise him.

And then he thought of Mark Delaney. They had first met while both at the Embassy in Damascus. Then, by coincidence, Delaney had turned up at the Embassy in Istanbul where Abbot had been Cultural Attaché. They had always got along well. Delaney was an MI6 officer; Abbot a counsellor specialising in trade matters. In that role he met many people in all walks of life and so had been able to help Delaney make useful contacts. He was a man with a mission, or rather many missions it seemed, but terrific company and a keen tennis player. (Abbot had a decent game of his own and they played every week on a variety of courts.) And Gillian and Delaney's wife had liked each other. Aggie had a good sense of humour, which appealed to Gillian. The two couples socialised together, played doubles, picnicked, swam and had generally enjoyed themselves in their off-duty moments.

After Istanbul they had lost touch, but through a mutual acquaintance Abbot knew that the Delaneys were now back in London. Had Gillian still been alive, he and she would have been in touch by now, and probably started to see their old friends again. Abbot's failure to contact them so far was because of his wife's absence – seeing them would just remind him, as so much else already did, of how much he was missing her. For their own part, the Delaneys' silence seemed to show that they understood his feelings.

As he worked his way through Oxford's one-way system, which deserved its description as the unique creation of warped minds, Abbot wondered whether he could really bother Mark with the problem of Jia Hao. Maybe left alone it would simply go away. But then he recalled what Nina Pierpont had just said about Jia Hao's sudden return home, and decided then and there he would go ahead and ring his old friend. After all, he remembered from the student's file that Jia Hao was an orphan. And what kind of orphan has a family emergency?

Mark Delaney couldn't have been friendlier on the phone, even when Abbot explained that it wasn't purely a social call and that he had something work-related he wanted to talk to him about. Delaney was busy that day – there was some crisis in Lebanon – but late the next morning Abbot disembarked at Paddington, took the Bakerloo line to Oxford Circus and crossed the river on the Victoria line. At Vauxhall he got off and found his old friend waiting for him at the top of the Underground station's steps.

'I thought we'd have a quick lunch. There's a nice bistro down the street.'

As they walked south they chatted. Delaney said how sad he and his wife had been to hear about Gillian's death, but otherwise kept off the subject, to Abbot's relief.

He was pleased to see that Delaney was the same as ever. Tall and athletic, now with some grey streaks in his dark hair, he walked with the springy steps of the tennis player he had always been. Abbot asked if he was likely to be going abroad again, but Delaney said no, he would be in London for the next few years. His children were happily settled at school here, and Aggie had found herself a job that she was really enjoying. He was interested in Abbot's new life in Oxford, and rather envious to hear where he was living. He had loved his time there as an undergraduate, over thirty years before.

Turning off Harleyford Road, they went down a little side street to the bistro. Delaney must have been a regular here, thought Abbot, since the owner greeted them with a big smile and led them without any prompting to a table in a quiet corner at the back.

It was only as they finished ordering that conversation turned to the matter at hand. Delaney's expression sobered slightly and he said, 'Now tell me what's up.'

He listened to Abbot's account of Jia Hao's letter in his pigeonhole, the conversation with Professor Cole, his visit to the Elm, discovery of the student's empty room and the conversation with Ms Pierpont.

When he finished, Delaney sat still for a minute, then sipped from his wine. Putting the glass down, he said, 'Thanks for getting in touch and telling me about it; you did the right thing. We've heard of this sort of thing going on in universities all over the Western world, but not here so far. The Americans are taking a particular interest in it, and I'd like to mention it to my counterpart at the London CIA station. I think he would be very interested to hear your story. Would you be happy for me to share with him what you've told me?'

'Yes, of course,' said Abbot, looking relieved. 'I'd be delighted for you to do that.'

'I'd better warn you now: we may need your help in pursuing this.'

8

David Saunders was head of Counter Intelligence for the CIA in London and had been in the UK for five years – an almost unprecedented stint in the post, and evidence of how well thought of he was. On first encounter he cut an unprepossessing figure – he was short and wiry and looked more like a building society manager than a high-ranking CIA officer, one who did hill walking as a weekend hobby. But as Delaney had long ago concluded, behind the modest façade lurked a formidable brain.

Saunders was dressed today in a dark blue suit, its formality relieved by a bright yellow tie. Delaney wondered if he had been lunching out, since his normal office wear did not run to suit and tie. His office, on one of the higher floors of the new American Embassy at Nine Elms, faced north towards the river. It was Delaney's first visit there and Saunders showed off the view of Tate Britain, with the Houses of Parliament looming in the distance, and in between a glimpse of the large squat building with a copper roof housing Britain's domestic intelligence service, MI5.

He ushered Delaney towards a sofa set against one wall of the room, and himself sat on a chair on the other side of a low coffee table. 'Have a seat and I'll send for some coffee. From what you said on the phone, I think we may both have stumbled on the same racket but it's best if you start right from the beginning and tell me what you know.'

Delaney did his best to keep his account concise, while Saunders made notes on his pad. The American listened carefully as Delaney described St Felix's College and its relatively new Institute of International and Cultural Affairs where his old friend Charles Abbot was the recently appointed Director. He went on to explain as clearly as he could what had happened after a Chinese student contacted Abbot to complain that he was under surveillance.

When he stopped speaking there was a short silence, and then Saunders asked, 'Who else knows about this letter Jia Hao wrote Abbot?'

'Well, Abbot tried to talk to his predecessor – the one who had founded the Institute – but when asked what he made of Jia Hao's accusations, the man dismissed them out of hand. What's more he accused Abbot of racism for taking the complaint seriously. The man is an old Hong Kong hand, and in spite of what has happened there recently is still very pro-Chinese. Abbot wishes he hadn't gone to see him.'

'Has Abbot told anybody else? Any of the authorities?'

'You mean the police?'

'I mean in the university, though actually anybody else at all. In fact, anybody who might inadvertently have spilled the beans about this letter.'

Delaney explained that Abbot was a widower, and felt a guilty pang as he said it – he and his wife really should have pushed more to see their old friend. He said Abbot had thought of going to the Principal – which was the title of the head of St Felix's – but the man was new in his post and, frankly, struggling a bit to win the respect of the Fellows. Abbot had said he couldn't see that there was anything the Principal could do about it – not without firmer evidence than he had.

Saunders nodded. There was a pause while he got up from his chair, took off his jacket, chucked it over a peg and said, 'I'm glad you came to see me about this. I want to take you into my confidence. I'm already talking to Wilson at Five – we're working together on a case that sounds very similar. A colleague of mine has just come over from Langley to work with us. You may remember her. She was very closely involved in the business of that MP who turned out to be a Russian spy.'

'Yes, I remember.'

'Anyway, I want to have her in so that we can talk further about how your story connects with what we're already doing. She's in the office now. I'll ask her to join us if that's OK?'

'Yes, I'd like to meet her. I remember the Robinson case, and I know Wilson well – we were colleagues once.'

Manon was still jet-lagged from the flight, but found as usual that plunging straight into work was the best way to fight the time-change fatigue. On the flight over she had worked her way through background material about St Felix's College, and an internal agency guide to Artificial Intelligence that she found hard going.

Now, when Saunders came into the little room she'd been assigned for the day, she was scanning an account of the Institute at St Felix's, written by its ex-Director, a man named Cole, in the college's alumni magazine, and was also wondering how she was going to approach Li Min, by now presumably settled in Oxford. Plus, Manon would need to find a place to stay there for herself. There was much to do.

'Something's come up,' Saunders announced, appearing in the doorway. He had welcomed her a few hours before when she had arrived, fresh from the airport, but then left her alone. 'Sorry about this, Manon – you've barely got your feet wet and you must be tired. I find jet lag is much worse coming this way. But I know you'll want to hear this. There's a guy from MI6 who's come to see me and I'd like you to join us in a little while. I won't say anything more than that since he can explain better than I can – but it could help us with this woman Li Min.'

It was half an hour before Saunders' secretary came to collect Manon, time enough for her to ponder what had happened to bring MI6 over to the US Embassy. She knocked lightly on the door to his office and went in, finding him standing by the window, talking to a lanky man seated on the sofa. She was relieved, given Saunders' formal garb, to see that the visitor was wearing a jacket and open-necked shirt, since Manon herself had not expected any meetings today and was dressed informally, in jeans and a light blue sweatshirt, with her long brown hair tied up in a ponytail.

Saunders explained to her that Delaney was from MI6 and had a story that seemed to relate very closely to what Manon was initially meant to be working on – investigating Li Min's sudden removal from Harvard and transfer to Oxford.

After giving the bones of the story, Saunders said, 'As you see, Manon, it's the same college both times: St Felix's. The Institute there seems to be a magnet to Chinese students.' Turning to Delaney he said, 'It looks as though, quite separately, we may have stumbled onto something.'

They went on to discuss how the two cases might connect. Delaney mentioned that Abbot, who had come to him with his concerns about Chinese spying at the Institute, was an old friend.

'I do wonder,' said Manon, 'why your man Jia Hao was also moved all the way across the Atlantic from Princeton to Oxford. It's a long way to go. Do we know what he was working on, or what their target for him at St Felix's could be?'

Saunders said: 'No, though I expect Abbot can find out. We may be looking at the tip of an iceberg. I'm interested to hear that Jia Hao thought he was being snooped on. It looks as though the PRC didn't trust him.'

Manon said, 'And perhaps they were right. His letter sounds unusually outspoken,' she commented to Delaney.

'Yes,' he said. 'You'd think they would have tested his reliability before they sent him all this way. I wonder if this man Chew found out about the letter to the Director. Why else would Jia Hao leave so quickly?'

'That must be the reason,' said Manon. She glanced at Saunders, waiting for him to speak.

There was a pause and then he said, looking at Delaney, 'I'd better tell you about the plan that's been discussed with Wilson at Five. Following up on Li Min's letter telling us that she would be at St Felix's College, we've decided we'd like to send Manon up there to try and get in on the action somehow.'

He looked at her and nodded, so she addressed Delaney. 'Now that you've told us about the Institute and your friend Abbot, I am wondering whether we could call on him for assistance. Do you think he's a man who could play a part in an undercover operation of this kind? You know the kind of thing I mean.'

Delaney thought for a moment then said, 'I've known him for years. He was a counsellor in the Foreign Office, and very helpful to me in some fairly dodgy postings overseas. He's discreet, and I think would be prepared to take part in the sort of operation you probably have in mind.

'Just let me know when you'd like to meet him. In the meantime, do you want me to give him your name?'

Here Saunders interjected, 'It will probably be an alias. We'll work on a cover, and then we'll let you know.'

Delaney smiled at Manon. 'OK. I'll tell Charles to wait to hear from Madame Mysterious.'

9

She had wanted to meet on Addison's Walk, behind Magdalen College, which she had recently discovered as part of getting to know her new environment. Li Min was diligent like that; at Harvard she had visited every one of the residential houses in the first four weeks she was there. She had some way to go in Oxford to match that, having only arrived ten days before.

But Deng had balked at her choice, seeming wary of meeting so near to one of the colleges. He had proposed the café at Blackwell's bookshop, not seeming to realise that there were few less private places in the city. Eventually they had agreed to meet in Holywell Cemetery, which was a ghoulish choice but one where their meeting was unlikely to attract interest.

She found Deng waiting for her at the far end of the cemetery, sitting on a bench near a towering Cedar of Lebanon. Even on this breezy day, he wore no coat, only his standard uniform of black suit, white shirt and unremarkable tie.

Li Min had been startled by the text message from him summoning her to the meeting, having expected to have a new controller based at the Embassy in London. But it seemed Deng too had made the transfer across the Atlantic and there must have been an important reason for that. Then with a start of surprise Li Min realised it might have something to do with her.

There was never any small talk with Deng, and his questions now were specific and to the point. Was she living in the Elm outside the city? *Yes.* Had she established herself in her department, and met with her adviser? *Yes*, on both counts; though he didn't seem very interested when she complained that the facilities at her new research lab were not what she was used to, and they had different approaches here to AI audio generation. She added that her adviser spent most of his time at the university's Internet Centre on St Giles' and seemed happy for Li Min to decide herself how best to move forward with her research.

Right, said Deng impatiently, and had she met other students in her field? Only a few so far, though there would be a drinks party the following Saturday for all the students in the Institute. And what about at the Elm? There she had been more socially successful. Living in such close proximity, she could not help but meet people, and it was easy to fall into conversation at mealtimes with her fellow Chinese.

He returned to the topic of her work at the lab, explaining that he would, as at Harvard, expect regular reports. 'On your progress,' Deng said specifically, and it was clear he saw this as being more important than the work other people were engaged on. But his instructions lacked the urgency they usually conveyed, and seemed almost cursory. Li Min wondered why.

'Now,' said Deng, with the air of someone finally getting down to business, 'have you been to see Professor Cole?'

She nodded but not happily. She had found the man both stiff and condescending. He had asked her about her work but not listened to the answers, and she had the feeling he was reluctant to extend any kind of intellectual respect to women. Something impish in her stirred as she recalled their introductory meeting. 'I thought he was a patronising idiot,' she declared.

Startled, Deng looked at her as if to check that he had heard her right. Then for the first time in their long if spasmodic acquaintance, he laughed – out loud, uncontrolled. And, just as suddenly, stopped. He said, 'I understand he is an idiot. But he is useful to us – a useful idiot. He will help you without demanding to know why. Remember that.' He looked at his watch, a habit of his which Li Min always found annoying. 'Now,' he declared, 'there is someone I want you to get to know.'

'At the lab?'

He shook his head. 'No, but she is living at the Elm.'

Li Min said, 'Is she Chinese?'

Deng replied: 'Not exactly. Her mother is, but the daughter is not really Chinese.'

There were Western students at the Elm, but they were there for the most part because they could not find more convenient, affordable accommodation in the city.

Deng continued: 'Her name is Washington. Sally Washington. Her father is American and she is from that country. I am not sure what she is studying – some social sciences rubbish,' he said dismissively.

So her work was not important to Deng, thought Li Min. Good; she was tired of stealing the fruits of other people's labours. But if this were the case, then why should she bother with this Washington woman?

'You just want me to become her friend?' she asked.

'Yes.'

'Is that all?' Had she really been forced to stop in her tracks, move across the Atlantic and possibly jeopardise her career prospects, purely in order to become the friend of some half-Chinese, half-American girl? It couldn't be the only reason for this upheaval in her life surely.

And when Deng hesitated, she knew she was right – something further would be required of her. 'No,' he said at last, almost reluctantly, and lowered his voice. 'But all in good time. I will explain in due course. After you have won this young woman's trust.'

Li Min left the meeting none the wiser, knowing only that she would have to continue to issue reports on her colleagues to Deng in London and, more urgently, find Sally Washington and become her friend. What if she couldn't contrive a way of meeting the woman? Worse, what if she did but the woman didn't like her? It all seemed indescribably vague, yet potentially difficult too. She wondered what the end game really was. Obviously something to do with this woman personally, not her work.

Li Min was now in the middle of town, halfway along the Broad, at the northern end of the mixed colleges and shops along the Turl. She went and bought some make-up in Boots, then stared through window displays at clothes she couldn't afford along the High Street. She looked at her watch and realised she had just missed the shuttle back to the Elm. Distracted by the shops, she had just missed the shuttle back to the Elm. There wouldn't be another for an hour, so still mulling over the baffling exchange with Deng, she decided to walk down to the river: across the High, down an alleyway the width of a big man's shoulders and then into Christ Church

Meadow. The path there ran in a circular loop of a little over a mile. She set out along it briskly.

When she reached the river, she paused only briefly to watch a couple of the eights setting out from the boathouses that dotted the bank, then continued on the little circuit, into the woods on the south-east corner of the Meadows. Here she saw only the occasional jogger, until walking at some pace, she found herself rapidly gaining ground on a couple of men ahead of her, and slowed down. As she did so she recognised one of them – a diminutive man, ebony hair cut short, wearing a black suit and city shoes.

Immediately she hung back. She didn't want Deng to think she was spying on him as he met another contact. If he saw her there was no obvious excuse she could give for being there.

Next to Deng, the other man was much taller, wide-shouldered too, and when he turned his head sideways to look at Deng, she saw that he was not only Chinese but familiar – from the Elm. What was his name? She had met him at dinner where he had complained about the cafeteria's alien Western food. Chou? Chang? Something like that… and then the name *Chew* flew into her head and stayed there.

10

The taxi dropped Manon at the flat she had rented in North Oxford. Once, not long before, she had stayed in a flat rather like this during a particularly stressful period of her life. It had been her introduction, entirely unplanned, to the world of CIA Operations, in which she was now a fully-fledged agent. She hoped that in any crisis, or while facing any physical threat, she would remain determined and calm, as she had been trained to be.

She had been lucky to find a flat now that term had started. The owner, who lived in a palatial house on Woodstock Road, had explained on the phone that it had already been rented once, but the tenant had changed his mind about doing graduate work, and, despite losing his deposit, had surrendered the lease. Hence its reappearance in the university's daily online information sheet, where to her relief Manon had found it.

The flat consisted of the ground floor of a two-storey red-brick Victorian house. Inside the shared front hall, a staircase led to another flat upstairs. Judging from the post that had accumulated on a side table in the hall, nobody had lived up there for some time. Good. Manon wanted a quiet place with privacy and no inquisitive neighbours.

Her flat turned out to be tidy, freshly cleaned and small, but then she didn't need a lot of space and had only brought one large suitcase with her. She had no idea how long she was going to be here, but could always go back to London for more stuff if she needed it. To the right of the hallway there was a little sitting room that overlooked the road. It was lined with bookshelves that were full of history books; doubtless a dumping ground for books the landlady had no room for in her own place. Down the corridor there was a bedroom, decorated simply in light colours that felt cheery. On the bed the landlady had left clean folded sheets and towels, happily supplied for an extra charge. Next door the compact bathroom had a shower head above the tub. At the end of the hall in the back of the house, the kitchen was petite but had all the basics, as well as a combo washer/dryer that would save her from making trips to the launderette. The room overlooked a strip of garden, in which Manon was glad to see a few hints of summer – a flourish of early peonies and buds sprouting on a rose bush that needed pruning.

It was all perfectly comfortable and ideal for a visiting academic. She was looking forward to seeing Charles Abbot in the morning at the Institute. They had spent a day together in the Embassy in London working on her cover story. Saunders did not want Manon anywhere near St Felix's until she was ready to arrive there in her new identity. Abbot had quickly understood this and had joined in enthusiastically. It was his idea that they might have met at a conference he had attended in America. 'And you might have been, let's say, a junior research librarian… something rather vague but that sounds reasonably high-powered? Let's say someone who used to work at the Library of Congress, but now, as actors like to say, you're "resting" so you're no longer on the accredited staff. And in fact, at the Institute we do have a large uncatalogued collection of books and papers, some of which relate to our foundation, given to us by scholars and academics. All in a terrible mess and needing to be put into some sort of order so as to be available to be used academically in the future.'

'That sounds like a good idea,' said Manon, 'but why would I have wanted to come all the way to Oxford to help you out with your problem?'

'Because you liked the look of me?' said Abbot with a grin.

'No, that won't do,' Manon said, laughing. She was beginning to warm to this man. 'We need something more solid than that! What if I wanted an excuse to take a sabbatical in Europe, but couldn't afford to pay for it myself? Are you offering me a salary for spending some time helping you at your Institute? I don't mean you really have to, but just for the purposes of this story.'

'Yes,' said Abbot, 'it sounds perfectly realistic.'

So that was what they had settled on, and both Saunders and the Operational Security team, who had to provide all the documentation needed to back up Manon's new identity, had agreed it sounded credible. Manon had spent a couple of weeks reading up about the practice of archiving and sorting out the details of her own background story: how old she was, her family members, where she had been at school, etc. The real Manon had grown up in western Massachusetts, where her father had taught American History at a small liberal arts college, and her mother – coincidentally in light of Manon's cover – had been head of their town's public library. The covers that were easiest to use were closest to the truth, so 'Judith Davidson', the name Manon would adopt in her new role, had a similar background to her real-life one, which made it easy to remember how old she was (twenty-nine), her family members and their names, and the schools and college she had attended. All the usual things that people ask when they first meet you. Now, as she settled into her flat, she was looking forward to getting on with the job.

11

The next morning Manon set out early for St Felix's, striding down the main thoroughfare of Woodstock Road as commuters' cars crawled along it in rush hour. She was at the college a few minutes before nine when she had her appointment with Charles Abbot and asked at the Lodge for directions to the Institute. Her route lay through an ancient quadrangle and out the other side of a narrow passage before crossing a wide expanse of grass to reach a new wing, cleverly designed so as not to quarrel with the original mediaeval buildings of the college. Inside Reception she was directed to some swing doors, then went up a staircase to a corridor where she found a door marked 'Director's Office'. She knocked and heard a cheerful call of 'Come in.'

As she opened the door Charles Abbot stood up from his desk and came forward to meet her. 'Come in and sit down,' he said. He was forty-six years old, Manon knew from Delaney, though in his blue cotton suit and open-necked shirt he looked years younger. He had wavy dark hair with streaks of grey in it. She'd liked his face when she'd first met him: a strong chin, dark blue eyes, a sharp straight nose. A handsome man, disarmingly rather than aggressively so.

He offered coffee, which she declined, and they sat to either side of his desk. 'It's nice to see you again, Manon,' he said. 'Though from now on, I must remember to call you Judith.'

She nodded. 'It's the easiest thing to slip up on.'

'When did you arrive in Oxford?'

'I came up from London yesterday.'

'Have you found somewhere to stay?'

'A flat off Woodstock Road. You thought that staying in the Elm would make me a bit conspicuous.'

'Wouldn't have been very nice either,' said Abbot, and they both laughed. 'Anyhow, I'm delighted you're here, and will take any help with the papers you can give. But don't worry about that side of things. I appreciate your priority is this student Li Min.'

'Have you heard anything more from the disappeared student, Jia Hao?'

'Not a peep, and I don't expect to. I just hope we can find out if his claims that spying is going on here are true. We really can't have that.'

'What about this Mr Chew he claimed to have seen rifling through his possessions?'

'He's still here, but I haven't felt able to ask him about it since Jia Hao is no longer around to tell his side of the story. Anyway, I thought I'd wait for your arrival.'

She laughed at his honesty, conceding that it would be hard to tackle Chew on the basis of Jia Hao's not altogether coherent letter. Abbot had sent a copy of it to Saunders at Delaney's request, and Manon had seen it. Jia Hao's accusations were alarming, but she wished he had been more specific or that he'd stuck around to give more details. 'Can you tell me anything much about this Mr Chew? What is his field?'

'Medieval History. Please don't ask me more; my knowledge stops right there – of both Mr Chew *and* Medieval History.'

She said, 'As Dave Saunders mentioned in London, we're interested in finding out more about the Chinese government's control of its students here – especially if that leads us to learn precisely what they're asking them to do. We're hoping to find at least one student who will talk.' She mentioned Li Min and their hopes of recruiting her and Abbot nodded, though he seemed deep in thought about something else.

When she stopped talking, he said, 'Sorry, I was just thinking of something. Obviously my knowledge of China, much less its government, is pretty limited. My predecessor here is a different story, however, and you should get to know him. His name is Arthur Cole and he still does the odd bit of teaching. I should add that he is not well disposed towards me – he was desperate to stay on as Director and is very bitter that it wasn't allowed. In fairness, I can't blame him – he was chiefly responsible for founding the Institute to begin with.'

'Will I find him in college?'

'Yes, but I suggest you approach him indirectly.' When Manon raised an eyebrow, Abbot explained, 'He can be a bit grumpy.' He paused. 'Especially with women. My late wife was not an admirer.'

A misogynist, thought Manon, who had dealt with plenty of them before.

Abbot said, 'But maybe I'm being unfair and you'll get on with him very well. It's just that he's…' He was searching in vain for the right words.

'Difficult? If not an outright woman hater?'

'Precisely,' Abbot said with relief. 'I tell you what – there's a Guest Night tomorrow evening for High Table. You could come as my guest and I'll make sure you're seated next to

Cole. That will give you an intro without having to seek him out on a pretext.'

'Thank you,' said Manon, wondering just how bad Cole could be.

'I'll put McCaffrey on the other side of you as an antidote. He's one of the History dons and can be very entertaining. You can talk to him about libraries.' Abbot said this with a straight face but laughed when she gave him a look of mock-horror. 'I'm sorry – I shouldn't tease you.' He stood up. 'Come on. I'll show you your office. It's downstairs but it does have a view.'

Settled in her new office quarters, her laptop open and some books on the desk, Manon surveyed what she was allegedly here to do. The room was full of boxes, presumably crammed with the archive Abbot had been talking to her about. In the distance, she could see a church tower bathed in pale spring sunlight.

She found herself thinking about Abbot; the boxes could wait. He seemed a curious man, not at all the stuffy diplomat she'd imagined. How long had he been widowed for? She admired the way he had at one point mentioned his wife, quite matter-of-factly, and she liked his sense of humour. Though she hoped he wouldn't go on teasing her – she had an older brother back in the States for that. Still, he seemed a gentle man, in the best possible way, with the gentleness coming from inner strength and a clear sense of who he was.

Enough with the psychoanalysis, she decided, and thought how best to move ahead with what she was here for – which wasn't to sort out a load of papers.

She pondered how best to approach Li Min. Having never actually met the student, Manon could hardly contrive to bump into her 'accidentally', either on the street or in college. And forcing an acquaintance would be difficult as well – if Manon went to the Elm for supper, hoping to wangle a seat near Li Min, she would stick out like a sore thumb.

The old-fashioned means of communication seemed the only plausible way forward and she wrote a note accordingly.

Dear Li Min,

I am a friend of Louise Donovan of Harvard who said you had recently come to study here at St Felix's. By happy chance, I am working in the Institute this term, and wonder if you would like to meet up for coffee sometime. I am living in North Oxford but come to college every day and have quite a free schedule.

Best wishes

Judith Davidson

She didn't post this note, or send it through the inter-college mail system, which was a skeleton of its former self, superseded by email. Instead, she put it into Li Min's pigeonhole in the Porters' Lodge of St Felix's. It would be difficult for anyone to pilfer it or pre-examine it there, with a battery of porters just a few feet away. Now the only worry was whether Li Min would reply.

12

LI MIN WAS MORE confident now that she would be able to do good work in Oxford. She would have to do it mainly on her own, she realised, as the university seemed well behind Harvard in the field of AI-generated simulations, audio or video. If anything, Oxford seemed suspicious of these developments, as Li Min found from almost the beginning. She asked another student in the lab, a girl from Leeds named Alicia, to sit for her and read aloud from a book Li Min picked at random – in this case it was a novel by Ian McEwan called *The Comfort of Strangers*. A few pages of audio proved ample, and two days later Li Min had an audio streaming file that had Alicia's voice talking for a good five minutes describing tourist sights in Oxford, moving from the Ashmolean to the eastern end of the Broad and the Bodleian Library. The words themselves were completely banal; with Alicia's help on film too, it should be possible to create a video simulation within the next few weeks. The result would be the production of Li Min's first complete deepfake – one that was utterly harmless yet a considerable achievement.

But given the audio file to listen to, Alicia had, to put it bluntly, freaked out. At first, she had been convinced she had somehow, somewhere been overheard and taped actually talking about Oxford – such was the uncanny accuracy of the fabricated speaking voice. Attempts by Li Min to reassure her that she had never actually said these words had only panicked Alicia more. She had gone to the Head of the Lab, Terry Harrison, in a complete state.

To his credit, Harrison had seemed more astonished by Li Min's achievement than disapproving. Referring to Alicia's reaction, he said, 'There are probably ethical issues involved here, but to tell you the truth, I think the problem is that it's scary… or at least she finds it so.' Li Min didn't know what to say; she found her work exciting – no one had found it frightening at Harvard, or raised any moral questions about it. Fortunately, she and Harrison had agreed on a compromise: Li Min could continue her work on AI-generated video and audio simulations of real people, but none of the 'real people' from the lab would serve as unwitting guinea pigs. Where she would find cooperative subjects was another matter and, as the lab manager made clear, something for her to sort out herself.

Before tackling that, however, Li Min had another problem to focus on, since only forty-eight hours after their rendezvous in Holywell Cemetery, Deng was texting her, asking if she had made friends yet with Sally Washington.

Li Min had already noticed the young woman with eye-catching blonde highlights in her brown hair. Strikingly pretty, she had wide cheekbones and pale hazel eyes.

On the Elm's website there was a page devoted to brief biographies of all the residents, sometimes accompanied by a photograph – that was voluntary, not every student wanted their picture up. Sally Washington was one of the abstainers, but Li Min was somehow confident that the talkative woman she'd spotted had to be her.

She was from the United States, her bio said, where she had taken an undergraduate degree at Pomona College in California. At Oxford she was studying for an MA in International Relations, though there seemed to be little that was international about her friends. At mealtimes she sat with a small group of what had to be Americans from the noise they made. They seemed to have nothing to do with the Chinese, or indeed any British or Europeans either. Li Min was afraid that if she tried to join them, she would either be rebuffed or seem too keen to get to know Sally Washington.

California came to the rescue, quite accidentally. A friend of Li Min's at Harvard had given her a sweatshirt for her last birthday, a rich red one that had, in the habit of American educational institutions, a name emblazoned in prominent letters on the front: *UCSF*. In a circle below was the crest of the University of California. When the weather cooled and she wore the sweatshirt one day, it made Li Min stand out vividly among her black-and-white-attired fellow Chinese students. And luckily, when she came into the dining hall one evening wearing it and joined the queue for the cafeteria-style service, she caught the eye of Sally Washington, two places ahead of her.

'UCSF!' the American woman exclaimed, her voice resonant with Californian tones. 'Wow, dude, are you from San Francisco?'

'Nah,' said Li Min, doing her best to sound relaxed and Californian herself. 'I was at Harvard.'

Sally nodded, but seemed impressed, though studying at Oxford put her in a trans-Atlantic Ivy League as well.

Li Min pressed on as Sally lingered, 'But I love California.'

'Me too,' said Sally. 'Listen, why don't you join us?' She pointed towards the tables in the hall. 'Unless you're eating with someone else?'

'Not tonight,' said Li Min, as if her social calendar was usually full. 'Save me a seat and I'll come over.'

She found a seat left empty among the small huddle of Americans, perhaps half a dozen of them. Li Min slid into it quickly, having put down her tray.

'This is—' Sally Washington started to say, and then looking at Li Min, laughed. 'You know, I don't even know your name.'

'I am Li Min.'

One of the boys, wearing a green T-shirt, with a ponytail and wispy beard, said, 'Are you from China?' He sounded incredulous, as if asking whether she had been to the moon.

Li Min nodded then added quickly, 'But I have been in the States. At Harvard.' She felt very alien among these Americans, a strange feeling since in Massachusetts she had known lots of Westerners and had friends among them.

The boy with the ponytail said, 'Can I ask you a question?' Without waiting for permission, he went on: 'Why won't the Chinese students here talk to us?'

Li Min's eyes widened. 'We think you won't talk to *us*.'

'Really? We figured you were forbidden to socialise with Westerners.'

'Forbidden?' No one had told her this. Even Deng had never tried to regulate her social life. It was work where he wanted her input, especially about her colleagues. He could hardly tell her to stay away from the people whose findings she was supposed to steal.

'By your government, I mean. No offence,' he added.

'No one has ever told me to stay away from the white devils.' She said this in a high-pitched, mock-official tone of voice, trying to make a joke of it. But there was silence at the table.

Then Sally laughed loudly and it seemed the ice was suddenly broken. After that conversation flowed more easily, and it helped when they stopped asking Li Min questions about China, and instead started talking in free-for-all fashion in the normal student way – about the Elm's food, and the unreliability of the shuttle bus to town, and whether in summer they could have parties outside in the adjacent field or if it were raining then in the barn on top of the hill. No longer the centre of attention, Li Min found it difficult to follow all their conversation. Despite her time at Harvard, she wasn't familiar with much of it – musicians and rock bands she hadn't heard of, talk about Major League baseball, some of the slang they used. She started to feel she was moving to the outer fringes of this circle of Americans and didn't know how she could reinstate herself.

After dinner they all got up to return their trays and Li Min found herself trailing behind the group, wondering where they were going and wishing that she was going there too. She had momentarily felt she had made good progress in following Deng's orders, but had also realised she was feeling lonely here. It pleased her for personal reasons, and not because of Deng, finally to meet some Western students socially. But now it seemed she would have to return to her room and spend another evening studying, with only the radio for company.

Sally turned round and called to her: 'We're all going to Luke's room. He has something he brought from back home. Want to come?'

And it was then in fact that the ice was not just broken but completely melted away. For the 'something' turned out to be several bottles of tequila. No drinker, Li Min had never had it – in fact, she wasn't entirely sure what it was, though she knew it was alcoholic – but she told herself she was breaking her teetotal ways for the sake of Deng. So she licked the salt Sally laughingly put on the back of her hand, closed her eyes and swigged, trying not to cough as the liquor went down. Then she bit the lime slice, a sour but effective antidote to the rawness of the spirit.

As the burning sensation gradually subsided, she felt a warmth moving through her limbs, and she was suddenly very happy to be socialising with people who had nothing to do with the lab. One of the boys put some music on, and in a corner the only other girl there besides Sally started dancing by herself. 'Do you like to dance, Li Min?' asked the boy with the ponytail.

The true answer was no, but she sensed that would sound churlish, even prim – the very traits that Westerners supposedly found in their Chinese counterparts. The bottle came round again and this time she took a big hit of the tequila, which no longer seemed to burn her throat so much. 'In China there are many kinds of dancing,' she said. 'Even old people like to dance where I come from.'

'Really?' said the boy and Li Min nodded. She remembered in her village an old woman, thought to be crazy by the villagers but actually, Li Min had concluded, suffering from dementia and the slight shakiness of Parkinson's disease in its early stages. On public holidays the woman would appear in the little square where, long ago, the village's inhabitants had come each day to draw water from a communal tap. Suddenly she would start dancing, to music only she was able to hear, moving in a kind of take one step then slide, take one step then shuffle, series of movements. People would gather round, laughing at this semi-grotesque tableau, but they were kind at heart and each time the old woman finished, they would applaud and she would smile.

Suddenly Li Min found herself describing these semi-ritualistic appearances by the old woman. Then, standing up, she began to demonstrate the bizarre dance. The ponytail boy laughed, Sally Washington laughed too, and Li Min grinned, happy in their company. Happier than she had been since leaving Harvard.

13

The next morning Li Min woke up with a headache unlike any she had ever suffered before. No lab today, she decided right away; she would be lucky to get downstairs to the dining hall without being sick.

She remembered dimly that, after dancing, she had enjoyed three more big glugs of tequila – or was it four? She couldn't be sure; nor could she be sure how she had got back to her room. Someone had escorted her, taking her by the arm. It had been Sally, she realised, who had somehow found her key and seen her safely into bed. How embarrassing, thought Li Min, suddenly mortified at her unprecedented behaviour; she had never been drunk before. And the dancing – what was she thinking? How would she ever look Sally in the face again? The girl must think her a clown.

She managed to take two paracetamol and got back into her bed. Gradually her dizziness subsided and she staggered to the loo, where she stared at her face in the mirror until the reflected image stopped moving.

She returned to bed and must have fallen asleep for she woke with a start to the sound of a quiet knock on the door. Who could it be? A Chinese student?

There was another quiet knock and Li Min decided to face the music and get it over with. 'Come in,' she cried weakly.

The handle turned; the door opened with the push of a hand. Sally Washington's hand. She stood in the doorway, holding a tray from the dining hall and wearing a big smile. 'A little bit under the weather, are we?' she said with a laugh, and came into the room, still bearing the tray. 'I've brought you lunch,' she said, and lowered the tray onto the bed while Li Min gingerly sat up. Sally had brought her a Coke (the old-fashioned kind, full of sugar), a bag of salt and vinegar crisps, and a packet of Haribo sweets.

'You are very kind. I am sorry about last night—' Li Min began to say.

Sally cut her off. 'Sorry? You were the star of the evening. You were *hilarious*.' And she gave a little shuffle, imitating Li Min's own imitation of the old woman's dance. 'I have to hand it to you, Li Min. You're not like the other Chinese here, that's for sure. Who'd have thought you'd be such a Dark Horse? Listen, if you feel up to it, come down to dinner with us. I'll save a seat for you.'

After this they became friends – good friends. Deng's instructions could hardly have been better fulfilled, thought Li Min, wishing he would show up and ask for a report on her progress. On second thoughts, she was glad he'd stayed away. Her friendship with Sally was a genuine one, and Deng's interest in it was increasingly unwelcome.

It was then that she received a letter from a visiting scholar, someone named Judith Davidson. It seemed she was a friend of Louise Donovan, the nice woman Li Min had met at a party during her last days at Harvard. At first she read the letter happily, pleased to think she might make another friend now – two in one week! Clearly, as the Americans liked to say, when it rained, it poured. But then doubts crept in. Louise had wanted her to talk with a friend – 'someone in Washington with good contacts' were the words she had used. This, after Li Min had impetuously expressed her frustration at being ordered to move to Oxford. Deng had surprised her by making her leave within days, so she had decided against meeting Louise's friend; it seemed too risky so close to her departure. The last thing she needed now was the Americans trying to interfere with her move – not when she had already made it successfully.

She decided to treat this new approach with the same caution. It was probably innocent enough – she doubted the letter writer had anything to do with Washington D.C. or the American government; that would be a coincidence too far, in Li Min's opinion. But why complicate things for herself? She was slightly wary of anyone contacting her at Louise's behest, since they might have been told of Li Min's unhappiness about having to switch institutions.

And she wasn't unhappy any longer. Her work was going well. There weren't as many people here engaged in the same kind of simulation creations as there were at Harvard – so much for Deng's original claims for the place. But there was a friendliness in the Oxford lab and a lack of competitiveness that were distinctly pleasant after the hothouse atmosphere at Harvard. And the English seemed better at adapting to their comparative lack of funding, using ingenuity where the Americans fell back on vast reserves of money to get things done.

So she wouldn't answer the letter from the Davidson woman, she decided, though she kept it in a drawer in the night table next to her bed. She felt a little rude and was uneasy about her failure to respond, but told herself that if she ever met the woman, she could always claim she had never received the message.

In any case, and not because of Deng, she had made a real friend in Sally. Li Min was confident that she was really Sally's friend, since for all her easy-going party girl antics, Sally Washington was showing signs of being a very private person who rarely talked about herself. Disclosures from her were rare, and usually guarded, which somehow seemed more English than American. One evening as they sat outside together, Li Min realised she was truly accepted by Sally when the girl suddenly said, 'You know I'm half-Chinese, right?'

'Really?' said Li Min, who knew full well that Sally's mother was a native of Langfang, a small city near Beijing.

'Yes. But it's so embarrassing that I don't speak Mandarin – or Cantonese for that matter. My mother's been in America for thirty years and doesn't want anything to do with her old country. She wouldn't let me learn anything about it either, including the language.'

'Why does she feel like that?'

'I guess once she met my father she decided to become as American as possible. I know she was worried that her being Chinese might hurt his career.'

Li Min was intrigued by this but tried hard not to show it. 'What does he do?' she asked casually.

'He works at the Defense Department. That's why I'm from Washington. Don't ask me any more – all I know is, he has something to do with submarines. It's all very hush-hush – he never talks about his job. I know sometimes he goes away and is actually *on* a submarine. I could never do that – far too claustrophobic for me.'

'Me too,' said Li Min, who in fact feared heights rather than enclosed spaces. 'Maybe he talks to your mom about it?'

Sally shrugged. 'Who knows? She'd never tell me if he did.'

14

'Dinner is served,' the man in the butler's uniform announced.

'Will you excuse me?' asked Charles Abbot. 'I had better collect my guest before he disappears in the scrum.'

'Of course,' said Manon, and the woman next to her, an English don from another college, nodded. They were standing with other diners in the Senior Common Room, where they'd drunk sherry for the last quarter of an hour. Abbot had made a beeline for Manon as soon as she had entered, which she'd found kind and supportive, even if he had brought her over to meet the English don, who had shown little interest in the Library of Congress, asserting petulantly: 'I dislike libraries – stuffy places.'

They moved into the Hall, a beautiful old room with a beamed ceiling and oak-panelled walls on which hung portraits of each Principal since the college's founding seven centuries before. Now the room was packed with undergraduates, waiting noisily for their food as the High Table diners came through to sit on an elevated dais at the end of the room. They all stood for a moment while a Fellow said grace ('*Christum Dominum nostrum*....'), then sat down to be served by waiting staff dressed in black and white. The noise level in the Hall rose and fell as speech gradually became replaced by the furious clatter of forks and knives.

At the High Table itself, dinner unfolded more leisurely, as a starter of smoked salmon was served with a delicate Riesling. As promised, Manon had been placed next to Professor Arthur Cole – she saw this from the name card at his place to her left. He nodded to her as they both sat down, but then turned to speak to his neighbour on the other side.

'Hello,' said a voice to her right, and she turned to a bulky, red-faced man who gave her a grin. This must be McCaffrey, the History don Abbot had mentioned, and it was – he introduced himself, speaking with an almost theatrically thick Scottish burr.

As they ate the salmon McCaffrey kept talking. 'Have you met the Principal yet?'

'No,' she said. 'Just the Director of the Institute.'

'Ah, Charles. Nice man; seems very capable as well. A rare combination, especially at a university. As for the Principal, you may just manage to catch a fleeting glimpse of him. Funny thing: his predecessor made a point of meeting everyone who visited us, whether it was for three days or three years. Sometimes he even greeted the occasional tourist who was just looking around.' McCaffrey took a long sip of his wine. 'The present Principal employs a different... *strategy*... if you can call it that. We see less and less of him at High Table. At this rate his next appearance at dinner will coincide with the announcement of his retirement.'

When he laughed Manon did too, though less loudly. Like anyone else she enjoyed indiscretions, especially comic ones, imparted in moments of humorous candour, but now she felt glad she was not, at least as yet, an enemy of McCaffrey's.

He turned to his other side, where a woman had been sitting silently. Deserted, Manon sat overlooked for a few minutes, staring awkwardly across the table at the portraits on the back wall, until at last Cole turned to her once more and said, 'I'm told you are Miss Davidson and that you are a librarian visiting the Institute from America.'

'That's right,' she said. It seemed gratuitous to reciprocate by asking who he was, since clearly he assumed she knew.

'We've never had a librarian at the Institute before that I can remember,' he said, not entirely affably. 'We've never felt the need for one. I set up the Institute, you know.'

Bully for you, thought Manon, unable to look impressed. Cole speared some salmon and examined it, then went on, 'Which library are you from?'

'None at present. I was at the Library of Congress for a while,' she replied.

'Hmm. Not an academic library then.'

Manon did not think it worth replying to this put-down and took a sip of her Riesling before changing the subject. She didn't want to be pressed on her credentials, aiming to make herself appear naïve, almost simple, in her view of the world. The less sophisticated the better, she decided, since she imagined this would elicit more unguarded opinions from Cole than any battle of wits between them would. She said innocently, 'One thing has surprised me, and that's the number of Chinese students in the College.'

'Oh,' he said dully, as if to imply: 'So what?'

'It did make me wonder: do they have trouble adjusting to life here?'

'No more than other foreign students.' He sounded defensive.

'But our ways are so different. At least, from what I gather about Chinese *mores*.'

He said sharply, 'Then I would urge you to "gather" their *mores* some more.' This was rude enough for even Cole to realise it. He said more mildly but expansively, 'You see, the Chinese are almost infinitely adaptable. It is one of the great strengths of their culture, and the advantage of being the oldest nation on earth. They have literally seen it all.'

'I understand. I suppose I was thinking of the prejudice they must encounter in the West. In America, for example, anti-Chinese sentiment seems to be growing.'

'America is a lost cause,' Cole said sharply. 'I remain more hopeful about my own country. And certainly, the impact of the Chinese here is for the good. Even to the level of this dinner. We are much more international now, and have a wider variety of guests... much more distinguished, generally speaking. It may seem comparatively insignificant, but I can't tell you the effect it's had on morale – the *positive* effect,' he said vehemently, in case she somehow got the wrong end of the stick.

'But can the UK really adopt a different policy towards China from the US? I take it that's what you mean.'

'We can stay clear of your country's madness, yes. The Chinese have so much to offer, it would be a tragedy if we joined with the forces of ignorance and shut our doors to them.'

To Manon, Cole sounded like an arch appeaser, circa 1936, arguing that Germany would see the sense of peace, if only warmongers in the UK did not unnecessarily provoke them. But she was not there to argue with the man, so merely nodded, trying to look thoughtful, though nonetheless unwilling to agree with him outright. Cole didn't seem to care much either way; she sensed that in his view she was just another mindless American, and a woman to boot. As the main course of beef was served and the claret poured, Cole turned again to his left, and soon moments later she heard him starting to tell his other neighbour at the table about his collection of Chinese ceramics.

Not such a good start there, thought Manon, but Abbot had warned her.

15

Someone had been in her room. Li Min could not say exactly how she knew this, but she was certain. She sniffed several times; there was a faint unpleasant smell that had not been there before. Sally had been in the room several times since the tequila débâcle. Her scent was of soap and the open air, and there was no possible reason for her to have been searching Li Min's room. This smell was sour and dank; the odour of a sweaty men's locker room.

Moreover, items had been moved; Li Min was sure of it. The books on her desk were in the same small stack, but too tidily so, too neatly aligned; the same for the pile of folders. She was not by nature particularly messy, but whoever had been in here clearly had higher standards of tidiness.

Who could it be? And how did they get in? Could it be that mean-looking woman, Pierpont? She would have a key. But why would she want to rifle through Li Min's room? What could she suspect?

That she was a spy – a spy for the Chinese government? Deng's silence since their meeting in the cemetery didn't mean he'd gone away, or that he wouldn't pop up at any time now and demand to know what progress she had made in getting to know Sally Washington. But he wouldn't have been searching her room, she was sure of that.

She realised with growing dismay that her friendship with Sally would never be entirely real, however much she wanted it to be. It would always be tainted by her subordination to Deng and to their government, and by their instructions to her to get close to the American girl.

Her thoughts circled back uneasily to her conviction that someone had been through her things. Could it be the Western authorities who suspected her? There had been an unpleasant incident at Harvard in one of the molecular biology labs, where agents from the FBI had come in and taken away a Chinese student in handcuffs. That had been in the previous year; the last she'd heard of him was that he was being held in a federal prison, waiting to come to trial. A frisson of fear ran through her at the thought that perhaps she was suspected – the woman Pierpont downstairs in the office always acted as if she had done something wrong and had never been friendly. And what if even Sally was working for the Chinese government? That would explain why she had let Li Min make friends with her so easily.

Whoever it was, she wondered if they would come back. She needed to take steps to identify the intruder, and opening her laptop she went onto Amazon, joined Prime with its promise of next-day delivery and found a bewildering range of kit to choose from. Eventually she found exactly what she needed. But Amazon scared her slightly, since her purchases could be easily traced. So late the following afternoon she took the shuttle bus, got off on Botley Road and went into a hardware shop. She bought the tools she was after and that evening skipped dinner downstairs, making do with a sandwich she'd bought from Tesco. By midnight she'd finished the installation.

Three days later, returning to her room from a day spent in the lab, she felt certain that someone had been in again. There was no smell this time, just a sense of recent disturbance in the usually stuffy atmosphere of the small living space.

She booted up her laptop, then synced it to the camera she had carefully positioned between the books on her bookcase, nowhere near the ceiling as a suspicious person would immediately check there for surveillance.

She scrolled rapidly through the feed recorded that day, but nothing changed in the captured images for the first five hours after her morning departure. Then at 3.15 the door must have opened – though it was out of camera range – and seconds later the image of a tall, well-built man passed by the camera lens. Li Min had turned on the audio capture and listened as the drawers of her dresser were pulled open, though at one point the man paused, as if he had found something of interest. Then he was visible again, going through her clothes in the wardrobe, feeling every inch of fabric for anything secreted there. He turned next to her bed – even checking under the mattress and inside the pillowcases. Finally, the bathroom, where she could hear him pulling back the shower curtain and rattling the mug she used to hold her toothbrush and throwaway razor.

When she heard the door close at last, Li Min exhaled; she had been holding her breath while she watched what had taken place in her room four hours earlier. She was still shocked by what she'd seen. She felt violated, stripped of her dignity and privacy. She would have been absolutely furious, had not she felt so numb – especially when she saw who had done the violating.

It was not the local authorities who were spying on her, not Nina Pierpont or the Fellows of St Felix's or the British police. It was one of her own countrymen. But what exactly was Mr Chew looking for? Almost simultaneously she thought of the letter she had received from Judith Davidson. It was in the drawer of her night table. He must have read it! But after all, there was nothing incriminating about it. Defiantly, for reasons she couldn't really explain to herself, she decided she would answer it, and right away.

16

Charles Abbot wanted to help Manon but he didn't know how. He had not seen her since he'd watched her from afar at High Table, where she'd seemed to be at ease with McCaffrey on one side and holding her own with Arthur Cole on the other. He'd hoped that after dessert she would stay on for coffee and they could exchange a few words, but she had left once the port had gone round twice. He had noticed she was not much of a drinker.

'Judith Davidson' – how he wished he could get to know her better, but in the circumstances that would be difficult. He liked her and told himself there was nothing wrong with that. Gillian too would have liked this woman. His wife had been highly resourceful; had in fact played a small part in an operation Delaney had been conducting in one of the countries where they had all been posted. He was sure Gillian would have wanted him to be friendly as well as helping Manon as much as he could...

Who are you kidding? he asked himself. He recognised that he was lonely, he missed female company and had liked Manon from the moment he'd met her, but since she was involved in an espionage investigation, he realised that he must stand back. His seeing too much of her might jeopardise her impersonation of Judith Davidson. She seemed focused on finding out why Li Min was here, and there was nothing useful he could contribute to that. Jia Hao, moreover, was now thousands of miles away; his letter alone was hardly enough evidence for anyone to act on.

Except perhaps for its mention of the mysterious Mr Chew. Abbot had looked him up in the Elm's directory of students and realised he had seen him in college. How could you miss him? He was enormous – six foot six at least, and heavily built; he must weigh eighteen stone, and none of it seemed to be fat. Young Mr Chew stood out – he would have done so anywhere, except perhaps in the scrum of the Oxford rugby team. It was hard to picture him with his head in his books, being genuinely interested in, say, the reign of Richard II. The guy seemed better suited to life as a hired thug, and certainly looked the part. Abbot had never seen him smile.

He looked up Chew's file. He was reading for an MLitt and was in his second year. He would have had to submit an extensive sample of written work at the end of the first year, and Abbot looked that up as well, curious to find out what topic he had chosen. To his surprise, he saw that Chew hadn't submitted anything; technically, therefore, he remained a probationary student, and had been granted a deferral of two terms before submitting any written work. Looking further back, he saw that Chew had been ill – with some unspecified ailment. There was a doctor's note supporting his application for a postponement, but when Abbot looked at the scanned document, he saw it didn't come from a local surgery but from a doctor attached to the Chinese Embassy in London. Was that really acceptable? It shouldn't have been in Abbot's view.

Also in the file there was a brief note from Arthur Cole, simply stating that he supported granting a deferral; he didn't say why, seeming to assume a simple endorsement from him would suffice. And finally, Chew's supervisor, Ian McCaffrey, had written at some length in his support, citing the calibre of his research and expressing confidence that once his health had been restored, he would submit written work of high quality. McCaffrey was nobody's fool, and certainly not inclined to favour the Chinese, so Abbot's scepticism eased a bit. Until he looked further at the file. There were seminars held each week for first-year graduate students throughout the year; attendance was mandatory. No formal marks were assigned for student contributions in the seminars; just a note from the Chairman of Faculty, someone named Bailey, confirming attendance. In Chew's case, however, there was no such confirmation, only a note in green ink that read: NA. Not applicable? Or No Attendance? Abbot wanted to find out.

Weird... it all seemed weird. A Chinese student studying medieval England was unusual enough, though that was no justification for outright suspicion. Failure to submit written work was serious, especially if explained on the grounds of illness – when the student was up and about and more than healthy-looking. The more Abbot pondered this, the more he wondered about Chew's academic attainments and true reason for being in Oxford.

At lunch he made a point of timing his departure to coincide with Ian McCaffrey's. He didn't know the man well – who did he know well in college? – but he had been among the friendlier of the dons when Abbot had arrived.

McCaffrey was wearing a green tweed jacket and a jolly red tie. He turned as Abbot followed him out of the SCR. 'I like that young lassie you have visiting. She's good fun. I hear she's a high-powered librarian. What's she here to do?'

'I met her at a conference in the States. She's actually on a sabbatical in Britain, but she's agreed to spend time helping me sort out the papers connected with the founding of the Institute and other things. Currently they're in a frightful mess, and nobody knows where anything is.'

'You old rogue, how did you persuade her to do that?'

Abbot tried not to show irritation at this and merely said, 'She was eager to spend some time in an Oxford college.'

'Pity she's not staying longer. I had an extremely invigorating time with her at the Guest Night dinner last week, all thanks to Arthur Cole. Rude old sod… he had his back turned to her for two courses. I felt it only polite to fill the gap for our new arrival,' McCaffrey said with a smile, then frowned. 'I hope Cole's not making your job a misery.'

'I don't see much of him.'

'Ah, good. Best to leave him to his pots. Our resident Sinophile.'

They were in the quad now, walking past the flower boxes, which now held tulips starting to open in the spring sun. Abbot said casually, 'Speaking of the Chinese, I had a question.'

'For me? Go ahead.'

'You're supervising a student from China, a Mr Chew.'

'That's right,' said McCaffrey. He seemed amused.

'I was intrigued. Are there many Chinese students of English Medieval History?'

'Not that I know of,' said McCaffrey. 'It takes all kinds, I guess.'

'I notice he didn't submit work for the graduate transfer.'

'No,' said McCaffrey, who suddenly seemed more alert. 'He was ill.'

'I see. Is he better now?'

'Decidedly so. Have you seen the man? He's a great big bruiser and a picture of health, I'd say.'

'He got an extension, yes?'

'He did. Arthur and I wrote on his behalf; that seemed to do the trick.'

'Do you think he'll take his degree?'

McCaffrey stopped walking. 'I can't swear to it, of course, but I retain a resolute optimism.' When Abbot looked him searchingly in the eye, he shrugged, like a small boy caught taking change from his mother's purse. 'Resolute, but possibly not realistic. Look,' he said a little impatiently, 'your scepticism is not unwarranted, but consider things from my point of view. The Chinese offered to pay for two full scholarships for graduate Medieval Studies – and I mean full, from day one of the MA all the way through the DPhil. This, moreover, in a field in which the Chinese are not conceivably planning to specialise, or *from* which they will learn much of value in their Xi-run society. And all they suggested in return – and I stress it was suggested, not demanded – was that we look favourably on the application of young Mr Chew. Who, I need not remind you, is paying the full whack of our extortionate fees for foreign graduate students. Will he get a degree? you ask. Sure, and fish will fly out of the Bodleian. But you know what they say about gift horses.'

'Yes,' said Abbot, impressed by McCaffrey's candour but not entirely surprised. 'They say that even when they added the pair of wings, Pegasus never got off the ground.'

17

There was something he didn't like about this new visitor to the Institute, Judith Davidson. Never keen on Americans, and not at his happiest in the company of women, Arthur Cole had found a double dose of antipathy difficult to stomach.

He had tried to be polite but inwardly cursed the seating plan that had put her next to him at High Table. She'd spouted the usual claptrap about the Chinese, but it was puzzling to him why she'd chosen China as the main topic of their admittedly limited conversation. She had once been a government librarian, so what was this all about?

Well, she would be gone before too long, so best to keep his distance in the meantime. She had seemed too interested by half in the Chinese portion of the student body, and doubtless would in time turn her attention to the Institute. And there were certain aspects, now historical, of the funding of the Institute he was not keen to be widely known. Abbot as Director might discover most of them in time, but he was self-confessedly bad with finance, and the Institute's accountant was a retired bookkeeper named Hills, who worked part-time, never rocked the boat and still came to Cole if anything tricky arose.

He got up and stood by his window overlooking the main quad of the college. He was dressed in a Harris tweed jacket, a sleeveless jumper, flannel trousers and a bow tie; by his standards this was casual, but he liked the warmth. He thought about how best to spend this last part of the day, and was considering a visit to the college library, where soon an exhibition of his best pieces would go on display, when there was a knock on his door. Three sharp knocks in fact, which irritated him. He thought fleetingly of ignoring the interruption, but told himself that whoever was there would just come back at an even less convenient time. 'Come in,' he called out crossly.

The door opened and Cole was confronted by an enormous man, tall and broad and quite frightening as he stood looming in the doorway. Then he recognised the figure; it was the Chinese student Chew, known in college as Mr Chew for reasons Cole neither knew nor cared about – to him Chew was a student, and thus in Cole's old-fashioned way didn't warrant the prefix 'Mr'.

'Ah, Chew,' he said, relaxed now that this monster-sized man turned out to be familiar. 'Were you wishing to see me?'

'Please,' said Chew simply. Cole remembered from their first meeting that Chew's English was not his forte; put frankly, it was substandard for someone supposedly doing graduate work in a field where language expertise was required. How did McCaffrey cope with him? Cole wondered.

'Come in,' he said, and Chew slowly entered. Cole pointed to one of the two armchairs and sat in the other one. As Chew sat down the chair seemed to disappear under his bulk, leaving only the arms visible.

'Now what is the problem?' asked Cole, enunciating each word carefully. 'Is it about your extension? I understand that it's been granted.'

'Not that,' said Chew.

'What else then? Are you having trouble with the sample of your work? Dr McCaffrey hasn't said anything to me.'

'My work is fine,' said Chew curtly, which Cole was pretty sure was a great big fib. Chew went on, 'I am assigned by the Embassy to do a task.'

'Oh, what is that?'

'They have instructed me to look after a new student, who has come from Harvard.'

'Is that Li Min?' Cole had only met her once, quite briefly, here in his room. She'd seemed competent enough, and doubtless intelligent, but he was surprised by the fuss made of her by the resident computer scientist. There had seemed nothing obviously extraordinary about the diminutive young woman he had spoken with in Mandarin. Though her English, when she insisted on switching to it, had turned out to be flawless.

'Correct.'

'I'm sure she will be grateful for any help you can give her. It can be very lonely for some students here.'

'Maybe,' said Chew, pronouncing both syllables with equal stress. 'But I am concerned.'

'Why?'

'She is not communicating so much with other Chinese students. And lately she has received a proposal to meet, from someone we are not sure is a suitable acquaintance.'

'Who is that?' asked Cole. This was sounding increasingly peculiar.

'A visitor named Davidson.'

'The American librarian?' Cole said. 'She knows Li Min?'

'She *wants* to know Li Min,' amended Chew.

'How do you know this?'

'She wrote a letter.'

'And Li Min showed you it?' asked Cole, genuinely curious. 'I have seen the letter.'

Cole understood at once. Chew had seen the letter without Li Min's permission. The man had been snooping. Ordinarily Cole would have been furious, and would have reprimanded any student for looking through the personal belongings of a peer. Not at all the way to behave.

But the Chinese were different. Their government took pains to protect their young people here with methods the West would not tolerate and did not understand. But Cole could and did understand them. The officials of the People's Republic had perfectly natural worries that their students would fall prey to Western influences that no one – certainly not Cole – could seriously defend. Sexual misconduct, drug-taking, 'rap' – Cole wasn't sure which was the worst, so he disapproved of them all equally.

And if in defending their students from these things, the Chinese officials overstepped the mark in Western eyes, so be it. Compared to Chinese generosity, the strength of their ancient culture, these infractions were mere bagatelles, ones Cole was happy to ignore. So he didn't press Chew on how he had come to see this letter. Unfortunately, Chew was equally unforthcoming when Cole asked him why he thought Miss Davidson posed any kind of threat. It was as if the mere act of writing to a Chinese girl was anathema, or perhaps it was that Li Min had been singled out for special protection by the Chinese Embassy in London. If that were the case, Cole didn't understand why, but decided he did not need to find out. Where he could help, he supposed, was in exploring the bona fides of Miss Davidson. In which case he had better put aside his mild animus, he decided as Chew left, and get to know the woman.

18

BACK FROM LONDON, WHERE she had reported to Saunders on her admitted lack of progress, Manon stopped in the Porters' Lodge to collect her post.

There was one sealed envelope which she opened, standing in the Lodge out of the sun. She saw at once it was from Li Min and read:

> *Dear Judith,*
> *Thank you for your note. It would be very nice to meet. Would you be free later this week – perhaps Thursday towards the end of the day? Six o'clock? I could meet you at the Varsity Club in the Covered Market – I am told it has excellent views from the terrace at the top. Let me know, please, and I look forward to meeting you then.*
> *Yours sincerely*
> *Li Min*

Bingo, thought Manon, carefully putting the letter back into its envelope and then her bag.

Li Min had given her email address, which Manon replied to, saying yes to the invitation. On Thursday morning she did a recce of the Covered Market, and after fruitless searching of the shops and stalls, at last found the entrance to the Varsity Club tucked away in one of the little alleys leading to the adjacent High Street. Despite its name, the Varsity was clearly not a members' club but a cocktail bar.

On Thursday afternoon Charles Abbot was still in London, and Manon spent the afternoon at home in North Oxford, enjoying the summery warmth that a high-pressure front had brought to the UK. There was a shed at the end of the little garden behind her flat, and she found a deckchair in it that she opened up and set down on the patio outside the kitchen. Sitting there in the sun, with her work notebook and a pen in her hand, she thought about the previous occasion she had worked in Oxford.

On that occasion too she had been required to recruit an agent, a Russian girl. The operation had been successful and, considering that at the time she'd had no training, remarkably successful. She hadn't suffered from nerves then because she had no experience of an operation going wrong – in fact, she had had no prior experience at all. Now, things were different. Would she be as successful this time? she wondered. Let's hope so, she thought, but she couldn't help feeling nervous. All the preparation only made her more aware of the possibility of failure.

Saunders was right in thinking that Li Min was a contact worth developing. Why would she have come here on her government's orders unless it were to do something for that government – or, more likely, find out something? Her masters were ruthless, this Manon knew; they would not have ordered Li Min here because it was good for her health. What could it be then? Manon wondered. Presumably something to do with deepfakes since that was Li Min's area of expertise. But what were they faking? Would it involve a specific individual – a person the Chinese would use as the object of their fakery? Who could that be? It was hard to imagine a target of value among the students at St Felix's or its Institute. And what use to the People's Republic would one of the Fellows be?

Only Li Min would know who was involved, which meant she was the one Manon must focus on, especially since the only other source – Jia Hao – was now somewhere back in China, presumably unwillingly returned and unreachable.

She remembered the point made by one of the instructors who had been schooling her group in the intricacies of agent recruitment. He had explained that there was no detailed guide on how to recruit and run an agent. To a great extent it depended on instinct and natural curiosity. He'd said, 'You want to know what the target knows, but to find that out you need to establish a personal relationship. You need to make them like you and trust you, and to do that you need to care about them.' Manon didn't have the faintest idea what Li Min was like or could be up to, but she was determined to find out.

19

As term proceeded, Li Min noticed that her fellow students in the lab, initially so friendly, were starting to avoid her. She thought at first that this was because she was new to the lab, and the first year's postgraduates had already made their friends. But as term went on, she realised that her fellow First Years were avoiding her too. At the college drinks party for students, including the Institute's new arrivals that year, she had found herself alone for much of the time, though the Institute Director Charles Abbot had noticed this and brought her over to meet a few of the Fellows. Despite this, the students seemed happy to keep their distance.

Li Min wondered if it had something to do with her being Chinese – since there was more than enough suspicion of her country in the West these days. But whatever initial prejudice she had encountered in the past, she had always overcome it. She had a friendly open manner, spoke excellent English and perhaps most important of all, never showed undue interest in other people's work or asked too many questions. Once at a party in Harvard a grad student had told her, after he'd had one too many beers, that no one could ever think she was a spy for the Chinese government, since she wasn't interested at all in what her fellow students were doing.

Though she was always willing to help her fellow students if they asked her, it was true that Li Min was very caught up in her own projects, and gradually she understood that it was her work that was distancing her from her peers. It had begun with the audio simulation, and the trigger had been Alicia, the girl who had read for Li Min but then objected so strenuously when she listened to the simulated result.

What had upset her so much? Li Min really couldn't understand it. Alicia's fright at hearing 'herself' speak words she had never actually put together seemed exaggerated. But it had certainly infected the other students in the lab and turned them even more against Li Min, especially after the lab manager had stepped in, forbidding her to use any of them as guinea pigs. That could not have come at a worse time. Li Min was on the edge of a breakthrough where she would be able seamlessly to combine automatically generated video and audio with footage taken from real life. But without a supply of raw material, she couldn't move forward. And as each day passed without any prospect of acquiring it, her frustration grew.

She could ask for volunteers from students not working in the lab, but she had little hope of recruiting suitable candidates, considering that it was unpaid, boring work that required three hours minimum of reading or just sitting there while being filmed. If only she had been living in college, Li Min might have made friends by now who would have helped. The Elm wouldn't do since it was so predominantly Chinese; she wanted Westerners to contribute the audio and sit for the video, since if she only had Chinese subjects, even if they spoke good English, she was worried her work would not get the attention it deserved here in the West.

And then a solution came to her, and she could have kicked herself for not thinking of it before: Sally Washington. She might be willing, especially if they did it in brief segments instead of a three-hour session. It was a sign of her confidence in their new closeness that she felt able to approach Sally that evening after dinner. And Sally had got it at once. 'Sure, I'll do it,' she said breezily. 'But promise me one thing.'

'What's that?' said Li Min, suddenly worried for the first time.

'That when you're famous, you'll make me famous too.' When Li Min laughed in relief, Sally said, 'I'm only half-joking. Somebody told Luke the other day that you're a genius.'

'I wish.'

'We'll see. Now when do you want to start? You're going to have to tell me what to do, you know. I'm not stupid, but they never told me I'd be working with an Einstein.'

20

The sun was still above the horizon as Manon left college a few minutes before six o'clock. It would not be dark for at least two more hours, she thought, but the warmth of the afternoon was gradually subsiding. She wore summery cotton trousers but was glad she'd thought to put on a sweater over her blouse.

She walked down the Turl, a thin medieval street with colleges and a small row of shops – including a second-hand bookshop, a café, an off licence and a vendor of bibelots and vintage jewellery. Narrowing by the side of a former church, now converted into a college library, the Turl ran smack into the High, the wide avenue that ran downhill from the centre of the city for half a mile to Magdalen College and the river. Manon waited for a trio of buses to pass, then crossed the High quickly, going straight into a small lane that ran off the other side of the much larger street, down towards the back of Christ Church and the cobbles of Merton Street. She had only gone forty feet or so when she stopped, waited for a few moments, then returned to the High. No one had crossed right behind her, she noted, and crossed back, reversing her route with growing confidence she wasn't being followed.

She entered the Covered Market through a passage at its western end. Before going into the corridors of the market itself, Manon stopped and opened a door, the entrance to the Varsity Club. She walked up the stairs to the bar on the first floor. The room was almost empty and Manon stood there for a moment until she was sure that no one had come in downstairs after her. Then she kept going, up to the roof terrace.

There were more people here, sitting at the tables, a mix of students and older-looking tourists, mostly couples or small groups. But there was one woman sitting on her own, next to the railings. From her photograph in the College admin files Abbot had given her access to, Manon knew this was Li Min. She looked lost in thought as she stared out at the view: the towering spire of St Mary's, the University church; the squat bulk of the Radcliffe Camera behind it; and to one side the pointed Hawksmoor tower of All Souls College. The view of this architectural tableau was unimpeded and made especially dramatic by the proximity of its landmarks.

'Li Min,' Manon said gently, reluctant to break the spell as she approached the table.

She looked up at Manon, startled, then got to her feet. She was short but trim and attractive, with a pretty face. 'You must be Judith,' she said, extending her hand. She wore a dark blue slicker and jeans with trainers – student uniform, thought Manon.

They shook hands, and Manon sat down on an adjacent side of the little table so they could both enjoy the view. 'This is amazing,' she said.

Li Min nodded. 'It must have sounded funny when I said the Varsity Club. It's really just a cocktail bar.'

'But a cocktail bar with a difference,' Manon said, gesturing again at the view. A waitress came and gave them menus, which turned out to be lists of beverages rather than food. Manon wondered if they did decent coffee here. She put down the menu, saying, 'Our mutual friend Louise asked me to send you her warm regards.'

'How nice of her. We only met one time but I enjoyed our conversation.'

'I know she did too.' Manon paused a beat, then said, 'But how are you finding Oxford?'

The young woman shrugged. 'It's different, I have to say that.'

'Not what you expected then?'

'I didn't know what to expect. I—'

She stopped, and Manon realised that if she went on Li Min would have to confess that her arrival here had not been her own decision. It was important not to try and move too fast, so Manon said, 'I like St Felix's, but I'm not living there, alas. How about you?'

Li Min explained she was living outside town in the Elm. She did not sound enthused about it. Manon said, 'Well, I envy you the company. It gets a bit lonely living on my own. And if you're doing a DPhil, you're going to be here a while, yes? Maybe next year you can move into college. I know some graduate students get rooms.'

'Maybe,' said Li Min, but she sounded sceptical.

She then asked Manon why she'd come to St Felix's. By now, Manon had it down pat – how she'd liked Oxford since briefly studying there; how she'd wanted a break from her own librarian job in the States, since she wasn't sure, to be frank, whether she was really cut out for it as a lifelong career. How during a visit a few months before she had met Charles Abbot, coinciding with his wanting to help sort out the Institute's archives. The two of them had just clicked – and, lo and behold, here she was, still getting her feet wet but enjoying it very much.

It was important to sound upbeat, Manon told herself, since by contrast it helped to magnify the target's own dissatisfaction. What had that same instructor said? *Once they're yours you want them happy. But it's misery that will make them yours.*

When the waitress came, Manon was going to order a cappuccino but let Li Min order first. 'I'd like a Margarita, please,' she said.

Wow, thought Manon, who had not expected her to drink. Because she was Chinese? Manon was starting to realise her preconceptions were often proving to be wrong. She said, 'I'll join you. Make it two Margaritas, please.' When the waitress went away, Manon said firmly, 'This is my shout.'

'Shout?' asked Li Min, puzzled.

'I mean, my treat,' Manon said, and as Li Min started to shake her head, added, 'I insist. You're my guest. After all, I invited you.'

'That's very kind,' said Li Min, and Manon realised she was probably on tight rations with her government grant. Though not tight enough to keep her from ordering an expensive cocktail.

They continued making polite small talk for a while, but when Manon asked her about her work, Li Min grew more expansive – she not only worked in AI, she was happy to proselytise about its manifold benefits, especially in medical contexts where it could accelerate both diagnosis and treatment, reduce waiting lists, and thus, in serious cases, save lives. Her work undetectably mimicking people's voices and even their appearance struck Manon as full of potential dangers, though Li Min clearly didn't think so, and the last thing Manon wanted to do was throw a dampener on the woman's zeal. She nodded occasionally as she tried hard to follow Li Min's rapid talk of data sets and analytics. Manon didn't understand it all, particularly the details of the analytics, but she certainly got the gist, and felt even more alarmed.

Their cocktails came, the glasses frosty from the freezer and rimmed with salt. As they sipped their drinks, Li Min said, sounding a little embarrassed, 'I didn't mean to go on so much about my work.'

'Don't be silly – I find it very interesting. And it's good to see you care so much about it. Not all the students do, I can tell you.'

'I know. My friend Sally says a lot of them just want to be able to say they've been to Oxford. They don't care about their work at all. Sally says: work hard *then* play hard.'

'Ha,' said Manon with a little laugh. 'That's fine so long as you get the order right. But who is Sally?'

'You don't know Sally? She is very popular.'

'I'm new. I haven't met everyone yet.'

'You'd like her, I am sure.'

'Maybe you can introduce us then. We could all have Margaritas together.' Li Min smiled. 'Where is she from?' Manon asked, wondering if the woman was Chinese and temporarily using a Western first name.

'Washington D.C. Funny, her last name is also Washington. Her father's something in the government.' Manon did not react and Li Min smiled. 'Sally says he is her "doting dad". She says her mother is not the doting type. She's Chinese.' Li Min went on: 'I think Sally would really like to come from California.'

'Oh, why's that?'

'She went to college there and fell in love with the lifestyle, I guess. She certainly looks like a California girl. She's got blonde streaks and light eyes and has a great tan.' Li Min sounded wistful.

'That's the classic California image,' said Manon. Life on the beach had its points, but she knew that after about three hours lying in the all-year-round sun, she would go out of her mind from boredom.

'Tell me something,' said Li Min, taking her hand and lifting up a bunch of her dark hair. She had let it grow long down her back and it was very straight. 'Do you think I'd look good with highlights? A lot of girls had them at Harvard.'

Manon laughed to herself. Li Min was a funny mix. Manon had scrutinised her file in Abbot's office, along with supplementary information about her background that Saunders had provided. Her work was said to be of the highest calibre, conducted at a professional level far more advanced than her youth would suggest – she was only twenty-four but had already published two papers in learned journals. Her references from the professors who'd supervised her were all outstanding. But socially she seemed a little immature, still slightly awkward.

Manon said, 'I think your hair's quite lovely as it is.' When Li Min looked disappointed, Manon quickly asked, 'Does Sally think you should put highlights in?'

'I don't know,' said Li Min, surprised. 'We've never really talked about it. Because of how she looks, people sometimes think Sally's a bit of an airhead, but actually she's very smart. And serious,' she added in case Manon was in danger of becoming one of Sally's detractors. Li Min took a hefty sip of her Margarita and suddenly grinned. 'Except when she's on the tequila.'

They each had a second Margarita (which Manon felt was one too many), then Li Min said she had to catch the bus back to the Elm. Casually asking if she would like to meet again, Manon was pleased by the young woman's quick agreement, and they arranged to meet for lunch the following week. They started to leave together, but on the first floor Manon excused herself, saying she needed the loo. In fact, she wanted to check that Li Min was not being followed.

Manon gave it twenty seconds, then went downstairs and into the Covered Market. Down the aisle she could see Li Min ahead of her moving along, stopping occasionally in front of a storefront to look inside. Though there wasn't much of interest to buy. The market seemed to consist largely of cafés and coffee shops, with the occasional stall selling T-shirts and souvenirs. Li Min stopped now in front of one of the exceptions – a fancy chocolate shop that was open late on Thursday evenings – and then went inside. Manon loitered well short of there, and it was then that she noticed a figure standing outside a key-cutting chain outlet.

It was a Chinese man, tall and well-built, wearing a dark raincoat. He was standing sideways to Manon, his back to the shop Li Min had entered. Why did he look familiar? And was it coincidence that he was here? He was industriously searching his pockets and looking at his watch, as if he had read a guide to conducting surveillance a little too literally. Suddenly Manon realised this must be Mr Chew.

She waited until Li Min came out of the shop and walked, quickly now, towards the exit on Market Street. Mr Chew walked the same way, but not as quickly, and Manon followed them both even more slowly. When she emerged from the market there was no sign of Li Min. But she was just in time to see Mr Chew turning into the Turl, apparently following the woman heading back to catch the shuttle bus for the Elm.

It was all getting too cramped, and Manon didn't want to follow him in case Li Min stopped and they all ran into each other like collapsing dominoes. It would be bad news if he saw that he was being followed, and even worse news if Li Min suspected Manon was tailing her. So Manon spun around and went the other way on Market Street, turning into Cornmarket – pedestrianised in theory, though the cyclists using it could be as lethal as cars.

She walked north towards home, stopping briefly on Magdalen Street by the line of bus stops, wondering if she should take a ride, tired from concentrating so hard on her meeting with Li Min. It seemed the lazy way out so she started walking again, briskly, trying to energise herself, wondering how she could best get Li Min to open up. The woman had said nothing about being forced to come to Oxford, and nothing to indicate any dissatisfaction with the government masters who had sent her here. Manon hadn't felt able to push her, and Li Min had been quite discreet, except when she had opened up about her relationship with Sally Washington. Maybe that was the way in, thought Manon. She would read the other girl's file when she went to the office in college the next day.

She was approaching the small side street where she was living. As she turned into it, she saw that a bus had stopped behind her at the shelter on Woodstock Road. An old woman slowly made her way down its front stairs, and then as the bus pulled away, Manon saw walking from the direction of the town centre a tremendously tall, broad-shouldered man. He was looking straight ahead, then seeing Manon standing on the corner, quickly turned to face the other way.

It was Mr Chew again, still wearing the dark raincoat. She realised now that he hadn't just been following Li Min. He was also following her.

He's trying to find out where I live, she thought. And I'm not going to let him. Looking round, she saw that another bus was coming along on her side of the road. She ran to the next stop further up Woodstock Road as this new bus passed by. Just in time, she reached the bus stop before the driver closed the doors. Breathless, she bought a ticket and sat down as they pulled away. I hope Chew has a long walk home, she thought, trusting he was none the wiser now about where she lived.

21

That Friday, Charles Abbot was disappointed that Manon was not at lunch. He felt he ought to talk to her about Mr Chew. But what was he going to say? He had no real evidence the man was anything but what he said – a postgraduate Chinese student working on English Medieval History. Unlikely, perhaps, but who could be certain?

Abbot might have continued with this optimistic assessment of Mr Chew's bona fides had McCaffrey not sidled up to him as he left the Senior Common Room after lunch. 'Would you have a minute to spare?' he asked.

'Of course,' said Abbot, and gestured to two leather armchairs in a corner, a short distance away from the sofa where the Fellow in Physics sat stolidly reading an issue of *New Scientist*.

'Could we go to your office?' asked McCaffrey quietly. Abbot was surprised. McCaffrey was never usually one for discretion. He could be counted on to relate the details of a fellow faculty member's divorce, juicy bits and all, or the unexpected pregnancy of the Bursar's secretary, at the top of his voice while standing in the middle of the front quad. This must be serious.

'Of course,' Abbot said and led the way. Once in his rooms, he motioned McCaffrey to a chair and seated himself behind his desk. 'Sorry, I can't offer you any refreshment. The party for the new arrivals has cleaned me out. Once they'd drunk the buttery dry, they went through all the bottles I had here. I need to replace them.'

McCaffrey gave a flickering smile then grew serious again. 'You remember the other day: we were discussing one of my students?'

'Mr Chew?'

'That's the one. Glad you remember.'

'Not a name to be easily forgotten.'

McCaffrey didn't react. 'The thing is, you were right to smell a rat as far as his credentials go.'

Abbot said nothing. McCaffrey continued almost wearily, 'By any standards, he has no business being here.'

'Yes, but you made clear the quid pro quo involved,' said Abbot, not unsympathetically since it was clear McCaffrey felt bad about it. And it wasn't any of Abbot's business to judge who was admitted to read History and who was not let in.

'I know, and I'm sure you think it a pretty tawdry kind of bargain. I do myself.'

Again, Abbot said nothing. He didn't want to add to McCaffrey's obvious anxiety about it, but nor could he bring himself to say he approved of the arrangement.

McCaffrey looked at Abbot, his expression a mix of unhappiness and guile. 'I wouldn't do it again, I assure you. I wouldn't want you to think otherwise.'

'I don't, honestly. And I'm sure the scholarships have come in very useful. They're a good thing to have come out of this.'

'There is that. But the thing is, there are some bad things too.'

'Oh?'

McCaffrey was looking to one side of him now, through the window and directly at the chapel tower. 'I should have paid more attention. I just thought it was run-of-the-mill gossip – scuttlebutt they used to call it – inspired by jealousy or something I wasn't privy to.'

Abbot didn't know what McCaffrey was talking about so he just waited.

The History don went on, 'I learned about it at a dinner in June. Of course there's always a dinner after final exams are over, but we have a smaller affair for the graduate students – in History but also English and the other humanities. I was sitting next to a boy called Howser – American but part-Chinese. He had wanted to live at the Elm in order to improve his Mandarin; it wasn't spoken at home – he was from Ohio or someplace like that. Anyway, we were talking and I asked him how he liked living there – it seems a perfectly awful place to me. I mean, it's so far away from college.

'But he said he'd enjoyed it – made friends with lots of the Chinese students and definitely improved his language skills. But as for the pure Chinese, he said they hated it to a man or woman.'

Abbot asked mildly, 'Because it's so far from town?'

'Up to a point. But the real problem, he said, is that the Chinese authorities are scared to death that the students will fall in love with decadent Western ways. That's why they like to house them outside town.'

'I know.' Was this all McCaffrey was here to tell him?

'And that's not all. They watch the students while they're here, very carefully. That was what this boy was really telling me. The Chinese students feel like they're walking on eggshells all the time.'

Abbot said, 'I suppose they're worried other students will report that they are somehow straying from the correct Chinese principles and becoming too Westernised..'

'No, it's more that there are a couple of so-called students whose whole *raison d'être* is to keep tabs on them. They're really security professionals – army or intelligence, it's not clear which.'

'Including Mr Chew?'

'I think it's probably safe to assume that. From what this Chinese-American lad said, it's pretty intensive surveillance we're talking about. Hacking into email accounts, checking mobiles for who they're ringing, even going into their rooms and searching them.'

'Not everyone, surely?'

'No, but those they suspect of enjoying life in the West more than they should.'

'It must be difficult to operate like that. This isn't China. Our authorities would not be best pleased to know this coercion is going on.'

'Agreed, but it happens just the same. It's said that the Chinese even have a couple of "police stations" they're running in London. And when they need to, they can sometimes secure the cooperation of English people.'

'To do what?'

'Help them with their surveillance – you know, report on people's comings and goings, that sort of thing. Lend them keys.'

'Who are these English helpers?'

'I don't know,' said McCaffrey.

'This is appalling,' said Abbot.

'It is,' said McCaffrey unhappily. 'And in the case of Mr Chew, I can only blame myself. I wanted to tell you that,' he said, still not looking directly at Abbot, who could see how much this admission pained the man. 'And I wanted to say that if there's anything I can do to help with this situation, then please let me know. If I sound guilty about this, it's because I feel guilty.'

22

There were cows on the newly surfaced narrow road that led to the Elm, and further on a small flock of sheep, some of which were still coming out of the dilapidated barn. Abbot remembered Arthur Cole telling him with delight of a group of Chinese newcomers and their excitement on seeing sheep in the flesh for the very first time. It was perhaps the one human exchange Abbot had had with his predecessor.

He passed the remaining livestock and, entering the grounds of the Elm, parked at the front. Inside the main building he went straight to the office on the ground floor. A young woman sat in Nina Pierpont's usual chair, talking on the phone. She hung up when she saw Abbot standing in the doorway.

'Is Ms Pierpont about?' he asked.

'I'm sorry, she's not. She's ill today and staying at home. I'm Amy – can *I* help you?'

'I don't think so. I'd better come back when Nina's feeling better.'

'Shall I tell her you want to see her? I'm sure she'll be in touch when she's back.'

It seemed a good idea. 'Yes, please.' He told the girl his name and her eyes widened. 'I could ring her now, sir, if you would like?' she said.

But he shook his head. 'It's nothing urgent.' Then he thought of something. 'Do you happen to know where she lives?'

'I don't, but if you hang on a second, I'll just look it up.' Amy worked her keyboard and stared at the terminal on her desk. 'She's in North Oxford. I'm afraid I can't be more specific than that. Data Protection, you know. But I hope that helps.'

'It does. But tell me, is that a database of addresses?' he asked. He knew of nothing like it in the Institute's main office.

'Yes.'

'And phone numbers?'

She nodded.

'Everybody's?'

'Everybody in the Institute,' she said.

'Really? Is that available to anyone who's a member of St Felix's?'

'I don't think so,' she replied. 'Like I said, Data Protection means I can't give out the actual address. Or phone numbers.'

He was thinking on his feet, following his instincts. 'Could you look up somebody's address for me then? I know you can't give it to me; I just want to know if it's there.'

She thought about this for a moment. 'I can't see it doing any harm. What's the name?'

'Judith Davidson.' If there were a database that for some reason he hadn't been told about, he wondered whether Manon's details would be in it – considering her recent arrival.

The answer turned out to be no. 'There's no address or phone number,' said Amy. 'Her name's there, but that's all – not even an email address. It just has question marks in those fields.'

'That's all right,' he said slowly, feeling stunned.

Inexplicably, Amy was grinning. 'Sorry,' she said, 'but it's funny. You're the second person to ask for her address today.'

'I am?'

'Yes. A student asked me just an hour ago.'

'Do you know their name?'

'It was a Chinese student. Mr Chew.'

'You're certain about that?'

'Of course. Even I know Mr Chew. He's pretty hard to miss, he's such a giant.'

Mr Chew again. Abbot nodded. 'What a funny coincidence,' he said, and Amy's smile widened. 'Tell me something: what happens when a student loses the key to their room? Do they come here?'

'Yes. There's a set of duplicate key Nina has.'

'There?' he asked, pointing at the desk.

'Yes, but the drawer's locked. You need a key to get to the key,' she said with a smile.

'Do you have it, this key to the key?'

'I don't actually. It's with Nina. She hands it over when she takes a day off and for the weekends. But I guess she didn't know she'd be ill today.'

'So what happens if somebody loses their key today?'

Amy shrugged. 'I don't know. Maybe Maintenance keeps spares. But otherwise, if somebody lost their key right now, then I guess they'd have to go to her house and collect the master from Nina. I don't have the key to the key.'

Abbot thanked Amy for her help and left the building. Halfway along the track back to the main road, he stopped to wait for the last of the flock of sheep crossing the road. He didn't mind the delay, still trying to sort out the puzzle he'd unearthed. How had Mr Chew got into student rooms without a key? The answer seemed to be that he hadn't; he would have had use of the master key. But how had he got that when it was kept under lock and key in Nina Pierpont's office? There seemed no other answer, he thought, as the sheep finally cleared and he drove on.

Nina Pierpont had given it to him.

23

That afternoon after lunch, Li Min caught the train from Oxford to Marylebone Station. It took longer than the trains to Paddington, but on arrival she would be within walking distance of her destination. She'd taken a raincoat with her as a precaution, since the sky was a threatening monochrome grey.

It was Li Min's first visit to Central London. Normally she would have felt excited by the prospect of seeing the capital city for the first time, and she would have enjoyed the journey – trains here seemed smarter and more reliable than those in America.

Deng had texted her mobile number the night before, using a burner phone as he always did for these meetings. She liked to speculate that there was a huge incinerator in the Chinese Embassy where people like Deng threw in their burner phones at the end of each day. When she rang him back, he was terse even by his standards, summoning her the next day without any explanation. He had texted instructions once she'd rung off, and they were clear enough.

On arrival, Li Min left the station through its front entrance and walked south to Marylebone Road, where she found a mix of pedestrian-packed pavements and a broad avenue full of speeding cars. She turned left and walked east along the north side of this road, passing a long queue of people waiting to enter something called Madame Tussauds. Who was she? A palm reader perhaps, or some supposed clairvoyant? Or was it a theatre, named for some actress? Li Min was curious but didn't have time to find out – there were only a few minutes to spare before her meeting. Maybe Sally would know; she would ask her at dinner that night.

After a few minutes, Li Min saw a green expanse of grass ahead on her left, and from Google Maps she recognised it as Regent's Park. She waited patiently at the lights, then crossed to the south side of the road, heading towards the sign for an Underground station. Next to it, a black railing ran in both directions, cordoning off a little square that was largely shielded from view by the trees and bushes planted inside.

At the square's far end, she turned right onto Park Crescent, and passed a small corner house next to a gate. The gate usually required a code to be entered on a keypad but had today been left ajar; Deng must have seen to that. Pushing open the gate, Li Min entered and walked along a path of packed gravel. She spied the bench mentioned in Deng's directions and went to sit on it, shielded from the road by trees in the upper corner of the square. There was a constant noise of cars from behind her, but otherwise it was a peaceful spot, and there was no one else in this part of the park.

Then she saw Deng, walking casually in her direction, wearing his usual black suit. He didn't look at Li Min, but when he drew near, he suddenly went straight where the path turned and came and sat down beside her. He was intimidatingly close; Li Min could smell his breath, which was starchy and sweet.

'You are on time,' he announced, which annoyed her. She was always punctual for these meetings, however much she disliked them. Almost as much, she realised, as she now disliked Deng.

'I followed your directions. Does this park belong to the Embassy?'

'No,' said Deng. 'It belongs to local residents. We pay a small subscription for its use.'

'It seems very private,' said Li Min.

Deng did not reply; he looked impatient to get past any small talk. 'Oxford,' he suddenly announced. 'You are now established at Oxford?'

Did he mean had she settled in? She supposed so, and nodded. 'Have you brought your report?' he asked.

'Of course,' she said, and reached in her bag for the print-out of pages. She handed it to Deng, who folded it and tucked it into his inner jacket pocket.

'I am making considerable progress,' Li Min said sharply. If Deng wasn't concerned about her work, then why had he forced her to come to this country?

'First things first. Are you now acquainted with Miss Washington?'

'More than acquainted. We are friends.'

'Excellent.' Deng seemed to have second thoughts about this praise. He was a worrier, Li Min thought with contempt. He said, 'She would consider you a friend in return?'

'It is a mutual friendship,' Li Min said, her voice level and cool. 'She has even helped me with my work.' Just the night before, Sally had spoken impromptu and unrehearsed to camera for forty-five minutes in Li Min's room. She had given a long and hilarious account of that American staple – the summer camp. A counsellor in his early twenties had taken a shine to Sally when she was just thirteen and not yet interested in boys. Sally had recounted her methods for first evading and then tormenting this inappropriate suitor, and Li Min had laughed until her stomach ached. It ended with the pervy counsellor stranded on a small island in a large New Hampshire lake, while Sally ignored his shouts and calmly canoed back to the camp.

Not that she would tell Deng any of this. She said curtly instead, 'Her assistance is detailed in my report.'

Deng took the pages from his pocket without any indication that he had been too hasty in stowing them away. Li Min sat repressing her disdain for this man while he read her words.

She had split her account into two. The first half outlined technical aspects of her work, most recently her design of a prototype for AI-generated video and audio simulations of people from real life. Deng skimmed this quickly since he wouldn't understand any of the detail. Presumably AI experts in Beijing would examine it once he'd sent it back.

The second half, which she had intentionally kept to a bare-bones account, simply stated that she had made contact with the subject (Sally W) and now saw her frequently. Li Min ended by saying she awaited further specific guidance as to how she should progress the relationship. She had not written that they were friends, and now regretted telling this to Deng. She had been boasting, she realised. She didn't think he would have any friends. Certainly no Westerner in his right mind would want to be friends with Deng. His English wasn't good enough for a start, and there was nothing winning about his personality.

'Finished reading,' Deng said abruptly. 'Tell me about Miss Washington, please. You give a very brief account of her here.' He waved the pages like a fan.

'There's not much to tell. I see her most nights at dinner.'

'With others present?'

'Yes.' This was true enough: the little group of Americans ate together every evening. Li Min was the only outsider to join them. There was something about Deng's interest now that she not only didn't understand but found threatening. Not threatening to herself, but to her friend Sally. What was this interest in her about?

She decided to ask. 'Why was I told to become friends with Sally Washington?'

Deng hesitated. This was a new, more forthright woman he was dealing with, he seemed to think, and he did not like it. 'We want a simulated film of an American female. It is important she be American, not English. I will soon come to Oxford and instruct you in what this film should show. You have said yourself you can no longer enlist people in your lab, whatever their nationality. This woman will do nicely for our purposes.'

'What purposes are these?' Li Min asked. She sounded suspicious, she knew, but she had reason to be. Deng was never straightforward. You could always guess at his agenda, but even if you were right, he would deny it and concoct some implausible alternative. It was like working with jelly.

She only hoped it was pure coincidence that she was already using Sally Washington as the guinea pig for her artificial video constructions. Sally normally would have told half the world that Li Min was filming her – she was the kind of person who let everyone in on her day-to-day life. But she'd understood when Li Min explained that she was not allowed to use her fellow students in the lab since Alicia had made such a fuss, and that she didn't want to risk a repetition of that. Fortunately, Sally had taken this seriously and earnestly swore not to tell anyone how she was helping Li Min.

Deng said now, 'The purposes will be clear in time.'

'You always say that,' Li Min cried out, exasperated. Deng sat up straight on the bench, taken aback by this outburst. But Li Min was tired of his obfuscating. She went on, 'This girl is not harming anyone, and certainly not China. Otherwise she would not have become my friend. But I tell you this: if you have even the remotest idea that she would spy on our behalf, spy for China, you are completely mistaken.'

Deng seemed unperturbed by this, worryingly so to Li Min. 'Whatever she does,' he said slowly, 'its consequence will not be known to her.' He turned to look directly into Li Min's eyes. 'Not unless you tell her.'

Li Min did her best not to blush. 'I will do nothing to hurt my friend.'

'I am not asking you to hurt your friend. I am telling you to help your country.'

Li Min shook her head. She returned Deng's gaze, saying, 'And if I refuse to cooperate?'

'What do you mean?' He looked surprised.

'If I will not do as you ask – film Sally in the manner you want – what will happen then?'

Deng picked up his mobile from the bench and spoke quickly, saying only, 'Now, please.'

Puzzled, Li Min looked at him questioningly, but Deng ignored her and stared along the path towards the middle of the park. Turning her head, Li Min saw why: two men, both Chinese, had emerged from behind a stand of trees and stood uncertainly about fifty feet away on the path. Young and strong-looking, they wore black T-shirts and dark loose trousers. They were waiting for Deng's signal.

'Are those your thugs?' Li Min demanded.

'That is no way to speak of two servants of the People's Republic,' Deng snapped. 'If you continue your disobedience, they will take you to the Embassy. It is nearby. Only two blocks away, as the Americans say.'

'What if I don't want to go there?'

'I have heard enough about what you want. They will take you there if I tell them to, regardless of your wishes.'

'And then what?'

'You will be returned to the homeland.'

She scoffed. 'What, are you going to smuggle me out in a diplomatic bag?'

'That will not be necessary,' said Deng, literal-minded as always. 'A doctor is waiting at the Embassy. If you persist in this refusal, he has authorisation to give you an injection. Those two,' he said, nodding towards the waiting thugs, 'will be available to assist if necessary. After that, the next thing you know you will be landing in Beijing on a private airplane.'

'You can't kidnap me in broad daylight and send me there against my will.'

He looked at her; they both knew she was wrong. 'We have done it before,' he said. He added meaningfully, 'Quite recently in fact.' Deng went on, 'I would prefer not to, I assure you. I would much rather you saw sense and did as I say. It will help our country – and it will help you to finish your studies. I know that great things have been expected of you, so do not spurn us when we ask for a little assistance from time to time.'

Li Min sat still, trying to think carefully while subduing her sense of outrage, not trusting herself to speak right away. Here again was the threat of a forced return to China, the end of her career, the termination of the work she loved so much and of all her hopes. Perhaps using Sally would prove to be as innocent as Deng suggested; perhaps her friend would never know how she had been compromised, made into an invisible pawn in some larger game.

She knew she was kidding herself. Deng meant her friend no good. He might not be intending to harm Sally physically but he had something unpleasant in mind for her. Whatever it was, he needed Li Min's assistance to accomplish it. She didn't know what they were intending to do with Sally, but whatever it was, it seemed they couldn't do it without her help. There was no point in resisting at this stage, but she was determined to thwart them and now knew the best route by which to do so.

'I need your response,' Deng said abruptly, interrupting Li Min's back-and-forth internal argument. 'We cannot stay here any longer or we will be noticed.'

'Call off your dogs then,' she said, capitulating. Then she added in tones of weary resignation: 'I will do whatever you want.'

24

The library of St Felix's was a remodelled chapel that had been converted to secular use in the 1960s. Inside it, a room had been set aside for exhibitions, and it was here that Arthur Cole found Judith Davidson, on time and ready for him to show her the display of his Chinese pieces. He didn't really care what this Davidson woman thought about his collection, but proud owner that he was, Cole couldn't help but fuss over the exhibits, and had already looked in during the morning to make sure that all was shipshape.

Davidson had her back to him, examining an explanatory card. He had written them all by hand in his neat italic script rather than having them typed. It gave a personal touch, he thought, but then it was a personal collection.

He was wearing an old sand-coloured corduroy jacket and grey flannels that broke tidily over his brown brogues. She was well dressed in her grey skirt and scarlet blouse under a light leather jacket. He found this woman unsettling. He wasn't quite sure what a junior librarian from the Library of Congress should look like, but somehow he felt it wasn't like this.

Turning round, she saw him and smiled. He did his best to smile back. 'I see you've already begun,' he said.

'Just a quick look,' she said cheerfully. 'I've only just arrived.' She pointed to the case. 'I didn't know the Chinese invented porcelain.' Manon prayed that she was not even half as stupid as she was pretending to be.

Who did she think did – the Eskimos? Trying to hide his irritation, he said, 'People forget what an old culture China has. And how much the Chinese invented – everyone knows about gunpowder but not much else. People talk about the Greeks all the time instead, as if they invented everything from the sun to the moon. A little reading would soon disabuse them. If one ancient civilisation can be said to have laid the groundwork for all that followed, it was the Chinese.'

'I'll remember that next time I have dim sum,' Davidson said lightly.

Cole ignored this but inwardly was made even crosser by the woman's levity. How could any educated person make light of such greatness?

She followed as he went over to a long table holding an array of beautifully wrought pottery and porcelain bowls and plates. He had a standard little speech which he gave her now, pointing out the major differences between the dynasties on show – from Han to Ming and beyond.

Davidson seemed particularly struck by a Sancai-glazed earthenware horse. 'Do you ride?' he asked, since he doubted she understood the artistry behind the work, but felt he had to take note of her obvious admiration for it.

'I did as a girl. But that's not why I like this. The detail is so remarkable. Look at the saddle. I love the lightness of that brown.'

She was right, he thought grudgingly; perhaps she wasn't an absolute dolt after all. She was now looking over at the table in the corner, with its odd array of assorted pieces. 'What are those things over there?' she asked.

'Ah,' he said, walking closer to the table. 'These represent different dynasties, just like the other pieces do. But they also have something else in common.'

He paused until the woman dutifully asked, 'What's that?'

'They're all fakes.'

To his surprise, Davidson laughed, and after a moment he found himself laughing too. 'They could pass as authentic,' he explained. 'And in the past many of them have. Until I came along,' he said proudly.

'You must be a great expert then,' Davidson said.

'That's not for me to say.' Though it was clear he liked hearing this nonetheless.

He took her round the rest of the exhibits then, and after ten minutes had pretty much covered them all.

'It's quite a compact collection, isn't it?'

'You think so?' He was clearly irked. 'Come with me a minute,' he said. Leading her out of the library, he went across the quad to another of the college's original buildings, which was due to be converted to dons' rooms and student bedrooms. He said, 'This used to be the Senior Common Room. Follow me.'

Inside the building, he unlocked a door and led her down one of the staircases, which culminated in a subterranean corridor badly lit by a series of dim lightbulbs. At the far end another door blocked their progress.

'Fear not,' said Cole, 'I have the means of ingress.' He held up a key in his bony fingers, then worked it into a steel-plated door until the lock suddenly turned and the door opened.

'Gosh,' said Davidson, stepping forward as he held the door open for her. 'And what did this use to be?'

'The wine cellar.' Against the far wall, racks extended from floor to ceiling; they would have held thousands of bottles.

'It's not used anymore?'

'Not for several years. We started having moisture problems that even repeated damp-proof coursing couldn't stop. We haven't had any rain recently or else we'd be standing in six inches of water. Even without rain, you can smell the damp,' he said, sniffing.

'Where's all the wine now?'

'Under the Bursar's room.'

'Can't you use this space for something else?'

'It is used, and for something better than wine.' He led her across the anteroom to another door. This one was also locked, but when opened revealed a cavernous room, much drier than its neighbour. Another wall of wine racks could be seen, but only partially for in front of them stood dozens of wooden crates, neatly stacked.

'Is that wine?' Davidson asked, pointing to the crates.

'Hardly.' In them Arthur Cole kept the less valuable odds and ends of his collection. 'There are twice as many pieces stored here as there are on display in the library. But they're not as interesting or as good.'

Davidson made suitable noises to show she was impressed and Cole closed the door. 'If you're at all interested, I can lend you the key. Though it's a bit gloomy down here, I'm afraid.'

She looked unwilling to contest this and merely nodded. Enough, he thought, suddenly impatient to be rid of this woman, who was obviously unimpressed by what had been the work of so many years. He led her out of the anteroom and then the corridor, locking the steel door behind them. When they emerged on the ground floor and went out into the quad, he pointed back towards the cellar and said, 'Now you've seen the collection, warts and all.'

'Thank you very much,' she said. 'I hope this wasn't too inconvenient for you.'

'Not at all,' said Cole, his mood lightened by the prospect of being rid of her. He didn't know why he disliked this woman, or what it was about her that nagged at him. He had known librarians all his professional life, enough of them to know that stereotypes are never uniformly accurate; that some are prettier than others; that it takes all kinds to make a profession. But this woman didn't resemble any librarian he had ever encountered. Why? And how could he discover who she was?

Then something came over him, something impish and – he told himself – harmless. He said, 'If you have any interest in modern China, you'll know the work of a great friend of mine. He's Chinese but went to the States years ago. He teaches at Princeton.'

'Oh, who is that?'

'Zimo Yuhang. He wrote that book about Kissinger's secret trip to China. You may know it.'

'Of course,' said Davidson, who looked slightly uncomfortable. 'It's something of a classic in the field.'

Cole looked at his watch. 'Goodness, we've gone and let time run away with us. I mustn't keep you any longer. But do have another look in the library sometime. And as I say, if you're really keen, I can lend you the key to the store room.'

'That's very kind. I've enjoyed this very much. It's been fascinating.'

I'm sure, thought Arthur Cole sourly as he said goodbye. She might think Zimo Yuhang was a famous Princeton writer on China, but actually it was the name of a young waiter Cole had once befriended in the province of Guizhou.

If, as she claimed, this woman had worked as a librarian in America's most prestigious public library, she would know better than to claim knowledge of an author who didn't exist.

25

On Monday morning, following his visit to the Elm, charles Abbot was late arriving at the Institute. He'd had to wait at his flat for an electrician to come and sort out a smoke alarm that had been ringing throughout the night. It was 10.30 by the time the man arrived. He had not seen Manon for a few days and wanted to tell her the various things he had learned. So he went straight to her office to see if she was there. He knocked and was relieved to hear her call, 'Come in.'

She was sitting at her desk with a box open in front of her and papers spread out over her desk. She looked up. 'Oh, good morning, Charles. I'm really pleased to see you. I've been looking at some of this stuff connected with the founding of the Institute and its funding, and there's something very odd about it so far as I can tell.'

'I'm not surprised to hear that,' he replied. 'It strikes me that there's a lot that's pretty odd going on around here. But I've also got something to tell you. It's such a lovely morning, why don't we go for a walk around the grounds and I'll fill you in.'

Manon locked her office door, leaving the papers where they were, and they set off across the grass dividing college from institute. Abbot said, 'I've had an intriguing conversation with McCaffrey, the don you sat next to at the dinner the other night. It seems he's been colluding with the Chinese, letting in people who have neither the qualifications nor the intent to study here. As we suspected, they're spooks of some kind, just here to keep an eye on the students. He seemed ashamed of what he's done, and I should think he ought to be. He says the Chinese funded a couple of scholarships in return for his turning a blind eye. It was all a bit garbled, but he was pretty firm about the spooks. Though he said there's only one still here that he knows of.'

'My God,' said Manon. 'I bet I know who that is. It's got to be Mr Chew, doesn't it? He's been following me around, and the other night was trying to find out where I live. But I made sure he didn't see me going into my flat. He's obviously suspicious of me. Or someone else is and is having him follow me.'

'That's interesting,' said Charles. 'I was out at the Elm yesterday and happened to stumble upon a database of staff and students that Nina Pierpont seems to have compiled for herself. She was off ill, but someone called Amy was taking her place and mentioned it to me. Just as a trial, I asked for your address.' He paused, seeming mildly embarrassed. 'Since you've only just arrived, I was interested to see if Pierpont kept the database up to date.'

'I don't think she'd know my address in any case. No one in the college would. I rented my flat from an agency.'

'You're right, she didn't have it. But that's not the important thing.' He paused, seemingly unsure how to word what came next.

'Oh?' prompted Manon.

'It seems I wasn't the only one asking for your address. The woman who helped me laughed at the coincidence.'

'Who else was asking then?' It must be Li Min, she thought.

'Mr Chew.'

'I see,' Manon said calmly, but her stomach suddenly felt like it had dipped.

'I'm not trying to scare you,' he said gently. 'But I thought you should know.'

'Thanks,' she said a little dully. 'I wonder if Pierpont is in league with the Chinese?'

'She may well be,' said Abbot. 'I don't like it at all.'

The walk had taken them to a spot where there was a picnic table and some chairs. Abbot said, 'Let's sit down.'

As they did, Manon saw, walking along the path to the Institute, the figure of Professor Cole. 'Here comes someone else who's got a lot to hide, I suspect,' she said. 'He showed me round his exhibition yesterday. I could tell that he was trying to find out whether I really am who and what I claim to be, and what I am doing here. I'm not surprised he's suspicious. I reckon he's got a good deal to hide himself. I think he's probably in pretty deep with the Chinese. And from what I've seen in those papers, there's something dodgy about the Institute's funding. The Norwegian company behind the Oslo foundation that helped found it in the beginning, was bought out five years ago. It took me some time to trace the purchaser – there were half a dozen shell companies involved, half of them in the Cayman Islands. But guess where the trail ended?'

'Don't tell me: Beijing?' He looked thoroughly shocked.

'Close enough. It was actually Shanghai.'

At lunchtime Manon caught the train to London. As usual it was crowded but she managed to get a seat next to a student who was eating a ghastly smelling burger from a cardboard tray. She was glad when they reached Paddington and she was able to snatch a few breaths of fresh air before catching the Underground to Nine Elms and the American Embassy.

Saunders, dressed today in his usual informal office gear, was waiting for her. As she came in, she noticed there was someone else in the room. A man in a smart blue suit and black shoes, with dark hair neatly cut and large friendly eyes.

'Manon, I don't know if you remember Hugo Wilson? He is the Director of Counter Espionage at Five. He was involved in your last operation here.'

Manon hesitated and Hugo broke in to say, 'I remember you, Manon, and your heroic performance in that operation in Oxford. I gather you are back there again.'

'I've brought Hugo up to date,' said Saunders. 'So he knows why you're there and your cover story. Perhaps it would be best if you tell us where things stand now. I got your message about Sally Washington and her family, and I'll tell you about that when you've brought us up to date with your end.'

'OK,' said Manon. 'Well, I've made contact with Li Min. I wrote to her and she agreed to meet me. She didn't say much when we did, though she did mention that she'd made a friend, an American girl called Sally Washington, and that she was enjoying herself. As I was leaving, I noticed we were being followed by a Chinese student I have since discovered is a spook, but I'll tell you about that later – I didn't let him find out where I live. I have made another date to see Li Min, when I'm hoping to make more headway.

'Charles Abbot has done rather better than me. He has made friends with a don called McCaffrey who confessed to him that he has colluded with the Chinese to let in a couple of security officers disguised as students. One of them is the guy who followed me home. His name is Chew – or, I should say, Mr Chew. That's what everybody calls him, and I suspect it shows they know he's not a student but state security sent to spy on them. Also, there's an awful place called the Elm where the Chinese students all live, and it seems their rooms are regularly searched by this spook. Essentially, it seems the Institute is pretty well infiltrated by the Chinese, and their students are all under Party control.

'I have also been looking at papers connected with the founding of the Institute. The funds ostensibly came from Norway, but I have tracked them back to a government-run bank in Shanghai. The original Institute Director, a man called Professor Arthur Cole, taught for years at the University of Hong Kong, and seems somehow in hock to the Chinese. This is all going to take further unravelling and I'll write you a more detailed report in due course. But what I intend to do next is to try and gain Li Min's confidence and get her to tell me what her role is. I think the lever to persuade her to cooperate with us may be that she is beginning to have fun, and her friendship with Sally Washington is becoming a real one.'

'Thanks, Manon,' said Saunders. 'That's all going pretty well so far.'

He looked questioningly at Wilson, who said, 'This is the first time we have had actual evidence of Chinese infiltration of a British university, so I am keen to see how it develops. I'm happy for you to proceed along the lines you suggest, but please keep us closely informed. When this unravels there may be a big stink, and the government's relations with China are already delicate. I'll have Kenton assigned to keep in touch with you for day-to-day contact,' he said to Saunders, 'but obviously I am always available as well.'

'From our angle,' said Saunders, 'we have been doing some research into this American friend of Li Min's. It seems that Sally Washington's father is a senior scientist in the Department of Defense. He's in a small strategic unit that reports direct to the Chiefs of Staff and the Secretary of Defense himself. Top Secret stuff. His specialty is sub-aquatic missilery. You know, nuclear submarines, equipped with nuclear missiles.'

'Well, that would certainly make him of interest to the Chinese,' said Wilson. 'But what's it got to do with his daughter? And what about Li Min? Don't tell me she's studying English literature?'

Manon laughed. 'No, she is an expert in AI. So far as I can gather it's to do with fabricated simulations – these deepfakes we're starting to hear so much about. But maybe it's not the daughter the Chinese are interested in, but her father. Though in that case, I am simply not sure how and why the daughter would be involved.'

They sat quietly for a minute. At last Manon said thoughtfully, 'It's just a feeling, but I got the distinct impression that Li Min is trying to spread her wings. We know she wasn't happy to go to Oxford, but rather than sulk about it, she seems determined to have some fun. She's still committed to her work – that's her passion – but she made a point of indicating that she wanted to have a good time as well. She's got a Western friend in Sally, probably the first one she's had, and she's discovered Margaritas.'

'I get that, but what do her masters want her to do?' Wilson asked.

'I don't know yet, and I don't think we will know unless she rejects them and decides to talk to me. I suggest that's what I should concentrate on.'

'What are the chances of her opening up to you?' asked Saunders.

'I'll know better once I've seen her again. I think it's time I pushed her a bit. She is clearly unhappy with her Chinese masters, but she may not realise she has an alternative.'

'OK,' said Saunders. 'But I want you to be careful. I don't like the sound of this Mr Chew.'

'Nobody does,' said Manon glumly.

26

Back from London, Manon found Abbot in his office, looking pensive and tired. But he smiled brightly when he saw her in the doorway. 'Come in,' he said. 'The first person I've been pleased to see all day.'

'That bad, is it?'

He shrugged. He had nice eyes, thought Manon, then told herself not to be ridiculous. 'Not really. It's the time of year we agree the list of people we want to invite as Visiting Fellows. It's always a bit of a bunfight apparently. I must have had eight different Fellows here, each touting the virtues of someone they want invited. But I shouldn't grumble. I get to make the final decision.' Manon laughed and he gave a small smile. 'But listen, I'm glad you stopped by – I was about to come looking for you. I have done a little more digging of my own and have to tell you that our suspicions about Mr Chew seem justified. I can't prove it, but from talking to McCaffrey again, I think it's clear that Chew is no more an authentic student than the Head Chef is.'

'I'd guessed as much, but it's good to have it confirmed.'

'Please be careful,' he said.

What was this? Did all men think she needed looking after? 'Me in particular or is that a more general instruction?' she asked, trying to lighten things.

But Abbot's expression remained sombre so Manon tried to reassure him. 'Don't worry, I'll be extra careful from now on. With any luck, Chew still doesn't know where I live.' Then she brightened. 'I've been in London talking to the Boss.'

'Anything you can share?'

'Absolutely,' she said. 'That's why I'm here.'

'Then take a pew and tell me all about it.' He pointed to the chair across from him. 'I'll get us some tea first.'

Manon sat while Abbot went out to the pantry next to his office where there was a little fridge for milk and a kettle for tea and coffee. She saw on his desk a framed photograph of a woman, sitting posed for the camera. She was striking, with clear, sharp features and a lovely mane of golden hair. It must be his wife, thought Manon, suddenly saddened. She perked up when Abbot came back with two mugs of tea. 'Little milk, no sugar, right?' He handed her a mug.

'Got it first time,' she said as he sat down facing her across the desk. As they each sipped their tea, she told him about her discussions with Saunders and Wilson, then her recent meeting with Li Min and the student's friendship with Sally Washington.

'So what's your next move?' he asked.

'I'm seeing Li Min again, and I need to try and move that along. I'm worried I'll scare her off, but I can't wait too much longer to make a pitch. I don't know what schedule her superiors are working to, but if they moved Li Min here all the way from Harvard in order to do something specific, then there's no reason to think they'll want her to take her time doing it.'

'Speaking of time,' said Abbot, glancing at his watch, 'I'm afraid I'd better be off. We could continue this tomorrow, but I'm due at the neighbours' for supper tonight. I seem to have become a pet project of theirs.'

'I'll walk out with you. I'm heading home myself.'

They left college and crossed the Broad, then headed north along St Giles', past the honeyed stone walls of Balliol and St John's. Manon was still new enough to Oxford to note the beauty of her everyday surroundings and said as much to Abbot.

'Me too,' he said with a nod. 'I keep waiting for it to wear off, but it hasn't yet.'

St Giles' split after a few hundred yards, where Manon would go up the left branch on Woodstock Road. Abbot hesitated. 'I'll walk a little way with you,' he said.

'Don't you live near the Parks? I don't want to take you out of your way. Especially if you've got a supper party to go to.'

'I wouldn't call it a party,' he said. 'More a charitable intervention – you know, "We'd better have the widower round."' He seemed to regret saying this, for he added almost immediately, 'Sorry, that's not charitable of *me*. They're nice people and mean well. I shouldn't be so snide.'

'That's all right. I know just how you feel. It's what my parents used to call "duty dinners".'

'Did they have lots of them?'

'Tons. My father was a History professor and very kind to his students. Both his parents – my grandparents, though I never knew them – died when he was little and he was raised by an aunt. A classic Yankee spinster – children should be seen and not heard. Or if heard, should be sent to their room without any supper.'

'Sounds ghastly.'

'It was, I think, though he never said so – and always praised her for making sure he got a good education.

Anyway, it made him very nice to his kids – my brother and I got away with murder. In our father's eyes we could do no wrong.'

'That explains it.'

'Explains what?' asked Manon, startled.

'Well, you've picked a profession that requires immense amounts of nerve, and a good deal of self-confidence.'

'I don't know about the self-confidence. I suffer as much as anyone from impostor syndrome.' She laughed. 'And here I am, actually being an impostor.'

Abbot gave her a knowing smile. At the next corner he stopped. 'I'd better leave you here, if that's all right.'

'Of course. I might write up what we discussed. If you don't mind having a look, I'd be grateful.'

'Gladly. I'm in all day. Come round anytime. If I'm in a meeting, just try again. Is that OK?'

'Of course. See you tomorrow then.'

But Abbot made no move. Looking down at his feet, he shuffled them slightly awkwardly on the pavement, then said, 'I tell you what. Perhaps if you were free sometime next week, you could come over. I'm not precisely cordon bleu, but I can make a decent pasta.'

Was this an invitation to supper? she thought at first, then realised that of course it was. 'I'd like that very much. Let me bring a bottle. What day were you thinking of?'

'Any day you're free?'

This could take forever, thought Manon, so she took the plunge. 'Thursday?'

'Perfect,' he said.

This time Manon moved first. 'See you then,' she said, going past him.

'No,' he said, and she turned, startled. He explained: 'See you tomorrow.'

A few minutes later, Manon was approaching the turn to her little street with a light heart, until further along she saw a police car parked in front of her flat.

She saw the front door was wide open as she neared the house. There were two officers inside, a man and a woman. They were polite to her but stiff and formal, until she found her Judith Davidson passport in the bedroom and established who she was. 'We had a call from the lady next door,' one of them explained. She looked younger than Manon, tall with blonde hair tied back in a long braid.

'What did she say?'

The woman's partner spoke up now. He was a little older and presumably more experienced; this call, he made clear, was not a significant event in his day. He said, 'She heard glass breaking. In the kitchen,' he added, jerking his thumb towards the back of the house. 'Unfortunately, she didn't think much of it; she just thought someone had broken a glass. But a while later she went out into her garden in the back and saw the window. Or what's left of it.'

They led Manon back to the kitchen, then stood aside so she could see the damage. The window overlooking the strip of garden had been almost totally shattered; only a few remaining shards jutted from the wooden frame. The rest littered the sink and the floor in countless fragments.

Manon went and tried the back door. 'It's unlocked. And I always keep it locked,' she said.

The woman police officer said, 'I reckon the burglar came through the window, went around the house, then left through the back door.'

'Taking the key with him,' Manon said crossly.

The police pair waited while Manon went through the flat room by room. Nothing seemed to have been taken. Whoever the intruder had been, they hadn't been here for cash-convertible booty, or even for cash itself – there was a twenty-pound note still lying on the mantelpiece in the sitting room. Though they had quite thoroughly ransacked the flat. The worst mess was in her bedroom, where drawers had been pulled out willy-nilly, their contents, mainly clothes, strewn across every surface. A bookcase in the sitting room had been emptied of books, which lay jumbled on the floor. In the bathroom, the caps were off her bottles of shampoo and conditioner; even the toothpaste tube had been unscrewed. Why? Had the 'burglar' been looking for microdots, or some supposed espionage *accoutrement*? It seemed weird. And her jewellery, the few pieces she had brought from the States, lay untouched in its box on the top of her dressing table.

'They haven't taken anything,' she said to the police officers, trying to sound surprised. Was she? No: someone was looking for evidence rather than money or goods; someone suspected she wasn't the librarian she said she was.

The male officer yawned, and his partner said, 'Can you stay somewhere else tonight? The back door's not secure – neither is the window for that matter. Unless you know a builder who will board it up for you tonight, and a locksmith for the door, then I'd advise you to spend the night elsewhere.'

'That's right,' said the male officer. 'We'll be off in a minute. Let me give you my card. You can ring us if you need anything more.'

'What about evidence? Aren't you going to check for prints?'

'Fingerprints?' the male officer said, as if she had asked for the moon.

'Yes, fingerprints. I'd have thought that was standard procedure for a burglary.'

'Not anymore,' he said, as if Manon were a walking anachronism. Just then his mobile rang and he quickly answered – as though relieved to escape from this demanding victim.

Manon heard another man's voice at the other end of the line, speaking calmly but seeming authoritatively – the male police officer was calling him 'sir'. When he finally rang off, the policeman seemed galvanised. 'Right, we're not going anywhere,' he announced, looking at his partner. He turned to Manon. 'We'll camp out here tonight if that's all right with you? Someone from Forensics will be here shortly to take prints. But just ignore us; we'll be gone in the morning.'

Manon suppressed a sigh. Saunders' British connections must have been at work, and extended as far as this previously uninterested policeman. Some alarm bell at the police station must have gone off when the neighbour reported the break-in, no doubt triggered by her address, which Saunders would have had transmitted. That was fine, but Manon hoped her cover wouldn't be blown by special treatment.

There was a lot of cleaning up to do, but at least she knew that if the intruder was stupid enough to come back, he'd find these two waiting for him. 'I'll go and put the kettle on,' she said. They might as well make themselves at home. 'Would you like coffee or tea?'

27

Manon waited until morning and the departure of her police companions before ringing Saunders. He was concerned, though she was confident he had already been informed of the break-in. 'Are you sure you're all right?'

'Absolutely. It's just a bit of a bore. I can't go into college until a glazier comes and fixes the window, and a locksmith's arriving at lunchtime to put a new lock on the back door.'

'And you say nothing was taken?'

'That's right. Whatever they were looking for, they didn't find it.' Manon had been making sure to follow the procedure she had been taught, and to leave nothing in the flat that might indicate her true business. Her laptop either accompanied her or was locked in her desk at St Felix's; it was heavily encrypted in any case.

Her hope that fingerprints might help the police catch the culprit had faded when the technician said there were almost a dozen different prints on the window frame and latch, and nothing but a blurred mass of indistinguishable ones on the handle of the kitchen door. If the burglar were even semi-professional, they would in any case have worn gloves.

'I really don't like the sound of this,' said Saunders now, 'especially since you thought this Mr Chew was going into student rooms. I think you should move, Manon.'

Was this an order? Moving was the last thing she wanted to do. She liked her flat, and in the middle of term it would be difficult to find a place even half as nice or convenient. She said vaguely, 'I'll start looking.'

'Do that,' said Saunders. 'If you need money for a deposit, just let me know.'

'I have to tell you, if they found me here, they'll find me in the new place as well.'

'Look for another place anyway. Then when you find something, we can argue about it.'

She sensed a concession on his part, so didn't push things. He said, 'When are you seeing Li Min?'

'The day after tomorrow. We're meeting for lunch. Everything should be fixed here today.'

Like Saunders, Charles Abbot was upset when Manon arrived in his office and told him about the break-in at her flat. He was also angry and showed it. Manon did her best to calm him down, and promised to let him know if there were any signs of a repeat performance from the intruder.

Once Manon had left his office Abbot sat down, still agitated but thinking hard. It seemed almost self-evident that the Chinese were behind this, but how had they got wind of Manon's real position and reason for being here? As far as he knew, he himself was the only person privy to her secret, and even if he had been less careful than perhaps he might have been in terms of the amount of contact between them, he knew he had not confided in anyone about her, or possessed anything in writing that might have been intercepted and read.

He wished there were an easy way to get rid of Mr Chew, who was at the heart of the problem – though he was almost certainly following the orders of more senior Chinese, probably in London. But the extension granted Chew for his thesis gave him protection from any steps Abbot could take, even with McCaffrey's help. The question now was, was anyone else helping Chew?

Having sorted all this out in his mind, he climbed into his car and set out once more for the Elm.

There was a pinched, drawn look to Nina Pierpont's face, even before she saw Abbot come into her office. Her eyes were rheumy and she coughed convincingly; he was prepared to believe she had been ill.

'Mr Abbot,' she said. She wore a grey wool dress today, buttoned at the neck. 'Back again. What can I do for you?'

'Call me Charles for one thing,' he said, trying to sound friendly. 'And I'm just following up on the complaint I had from our friend Jia Hao. He's chasing me for an answer.' A lie, of course, though how would Pierpont know any different?

'I gave you the best one I had. He was beaten to the post by Mr Chew in a matter of the heart. If you ask me, he's pursuing a vendetta because of that.'

'Could be,' Abbot said mildly. 'But for the sake of argument, if Mr Chew was going into student rooms, how did he manage it? I'm told there's a master key, but you are the sole holder of it.'

'Technically speaking, Gillroy has one too, though since he's always borrowing mine, I think it's reasonable to suppose he mislaid his. Or else someone borrowed it and forgot to give it back. But that's no reason to think it ended up with Mr Chew.'

'No, it's not. And if they borrowed your key, they must have returned it, yes?'

'Since I have it currently, then yes,' she said patiently, as if she weren't sure whether Abbot was truly stupid or just acting the part.

'Sorry to be slow,' he said. Which his wife had always claimed was a red flag in their conversations, a warning to take cover, because it meant he was ready to pursue an argument to the bitter end. 'But if someone borrowed your master key, couldn't they go and get a copy made in town?'

'You can't do that with a master key. No locksmith will copy one without authorisation from the primary registered holder. *I* couldn't even get one copied – not without a letter of authorisation.'

'From me?'

'From the Principal,' she said emphatically. 'The Institute leases the building but the college owns it – and the land. It has for years. Before that it used to be a farm.'

That puts me in my place, thought Abbot. It also explained why the decrepit barn was part of the property.

Pierpont shuffled some papers on her desk and asked, 'Is there anything else, Director? Because if not, I have a meeting with the Maintenance people.'

'No, I'm all set.'

She nodded and got up from her desk, and as she left he followed, more slowly. She was halfway down the hall when he called out his thanks. She flapped a hand in acknowledgement but kept going.

He waited for a solid minute, then walked to the building's front door, opened it and looked outside. No one about. Coming back, he scanned the corridors leading to both wings. No one again.

Five seconds later he was behind Pierpont's desk, scanning her computer, which she had left open and logged in. It took three false starts with Word documents before he found it listed as an Excel spreadsheet – entitled simply *NP List*.

Judith Davidson was sixth in the alphabetical list, following Bittelman and Bosanquet. There still wasn't any phone number listed for her, which came as no surprise to Abbot. To his dismay, however, the spreadsheet now showed her address – in North Oxford, just a stone's throw off Woodstock Road.

He forced himself to stop staring at the screen, close down the spreadsheet and get up from the desk. He left the room and went straight out of the front door without looking around. If challenged, he would have said he had come back to retrieve something he'd left behind – though God knows what. But either no one saw him leave or, if they had, didn't think it remarkable.

As Abbot drove away, his fury returned. He was confident he knew how Manon's address had suddenly appeared. It wouldn't have taken Mr Chew much effort to discover it, not if he had followed Manon more successfully on another occasion. And handed her home details straight over to Pierpont.

28

This time Arthur Cole refused to have the young man in his rooms. It was too risky by far.

Instead, he walked down the Broad and past the array of bus stops on Magdalen Street, outside the cinema. He no longer drove, accepting that his reflexes were slower, his eyesight poor even with the annual checks and expensive updating of lenses. His car, an ancient saloon, now sat on the driveway of his extraordinarily dull nephew Alan, a computer marketeer living in Swindon. Perhaps he should give it to him, he thought, since that way Cole would never have to retrieve it. Or see Alan.

It wasn't long before the double-decker Park and Ride bus came along. It was a little before three o'clock and the bus was virtually empty. He managed to climb the awkward metal stairs and find a seat in the rear of the upper deck.

The bus progressed up Woodstock Road, stopping only for the odd passenger getting off or someone flagging it down. None of them ventured upstairs. Cole looked west out the window, where teenage students were emerging from a sixth-form college – known as 'crammers' in Cole's day. A group of young Chinese students was walking south, and it heartened Cole to see them. What a fine addition they made to the ranks of their pallid English peers. They were so polite, gracious, charming even. He felt pleased to have brought so many of them here to study and live.

After the next stop a Chinese face emerged from the staircase near the front of the bus. A familiar visage: Mr Chew, who had to duck his head as he came down the centre aisle to sit next to Cole, all done without acknowledging his presence. Such was the man's muscled bulk that Cole found himself half-squashed against the window. Sitting so close to him, Cole noticed for the first time that Chew had a long scar on one side of his neck, thin and raised and the palest pink.

Three teenage boys had also boarded the bus and now bounded up the steps. Instead of sitting down they roamed around the front half of the upper deck. Seeing Chew, one of them whispered to the other two. Then, clinging to the metal pole as the bus accelerated, the boy cried out in a caricature sing-song voice, 'Spring rolls for sale, spring rolls for sale!' The other two boys cackled.

Cole was appalled by these hoodlums. He was about to remonstrate with them when Chew grabbed the back of the seat in front of him and pulled himself to his feet. He had to bow his head slightly beneath the low roof of the upper deck. From Cole's vantage point, the man was enormous, and the three boys looked visibly taken aback. Chew said, 'You wish to speak with me?'

The boy who had taunted him swallowed hard and said nothing. His mates were no longer laughing. Chew said, 'Take yourselves downstairs.' When they hesitated, he said, 'Now,' and made to move into the aisle towards them. The boys didn't think twice and hurtled down the stairs in a rush.

Though they now had the upper deck to themselves, Cole and Chew talked quietly, almost in whispers. 'Have you made progress with Li Min?' Cole asked.

'I thought first I should pursue the other end.'

Other end? 'What do you mean?'

'Li Min is smart and accustomed to the close supervision of her Chinese betters. It will be very difficult to catch her out since she knows she will now be watched carefully.'

So he hadn't followed up with her at all, concluded Cole. What on earth had this man been doing instead?

Chew seemed to read his mind for he said, 'I have been pursuing the new acquaintance of Li Min.'

'Another student?' He had seen Li Min from afar two days before, walking with a young woman with streaky blonde hair. He had noticed it particularly since the Chinese usually stuck with their own while at Oxford.

'No, though she will be next as the focus of my attention. It is the new arrival, Miss Davidson, who I have been watching.'

'And have you discovered anything of interest?' asked Cole, his curiosity piqued. It seemed Chew shared his suspicion of the Davidson woman.

Chew was silent for a moment, discomfited it seemed. 'Not precisely. Not yet,' he added more positively, which suggested to Cole that his answer was a resounding no. Chew said eagerly, 'I know where she lives,' and stated the number of the house and name of her road. Classic North Oxford, thought Cole, slightly annoyed that a junior librarian could afford to live in such a good part of town. If she were in fact a junior librarian…

Chew was watching Cole now, turning to look down at the older, slighter man. He seemed to have expected a more enthusiastic reaction to his proclamation of Judith Davidson's address. He said with a note of triumph in his voice, 'I have been inside.'

'How's that? She asked you in for tea?' said Cole witheringly.

'She was not present when we inspected her residence,' he said, with an air of defiance.

'You don't mean to say you broke into her flat?'

Chew mistook this amazement for approval. 'I did not myself do that. I went in through the front door.'

'While someone else broke in?' asked Cole incredulously.

'Something of that order. It would not do for me to be seen doing something unusual. Not in this town where I stick out like – what do you say?'

'A sore thumb,' said Cole wearily.

Oh, no, he thought about this news, but curious despite himself, asked, 'What did you find?'

'She is very careful, this American lady, very professional. She left no evidence of ties to the authorities here or in America.'

In other words, he had found nothing. What a gamble he had taken – Cole happened to know that street; he had been to dinner just the year before with an academic couple who lived two or three houses along from Davidson's place. And it was a dense, crowded area, full of small detached houses with very little space between them. Neighbours kept an eye out for anything and anyone strange; Neighbourhood Watch signs abounded. Someone of Chew's size and race would hardly pass unnoticed in those white middle-class environs. He was very lucky not to have been caught. And all for what? Nothing.

The bus had reached the top of Woodstock Road and was queueing up short of the roundabout there. The terminus was just a little way north of them at Pear Tree, but that didn't matter – he and Chew would just stay up here and ride it back to town.

Cole supposed that Chew knew his business, and that if there were anything to be found in the flat, he would have found it. In a slightly perverse way, Cole couldn't help but find the utter absence of anything out of the ordinary suspicious in itself. Far from removing his doubts about Judith Davidson, it strengthened them.

But he couldn't have Chew going round like a bull in a china shop (he winced at his own choice of words). 'You have done very well,' he said, starting with a carrot, but holding a metaphoric stick in reserve. The Chinese man smiled, gratified by the praise. Cole went on: 'But for now it would be best to leave the woman well alone. Please do not follow her, and whatever you do, don't go within a million miles of her flat again.' He could see that Chew was puzzled by these instructions, and by the fact Cole felt he could give them. Cole continued, 'I will be seeing your superiors in London next week.' Chew's eyes widened. 'I will be sure to tell them of your excellent work in this matter. So I am sure you will do as I ask, and keep your distance from Miss Davidson.'

29

WHEN THE SHUTTLE DROPPED Li Min off at the Elm, she was the last one to disembark. She stood for a moment by the bus, gathering her wits since she was tired and had fallen half-asleep on the journey from town. She was working hard, and had more work to do this evening, filming Sally.

Then she heard someone whistle, a high quavering sound, and looked around her. In the adjacent field, near the aluminium-roofed barn that seemed about to fall down, she saw a figure. He waved as she stared out at him – it was definitely a him, Chinese too. And all too familiar.

What was Deng doing here? she wondered, groaning inside. He had not told her to expect him. Li Min was religious about checking her emails and WhatsApp messages, precisely because she didn't want to be caught out, unprepared. Something must have happened to bring him here unexpectedly.

He was gesturing for her to join him, so she trudged over, climbing the low hill that was crowned by the barn. Someone should put a house there, thought Li Min, since unlike the position of the Elm, the site was high enough to overlook Oxford, its towers and spires, and these days its many construction cranes, all settled in the bottom of the bowl-shaped Thames Valley. Outside the city green fields lay like supine dominoes, and in the eastern distance one could make out the beacon where the motorway climbed up through a chalk cut towards London. Li Min still found it amazing how much countryside remained unspoiled in such a densely populated country.

'Come with me,' Deng said as she approached. Always so gracious, this man, but she followed him through the barn's entrance. Inside on a cracked concrete floor lay a loose hillock of hay with some stringed bales next to it, a couple of pitchforks and a spade, and, in the back of the barn, an ancient Land Rover.

'Have you been waiting long?' asked Li Min, feigning concern.

'No. I have other business but thought I would kill the many birds with the stone.'

Li Min kept herself from laughing. Deng was proud of his English language skills, unaware of how he sometimes mangled its idioms.

There was a noise at the doorway and a man appeared. It was the Head of Maintenance. A frequent presence in the Elm itself, but Li Min was surprised to see him here. He must not have expected them, for he too looked surprised. Deng said shortly, 'We will not be long.'

The man gave a casual wave of his hand. 'Not my business, sir. I just left my fork.' He collected a pitchfork standing against the wall and left without looking at them again. Perhaps Deng had something on this man as well, Li Min thought.

'So what do you want from me?' she asked with a new bluntness to her tone. There was no use pretending she was Deng's equal, or didn't have to follow his orders, but she was not going to be docile about it. She was no longer his hi-tech puppet, she realised; she must be valued or this annoying man would not be so present in her life, such a thorn in her side.

He seemed to sense the change in her. He said, 'I too take orders, you know.' His voice was different; sickly, almost syrupy. And to Li Min utterly unpersuasive. He continued, almost as if wooing her, 'There are things even I cannot question. Even when they do not seem to make good sense.'

Something he wanted was about to be specified, Li Min sensed; hence this nauseating preamble. Sure enough, Deng said, 'From your report it appears you have substantial footage of the Washington woman.'

Li Min waited, unwilling to give him the satisfaction of an answer. He knew it anyway; her last report had rather crowingly stated there was ample material now. But for what? Was he going to tell her? It must be something she would find unpalatable if he were beating round the bush like this.

'We are now instructed to add a person to your… data.'

What did this mean? thought Li Min, annoyed by the use of 'we'. As if Deng and she were jointly suffering at the dirty hands of their superiors.

'Who am I to add?' she asked sharply, wishing he would get to the point.

'One of the Chinese students. You are acquainted with him perhaps.'

She thought for a moment. Could it be Wong, the quiet one? Who, though not in AI, was knowledgeable about computer science, and was using a range of analytic software in his biology research? He had seemed keen on Li Min, she remembered, but she had not reciprocated. And since befriending Sally and her American gang, Li Min hadn't given him a thought.

She uttered the name tentatively but Deng shook his head. 'No,' he said, sounding almost regretful. What was the problem then? Who could be so terrible that Deng was reluctant even to say his name?

And then she knew. 'Not Mr Chew?' she asked in a whisper that was both horrified and disbelieving.

Deng looked at her reprovingly. 'You have a prejudice against him?' He paused, and added, 'Because he is Chinese?' Li Min realised he was trying to make a joke, which for Deng was unprecedented. But it wasn't funny.

'Sally will never agree,' she said, thinking of the first reason to object that came into her head.

'You must get her to cooperate; in return we will not use Mr Chew. We will ask young Lee instead.'

Lee was tall and strikingly good-looking, but seemed appealingly unaware of this and had a modest manner. He acted very conventionally, at least on the surface, but Li Min decided to probe this with Deng. 'What if Lee won't do it? You know, maybe he won't want to be filmed.' She sensed that Deng had just outmanoeuvred her. Despite Li Min's best efforts, Sally was now involved; the only consolation was that Mr Chew wouldn't be.

Deng shook his head. 'He will do it, never fear.' He said this with such confidence that Li Min understood – Lee was under Deng's thumb as well, in the same way she was. He was not one of the wealthy Chinese students and would need the Chinese government's support to stay here. A negative report from Deng could have him packing his bags at the end of term. Deng continued, 'We need him and the Washington girl filmed together. I have the specifications here.' And he handed an A4 envelope to Li Min. 'They ask for conventional poses, nothing unseemly.'

Not yet, Li Min thought sourly. 'And here,' he said, handing another envelope to her. This one was small, letter-sized. It felt empty.

'What's this for?'

'Nothing. I mean, there is nothing inside. But you must show it in your filming.'

'But who has it in the video? Which one holds the envelope?'

Deng shrugged. 'That is in the script's specifications,' he said curtly; clearly he didn't want to answer.

He got up from the bale, sweeping strands of hay off the sides of his trousers. 'I must go now. Lee will come to your room at eight o'clock this evening. You should warn your Washington friend in advance. Text me at once on the new phone if she says she will not participate. We may have to make it worth her while.'

He was speaking to Li Min as if she were on his side. How little he understood, she thought. You could never bribe Sally Washington. If she did not want anything to do with Lee or filming, the woman would stand firm. Li Min knew her friend and was sure of this.

But that evening after dinner when they retired to talk in Li Min's room, Sally seemed entirely unperturbed by the news of Deng's request. 'No problem,' she said and laughed. 'I mean, the guy will be wearing clothes, right?'

'Yes, he will be fully dressed.'

'Maybe I should take mine off,' said Sally, giggling.

'No!' exclaimed Li Min, horrified.

'Chill, Min,' said Sally. 'I'm not being serious.'

When Lee appeared the filming proved to be entirely uneventful. Lee was quiet and professional, though he consulted notes he had brought along with him, presumably to ensure Li Min covered everything he was expected to be part of. It was cramped, for even though they used Sally's room, which was at a corner of the wing and slightly larger than Li Min's, Lee was so much taller than Sally that it was difficult to get them both in the camera's frame. Eventually Li Min used a fixed tripod and had Lee and then Sally move in and out of the lens' range.

As for the envelope Deng had made such a fuss about, Li Min had almost forgotten all about it when seeing Lee consult his instructions jogged her memory. She filmed the envelope held by Sally, then held by Lee, and finally placed on the chest of drawers, held by no one. What it was supposed to suggest Li Min could not begin to imagine, but she was glad to have remembered it.

When the near-mute Chinese man had left, Sally and Li Min both laughed at the sheer oddness of what had just transpired. Sally said, 'I was about to say I'd be happy to run into him in a dark alley, but actually I wouldn't be keen to run into him anywhere – there wouldn't be anything to talk about! That is one quiet dude.'

Li Min nodded and started laughing again. Nervous laughter, she realised. She sobered up when she thought of what use this film and audio material might be put to. Watching her friend relax, she kept that thought to herself, but Li Min knew there was a point to this exercise that went well beyond experiments in AI. She felt guilty that Sally knew nothing about it. But what could Li Min possibly say? What warning could she give her friend, when she didn't know herself what Deng and his wretched bosses had in mind?

30

There was just enough milk left for Saunders' coffee. They sat in the kitchen of Manon's flat, and she realised that in all the kerfuffle of the break-in she had forgotten to buy any more basics, like bread and milk. But Saunders seemed happy enough with the last inch from the carton and Manon drank her own coffee black.

They sat at the little table, Saunders facing the window, its panes cleaner (because brand new) than they had been for years. He wore a three-piece suit, white shirt and conservatively striped tie. Manon had never seen him in such a formal outfit, but they had agreed that he was here in the guise of benefactor of the collection she was cataloguing, a wealthy businessman with a keen interest in modern China. They had stopped short of having a driver bring him down to Oxford from London but it was easy to envisage him as a man accustomed to being chauffeured to his many important appointments.

They had originally arranged to convene in St Felix's with Abbot, and that meeting was still on the cards in less than an hour. But Saunders had asked to see her alone first and now he explained why. 'Point one, I'm concerned about your safety. I think we should consider at the very least moving you to safer turf – probably a hotel. Whether this man Chew is responsible for the break-in, I realise no one can say, but it's pretty clear it was no conventional burglary – you say they didn't take anything.'

'No. Whatever they were looking for, they didn't find it. As you say, this couldn't have been your average burglar, or they would have taken my jewellery.'

'This man Chew sounds the most likely culprit. Or an associate. Or maybe both – Chew might have had help since presumably he would stick out around here. And that's what worries me.'

Manon looked at him. 'What, are you thinking they'll be back? I doubt it – why would I have something they're interested in *after* they've already swept the place clean?'

'Maybe. I was thinking of your personal safety.'

'That's good of you,' she said, and meant it. 'But if they wanted to hurt me, they would have come when I was here. In the middle of the night, not in the middle of the day.'

'I guess so.' He didn't sound sure of this.

Manon liked her flat and had no desire to leave it, so she moved on, 'What was your second point?' Saunders looked momentarily puzzled. 'You said there were two reasons you wanted to talk to me alone.'

'Yes, of course,' he said, though Manon sensed he wasn't done with his concern for her safety. 'I've been talking with the Department of Defense people. They're always tight-lipped – they make us seem positively verbose – but eventually I went upstairs and put in a formal request for info about Sally's father. His name is Donald Washington and he's been with Defense for more than twenty years. As I mentioned before, his specialty is sub-aquatic missilery.'

'Why is that interesting to the Chinese, beyond whatever interest they have in our defence?'

'The South China Sea is why. We don't have a base in Taiwan anymore, but we are ramping up our presence in the waters around it. Frankly, we have to, or the Chinese would claim it as their own and fill it with their ships and submarines. Donald Washington's work is focused on how best to make our presence felt, without provoking World War Three. He is in charge of the military strategy – naval that is – for the whole area. Put it this way: if you wanted to know how many submarines we have there, what their working orders are, how they are meant to react if the Chinese attack Taiwan – then Donald Washington is the one man with all the answers.'

'OK. There is nothing in Sally Washington's background to make her, on her own, a target for the Chinese. From what you are saying, her father is a different story.'

'Yes. Keep thinking.'

Manon bridled slightly at the pedagogic tone, but then recognised that Saunders wanted her to reach the same conclusion as he had on her own. She said, 'They somehow want to use their access to Sally, through Li Min, to get at the father. When I say "get at", I mean that something Sally knows or does – or that they know about Sally – will persuade him to cooperate with them. Yes?'

'I can say yes, but it's not as if I know for certain any more than you do. I'll say yes anyway.' And he laughed. There was nothing pompous about Saunders, thought Manon, remembering his affable calmness during the ruckus of the previous year.

She said, 'I can't believe they'd threaten to harm Sally. Do you think that's possible?'

'No, I don't,' said Saunders. 'Even at the height of the Cold War that kind of thing didn't happen. The Russians were happy to execute any Russian double agents they caught but they never started killing Western Intelligence officers or members of their families. They knew where that would lead. And the minute the Chinese threatened to harm Sally, we'd make sure she was surrounded by armed guards and put on the first plane home. Then we'd sort out the Chinese agents here.'

'So assuming we're right that her father is the object of all this, how do the Chinese want to use her?'

'I'm not sure. Any ideas?'

'Well, it has to do with Li Min – that seems clear to me. That's why they've brought her to Oxford; otherwise it doesn't make much sense, since she was doing brilliantly at Harvard.'

'From what you say, Sally Washington doesn't know the Chinese are using her.' Saunders was looking at Manon searchingly.

'No, I don't think she does,' Manon said, 'and I don't think there's much point telling her. It would probably just lead them to abort their mission when we're getting close to discovering what it is. Do you agree?'

'I do.'

'Li Min is the key,' said Manon. 'If there's a deepfake involved – and why else involve Li Min? – then Sally is part of it. Though it's Li Min who knows how it will be used – I'd bet anything Sally hasn't got a clue.'

'When are you seeing Li Min again?'

'Tomorrow, for lunch.'

Saunders pursed his lips and nodded. He didn't have to say that this meeting would be critical. Time to press the young Chinese woman, Manon knew. And time for them to see Abbot, she realised, looking at her watch.

'How nice of you to come,' Abbot said loudly, for the benefit of his secretary. 'Your generosity is greatly appreciated.'

He closed the door to his office and lifted his eyebrows in a slightly mocking apology. Saunders gave a quiet laugh.

'Is she being stubborn?' Abbot asked, pointing to Manon. 'I think she should get out of that flat pronto.'

'I do too,' said Saunders.

'I don't,' said Manon. 'They're not after me. Whoever "they" are.'

'Mr Chew, I fear,' said Abbot.

'They may suspect me – though it's not clear of what. But I don't think they want to harm me.'

'Anyway,' Saunders said, seeing this exchange was going nowhere, 'we wanted to check in with you, Charles, let you know how we're getting on, and see how things stand with you.'

'Well, I have the benefit of an ace cataloguer,' he said, pointing to Manon, and they all laughed. 'But more seriously, I think the administrator at the Elm – it's a woman named Pierpont – may have got herself involved in helping our Mr Chew.' He explained that Pierpont's assistance seemed to be the only way he would have access to a master key, and thus to all the student rooms. 'I want to look into this a little more. We know from McCaffrey how Chew got here, but not how Pierpont also came aboard.'

Manon spoke up now. 'Would both of them be associated with Arthur Cole? I was just thinking: presumably he was involved in hiring the manager of the Elm – Pierpont – and I wonder if Cole was involved in getting Chew accepted as a student.'

Saunders said, 'I doubt that Chew's run by anyone here in the college. Whatever Cole's shortcomings or prejudices, he's not likely to be an agent runner for the Chinese. Even if he were willing, the Chinese wouldn't be.'

'A useful idiot,' Manon muttered. Abbot looked puzzled and Saunders explained: 'He's a sympathiser, is the point. He wouldn't in his darkest moments think of himself as working for a foreign power or doing anything treacherous in the eyes of His Majesty's government. It's worse than that – he thinks *we're* the ones who are blind. By his lights, we don't understand the wonder that is modern-day China, or that China should be viewed as our best friend, not as a lurking enemy. He will automatically sympathise with the Chinese point of view in any dispute, not because he's a traitor (even though arguably he is), but because he thinks that China is the victim of defamatory depictions in the Western press. If only we could be made to understand, we'd see China as the true beacon of the future he imagines it to be.'

Manon said firmly, 'So people like him are referred to as useful idiots, because they don't understand the damage they're doing. That's the concern with Arthur Cole. If the Chinese authorities are up to something – and we're confident they are – they'll use him whenever it suits them, to help hide their activities and keep any covert operatives – like this Mr Chew – from being exposed.'

Saunders spoke again. 'In some ways, it would be so much easier if he were an out and out spy for the other side.'

'I guess so,' Abbot remarked sceptically. 'Though having him under the same roof here, much less as my predecessor, gives me the absolute willies. I'm proud of the Institute; the longer I'm here and the more I get to know it, the better I feel about its prospects. But not if he's making it a halfway house for espionage. So how do we stop him?'

'First things first,' Saunders said emphatically. 'We have to focus on what Li Min is doing. But never fear: then it will be Arthur Cole's turn.'

31

ARTHUR COLE HAD ONLY previously been to the Chinese Embassy on Portland Place for social occasions. A lecture followed by small glasses of sweet white wine. A dinner when the Peking-born Ambassador to France had crossed the Channel in the wake of the French Prime Minister. A prize-giving ceremony for Chinese students studying in the UK (gratifyingly, two of Cole's own students had won awards).

At noon today, the atmosphere was different. Uncrowded and businesslike. The front door was unattended when he buzzed to be let in and explained through the speaker phone the nature of his business – he was there to see Yìchén, the Cultural Attaché.

The building was something of a Potemkin Village, since behind its elegant Robert Adam façade, the entire interior had been torn down and rebuilt in the 1980s in a grandiloquent Neo-Stalinist style that even Arthur Cole found hard to forgive.

Once inside he stood on the black-and-white marble floor of the vestibule, attended by a guard dressed like a doorman in a gold-buttoned greatcoat. A young energetic-looking woman, dressed neatly in a dark skirt and white blouse, came through some particularly ugly swing doors. For a moment he thought it was Li Min, then realised it was because she wore the same bobbed hairstyle and had a pair of equally expressive eyes.

'Mr Cole?' she asked in English, and they shook hands. 'Mr Yìchén will be with you shortly. Kindly follow me.'

She led him through into an enormous hall where he had been once before for a reception. It had an oddly low ceiling, with alternating squares of light and decorative panels. The effect was like having a huge chessboard hovering above your head. To either side cheap folding chairs were stacked, ready for use when the staff were called to all-in meetings.

They crossed this space and went through a door into a much smaller room, which had bright red sofas of fake leather lined against one wall. 'Make yourself comfortable,' the woman said, which seemed to Cole a very unlikely prospect.

He was nervous and realised it was because he felt *summoned* here, rather than invited. Previously, thanks to his status and appointment at St Felix's, he had always maintained a conviction that he was a free agent, independent, and, ultimately, though he cringed even at the thought, *not bought*. But Lau's successor had not shown even token obeisance to the usual social niceties; no, he had told Cole when he was expected and where, and left the grace notes for another occasion.

He did not have long to wait. The door opened and the Cultural Attaché came in, looking even younger than usual. Not much older than the postgraduate students who came to Cole for encouragement and advice. He wore a dark blue rollneck sweater, grey flannels and a blazer with gold buttons. He was considerably taller than Cole, or maybe Cole was shrinking, like so many of his older friends, as osteoarthritis took hold up and down their spines. I am an old man, he thought, wondering why the youthful attaché had asked him here today.

'Good morning,' Yìchén greeted him. Apparently he was known to many Westerners as Itch – since he said no one at Stanford, which he was very proud of having attended, could pronounce his actual Chinese name. Naturally Cole insisted on using his proper name.

They sat down at either end of one of the hideous fire-engine red sofas. Yìchén was a self-satisfied young man, who seemed to relish his life in the West; usually before proceeding to any business, they talked about films and plays he had seen, and he took great enjoyment in describing the many holidays he had spent in Europe. But today he moved rapidly to the agenda for this meeting. 'I understand you have met the new student Li Min,' he said in English – to Cole's irritation, since his own Mandarin was better in his view than Yìchén's English. Why, one time a Chinese woman who worked at the British Consulate in Hong Kong had praised his facility with her native language, saying he could easily be mistaken for Chinese. 'If they did not see what you look like,' she had added with a laugh.

He said now to Yìchén, 'Yes. Nice girl, I thought.'

'She is important to us,' the attaché said bluntly, making clear that her niceness was of no consequence.

'All our students are important to us,' said Cole feebly.

'I mean, important to the government.'

Really? thought Cole. Li Min was a pretty little thing – he would concede that – but it was hard to see her as being of any value to the authorities. But then Cole had never been very good with computers, never valued them much at all. He was confident that one day in the not-too-distant future, the world would see sense, and all this maddening fuss about IT skills would evaporate and be seen for what it was – an excuse for people, especially academics, to avoid the hard slog of proper research.

'We are slightly concerned that Li Min is not properly focused.'

'Oh, in what sense? On her work?'

'No,' Yìchén conceded. 'That remains excellent. So far. It is more her… attitude. And her associations.'

This surprised Cole a good deal. Virtually without exception, the Chinese students went about their business – the business of their studies, that is – quietly and without any problems of any consequence; they were so unlike their Western counterparts, especially the Americans who could be unreasonably demanding and very spoiled. The Chinese socialised quietly among themselves. They were not big drinkers, seemed utterly uninterested in drugs and had never in Cole's considerable experience attracted the attention either of the university proctors or, heaven forefend, the local police.

And what was he supposed to do about it anyway? His mission had been to invite the Chinese to study in Britain, welcome them, help them with any difficulties they encountered in the endless arcana of Oxford's academic life. In return, he had received funding for his beloved Institute and the Director's position. It had seemed a fair trade, and if morality entered into it at all, Cole was confident he had always stood on the right side of the ethical issues. It helped that the original endowment for the Institute had come, however curiously, from the Norwegians, a fact Cole had never wanted to investigate too closely. Recently there was the matter of

Chew's burglary of the Davidson woman's flat, but at least Cole hadn't known about it beforehand, and though he did wonder who had helped Chew, on the whole he preferred to forget about such an unfortunate incident.

He knew he was nobody's idea of a policeman. If this girl Li Min was going off the rails, she wasn't about to listen to an ageing bachelor, now retired. It would require representatives of the PRC to make any errant student see sense. They could frighten anyone, much less a young slip of a thing who happened to be good with machines.

The double doors at the end of the room swung open and another young man came in, approaching them rapidly. He stopped short of the sofa and made a little bow. Cole stood up awkwardly and gave a little bow back. Yìchén said, 'This is Deng. I have asked him to join us.'

Deng had none of the attaché's Europeanised savoir faire; his clothes were the anonymous Chinese ensemble of black and more black – black shirt buttoned at the throat, a black linen jacket, black cotton trousers and black lace-ups. Cole sensed at once that this man also had none of Yìchén's cultural attachments or interests. He had to be a member of the Ministry of State Security.

Yìchén spoke in rapid Chinese to Deng, repeating what he told Cole so far. Deng nodded almost imperceptibly and stared at Cole. It was the neutral gaze of someone who subordinated any display of feeling to cold professional assessment, and Cole, who prided himself on his ability to charm, found it unnerving. At the first break in Yìchén's account, he spoke up. 'Who are these new associates of Li Min, and why are they of concern?' Though remembering the visit from Chew, he had a pretty good idea.

Deng said flatly, 'There is a young woman from the United States. Her name is Sally Washington. Li Min and she are recent friends.'

'I see. And you are concerned about this friendship? I mean, I know it is not common, but I believe Miss Washington has a Chinese mother. So it's not so surprising. But perhaps you wish to discourage the friendship?'

'Not at all,' said Yìchén crisply. 'We have encouraged this association.'

'Then I don't see what the problem is.' Honestly, sometimes people could be so stupid, thought Cole. Even Chinese officials.

Deng held up a hand to silence Yìchén and said, 'There is another association we do not wish to be encouraged. A woman has come to work in the Institute, an American woman. She has made contact with Li Min and met with her on at least one occasion. We are concerned this woman may not be –' he hesitated '– that all may not be as it seems with her.'

Cole knew who they were talking about: Judith Davidson. He'd had his own suspicions, but more because he worried she was inflating her credentials and experience, which concerned him since the archival materials she was meant to be getting into shape would be the key constituents of any official history of his tenure at the Institute.

These men had different priorities naturally, but they didn't seem to realise that he was up to speed with their concerns. He thought of Chew's visit to see him, and then on the bus his confessing to breaking into Miss Davidson's flat. Did these two men not realise he knew all about it? He must put them straight. 'I take it you have been hearing from young Chew.'

'Yes—' Yìchén blurted out, before Deng could shut him up with an icy glare.

'Very well,' said Cole, ignoring the crossed signals between the two Chinese men. 'How do you wish to discourage this other friendship? Li Min's work is important, you say, so it's important that she stay in place. But Davidson is not a student; she is working for Abbot, my successor as Director of the Institute. I have no reason to complain about her; no grounds to have her fired.'

'It may require a more radical solution,' said Deng.

Despite his inward alarm (for he was not violent by nature, either directly or vicariously), Cole nodded wisely. 'I understand. But surely that is a duty more for the likes of our *Mr* Chew,' he said, adding the prefix to stress the gravity of the situation. 'Is he not trained to handle affairs like this?' He neatly avoided his private belief that Chew was little more than a buffoon – physically impressive, but cack-handed, borderline incompetent. He wanted no further involvement with the man, he realised, and certainly wasn't going to be shanghaied into helping him.

But it seemed this was not what Deng wanted in any case. 'Mr Chew is occupied with Li Min for now,' he said. 'He has hands that are full.'

I'll say, thought Cole.

'We thought,' said Yìchén, speaking for the first time since his mistimed outburst, 'that you should stay close to this Davidson woman. It may be an entirely innocent friendship she is developing with Li Min. But we cannot assume that. We need you to determine if something more sinister is at play.'

'I will happily do my best,' Cole said, hoping he could end this conversation soon. A graceful promise of assistance should hopefully keep them off his back in the weeks ahead.

'And then,' Yìchén continued, 'if we determine this American woman is endangering our interests – in this case Li Min – we will need you to act decisively.'

'Act?' said Cole, his voice rising in alarm. 'In what way must I act?'

It was Deng who delivered the blow. 'To make Judith Davidson disappear.'

32

Li Min glanced at her watch. She had been reading most of the morning in her room, but then Sally had knocked on her door and called, 'Are you in?' They often went into town together, where Li Min would head for the lab and Sally for the Bodleian Library. It was unusual for them both still to be at the Elm this late in the morning.

'Hi, Sally,' Li Min called back, getting to her feet. She was happy to be interrupted.

Their friendship had continued to grow – they had dinner most nights with the same small group of Americans, and unless one of them had pressing work to do, spent the better part of the evening together as well. Sometimes they also met in town: Li Min would walk down from the Science Parks and see her friend for coffee in the Middle Common Room of St Felix's, where the graduate students congregated, or occasionally at a café in the Covered Market.

Li Min was no misanthrope, and had had close friends before, but that had been in China. At Harvard people had been perfectly civil but not really warm or friendly; too often they seemed wary of the Chinese, and occasionally suspicious or even hostile. Given Li Min's own reserve, her initial nervousness about Western manners and conventions, she had spent most of her down time, out of the lab, alone. At Cal Tech before that, most of the Western students had seemed to view a social life as an unwelcome distraction from their work.

She could have fallen back on the company of other Chinese people at any of these institutions, but she had been determined to learn as much about the West as possible, and playing Mahjong on Friday nights with other Chinese students didn't seem a good way to go about it. Better to be on one's own than replicate life back home. Better still, however, was to have a new close friend – a 'pal' as Sally called her.

Li Min had not even got to the door when it swung open and Sally appeared in the doorway. 'Come in,' said Li Min, though her friend was already over the threshold.

'Were you working?' Sally asked. 'Hope I'm not interrupting,' she added entirely insincerely.

Li Min wanted to laugh. She was always amazed how Sally rode roughshod over so many of the Western social conventions – knock first, hold doors for people, etc. – that Li Min had tried to follow carefully. She said now, copying her friend's usual opening query, 'What's up?'

'Not a lot,' said Sally. 'My mom's threatening to come over for a visit.'

'That would be nice.'

'That's what you think,' said Sally with a laugh. 'But tell me, when are you going to make me a star? That would keep Mom quiet – she keeps asking me when I'll get my Master's degree.'

'What kind of star?' asked Li Min, slightly puzzled.

'A movie star of course. You have enough footage of me for two feature-length films.'

This was true. Li Min had gone on taking film of Sally well after she had enough to fill Deng's brief. One sunny afternoon they had walked up Cumnor Hill behind the Elm. Finding several flocks of sheep grazing on the pasture there, Li Min had started filming them too. When her friend wanted to be part of things, she filmed Sally running towards the sheep, this way and that, with her hair swept back in the wind as the ewes grudgingly scattered. Looking at the film later, Li Min realised none of it was likely to be of use to her work, or to that bastard Deng, but she was glad to have it nonetheless. It caught the gazelle-like freedom of her friend perfectly. It was private, she decided, and she would keep it that way.

'Have you decided what to do with all your footage?' asked Sally.

'Not yet,' said Li Min, thinking bitterly it was Deng who was going to do the deciding. She had once tried to explain the nature of her work to Sally but had soon realised her friend wasn't really interested. Li Min could only hope that whatever use she made of the Sally footage, and that of the obedient male student, her friend would never need to know about it. Right now, Li Min valued their friendship more than anything. Even her work.

33

Manon felt conspicuous waiting for Li Min outside the Covered Market. She tried to look interested in the window displays of the shops across the High Street from the market entrance, but the clothes looked like tat for the most part, and expensive tat at that, so she found it hard to feign much interest. Fortunately, the spring warmth had returned, and the sun was out for the first time that week, so at least she wasn't getting wet or cold.

Then Li Min arrived, slightly breathless. 'I am so sorry to be late,' she said, panting. 'I ran from the bus stop.'

'You're not very late,' said Manon, who knew her own punctuality bordered on obsessive, which made her more, rather than less, tolerant of other people's tardiness. 'Come on, there's a nice quiet place across the street. Let's go get a table.'

'I was talking with Sally and forgot the time,' said Li Min as they settled themselves in the rear of the restaurant.

'From the sound of it,' said Manon, 'you've become good friends with her.'

'I have,' said Li Min, nodding. 'She has even helped me with my work.'

'Oh, how's that? Is she working on AI too?'

Li Min laughed at the thought of this. 'No,' she said more seriously. 'But my adviser was unhappy when I used some of my fellow students at the lab as… how do you say it… guinea pigs?'

'That's right.'

'So I got Sally to stand in instead. Along with one of the Chinese boys.'

'Oh,' said Manon, trying not to sound too interested. 'What are you doing with the film? Do you extrapolate it along with audio?'

Li Min looked at her appreciatively. 'You understand what AI can do?'

'I think so. You can take basic raw footage and use it to make new film that shows the same person, only doing different things. And even saying different words. Is that right?'

'Yes. Though my adviser said it would be wrong to show someone doing something they hadn't actually done. He misses the point,' she added, with a note of contempt in her voice. 'AI can make real what have up to now been only dreamed-of possibilities.'

'I think he's just being careful. It's not clear what the legal status is – to be honest, Li Min, if someone gets upset about anything you produce, they won't sue you, they'll sue the university.'

'But why sue anyone?'

'It depends what you show them doing,' said Manon meaningfully.

Li Min looked startled. 'But I would never—' And she stopped.

'I know that, and you know that, but your adviser doesn't.'

Li Min thought about this, then shrugged. 'Maybe so. But it would not be a problem.'

172

She said this boldly but still looked uncertain. Manon decided to press her. 'Is your government interested in your work?'

Li Min looked away. 'Yes, they are,' she said reluctantly. 'Even if they don't understand it.'

'Do they take an interest in this filming you've been doing?'

There was a look of resignation now on Li Min's face. 'Too much so,' she said quietly.

Manon did not want to overdo it and derail their conversation, but she gambled anyway, asking, 'Do they tell you what to film?'

'Not really,' said Li Min, looking relieved.

Manon understood why. 'I mean, do they tell you what to *show* the people doing in the AI-generated film? Sally and the Chinese boy, I mean. Not what they are actually doing, but what you can make them look as if they're doing?'

There was a long silence and Manon worried she was pushing too hard. 'Not yet,' Li Min said at last. She seemed to be wavering for a moment, but then set her jaw firmly and stayed silent.

Enough questions about her work, thought Manon when Li Min did not go on. Manon said, her voice lighter, 'It's nice that you've got such a good friend as Sally. Have you met any of her family?' She had switched to using another kind of bait.

Li Min took it. 'No, I haven't, though she says her mother's coming to visit soon. Funny, because it's her dad she is closest to, she says. He's – how do you say it? – a big wig.'

'Bigwig sounds right. What does he do?'

'He's in the government, and something in the military.'

'A bigwig for sure then.'

Li Min smiled. 'He adores Sally. She says he lets her get away with murder.'

'But her mom doesn't?'

'Not at all. She's very strict. A bit of a tiger mother.' Here Li Min smiled, realising it was unusual for a Chinese woman to use the phrase, especially about another Chinese female. 'At least that's what Sally says. She's invited me to visit her in Washington. That is, if I'm allowed to go.'

'What do you mean? Would your parents object?'

'Of course not – they're proud of me, even though we live in different worlds now. My father runs a little shop – sort of like a newsagent here. My mother helps out when she can – she has my little brother to look after. No, I meant if the Chinese government lets me go.'

'You need their permission?' Manon already knew the answer to that.

Li Min looked her in the eye. She said flatly, 'I need their permission for everything.'

34

Charles Abbot managed to find a parking place outside a row of shops in Summertown, about a mile from his flat in North Oxford. He went into the M&S Food Hall. Keep it light, he told himself; it's only supper, not some grand feast.

So he bought fresh fettuccine, some pecorino cheese, fresh basil and pine nuts. Two large tomatoes for a salad on the side, a box of cheese straws and a small carton of mixed olives, a baguette, some butter and grapes for dessert, with a box of almond biscuits. There was red wine at home so he bought a bottle of Sauvignon Blanc. And he was done.

In the past he would have enjoyed this small collection of treats, looked forward to sharing them with his wife, while she told him about her day and he did the same for her. How could anyone ever take her place? He thought fleetingly that maybe he should cancel this dinner, claim illness or some semi-emergency. Manon would understand. She was sensitive; he could tell that.

But no, he couldn't do that, not on such short notice and out of nothing but simple cowardice. Abbot was a friendly, open sort of man, known for his considerate treatment of staff and his sympathy for other people's problems, but no one in the Foreign Office got very far if they wore their heart on their sleeve, and he was therefore by objective standards still more of a classic 'stiff upper lip' type. For any venting of his own troubles, he was used to an audience of no more than one – his late wife – and even she had been spared any long accounts of really serious upsets.

Yet some months after his wife's death, finding that time was not healing the wound at all, Abbot had at last gone to see a grief counsellor in London. He had gone reluctantly – the mere idea of seeing a therapist almost as alien to him as actually going to one. But he tried it nonetheless, thinking he had nothing left to lose after parting from the most important person in his life. And to his intense relief, the therapist had actually proved helpful, by not focusing on the awfulness of Abbot's loss but on the possibilities for his new life. There was one particular piece of advice from him that came to mind now. *When you're afraid to do something new, that's exactly when you should do it.*

So he told himself he'd just have to grit his teeth and get on with it. Then he cheered himself up by remembering how nice this new person to enter his life seemed, and how much he liked seeing her when she appeared in his office doorway. There was nothing wrong with feeling like that. Nothing at all, he told himself sternly. He was only being friendly.

35

Abbot's flat was less than half a mile from Manon's but seemed to belong to a different world altogether. A grander world, a more expensive one. On Norham Gardens, his road, the houses were tall and Victorian, with sharp Gothic gables of mellow dark-red brick. In the mist of early evening, the buildings loomed spookily and made Manon feel she was entering a club requiring membership she didn't have. She recalled how at the High Table dinner she'd gone to, McCaffrey had complained about the comparative penury of today's dons. 'Once, you made a fortune just through buying a house,' he declared. 'Remember Hazelton?' he asked of the little circle listening at table. When no one nodded, he said, 'An Economics don aptly enough – better than some, but hardly Maynard Keynes' successor. He looked after himself very nicely. Bought one of the mansions in Norham Gardens in the early sixties – paid ten thousand all in. He put down one thousand himself and secured the rest with an interest-free loan from his college. Those were the days, eh? I happened to see that it came up for sale last year, and the owner was asking a cool four million.'

So Abbot must be very well off, thought Manon edgily, already nervous about this supper invitation. What was wrong with her? she asked herself. Why should she care one way or the other about the state of Charles Abbot's finances? It wasn't as if this were a proper date, after all. It was just polite hospitality offered by the man who was pretending to be her boss.

She was relieved to see that there were four buzzers. So there must be four flats in this pile of a house, she thought with relief. He can't be that rich. The relief was matched by anxiety. It was still a date of sorts.

She pressed the buzzer labelled *Abbot* and a moment later the heavy front door opened. Charles had changed and wore casual dark blue cords with a light-coloured shirt that just peeked out above a blue jumper. 'Come in, come in,' he said. He led her down a communal hallway and through another door into his flat.

'Gosh,' she said, taking in her new surroundings. They were in a large through room with a kitchen area at the back and a work/dining table at the other end. Looking across the hall, she could see a living room – with a long sofa draped in throws, and comfortable-looking armchairs with bright cushions.

'This is lovely,' she said appreciatively.

'I'm glad you like it.' He went on, 'This used to be two rooms – I had it made into one. I didn't think I'd have much use for a separate dining room. When I need to entertain formally, I take people to High Table, which the great and the good seem to prefer anyway. I don't mind having the kitchen and the dining space together, though I imagine my grandmother would have died a death before she'd have let her guests see their dinner being prepared.'

Manon laughed. 'I think it's very smart.'

'Come sit down,' he said, pointing to an island at the kitchen end of the room with stools on either side. 'What's your poison? White wine? Red? Gin and tonic?'

She opted for the Sauvignon and he joined her while he put a large saucepan of water on the range to boil. 'How does pesto pasta sound? Do say if it's not appealing. Pesto is the Marmite of pasta sauces, I find.'

'Marmite?'

'Oh, sorry – it's a condiment of sorts. Looks like treacle but tastes completely salty. People either love it or hate it. The lovers put it on toast for the most part.'

'Bring it on,' she said. 'I don't know about Marmite, but I love pesto.'

He had set the table looking out over the street, where they sat with large white bowls full of steaming fettuccine and basil pesto. There was a side salad of lettuce and tomatoes, and a bottle of Chianti Classico. A simple enough supper but tasty, and Manon was impressed. 'Do you like to cook?' she asked.

'Needs must,' he said wryly. 'A cook doesn't come with the job.'

'Does this flat?' she asked, then wondered if it had been rude to ask.

'No. But I sold up in London, so could afford to move to this swanky part of town.'

'It's a lovely room.'

'Thank you.' He ran a hand through his hair; it was nice hair, Manon thought, then slapped her own wrist mentally. It was just supper, she told herself.

He cleared their bowls and returned with a wooden platter of cheese and biscuits and grapes. 'There's just fruit for pudding,' he said, 'but there's plenty of cheese. I hope this will do?'

'More than do,' she said, taking a small cluster of grapes, then cutting into the cheese.

'So,' he said, topping up their glasses, 'enough of me talking about me. Tell me, how did you end up in England? I always think of… I'm not sure what to say here… agents? Staff members? Well, whatever the word is, I always think you're all beavering away in the Middle East.'

'You're not far off actually.' And she explained that she had originally been an analyst specialising in the Middle East, though none of her work had involved travel in the region. He seemed impressed that she knew Arabic, though by some unspoken agreement they didn't converse in it, since it would have shown who had the superior skills. She admitted that she had worked on the Middle East desk for over three years. 'The analyst's lot,' she said. 'Utterly unglamorous.'

'Most important work is,' he said. 'But unless you've decided you really are here to catalogue the Institute's excuse for an archive, it's good that you're allowed to talk so openly about what you used to do. But you're not doing that anymore?' he asked, leaving the question mark hanging in the air. Manon just smiled. 'That's what we call a Mona Lisa smile,' he said.

'How so?' she asked.

'Enigmatic.'

'Before I forget – I saw Li Min today. The AI student.'

'She's said to be gifted. Unlike our mutual friend Mr Chew. How was she?' he asked.

'She seemed on edge, close to some sort of tipping point. I only hope it tips her towards us. Something's up, something to do with her work and her friendship with Sally Washington. I didn't want to push too hard. She's angry with her Chinese bosses but still scared of them.'

'Well, let me know if there's anything I can do. Or the Institute.'

'I will,' said Manon. 'She is probably scared of losing her funding, and that's when the Institute or one of its benefactors could step in to help.'

'Yes, though I would leave Arthur Cole out of it, in case you were thinking of talking to him.'

'I wasn't,' said Manon flatly. 'Don't worry.'

'The question I have,' said Abbot, 'is why would she lose her funding? The PRC ordered her here after all.'

'I know. I can only think they might want her to do something she refuses to do. Funding is the weapon they used to get her here; funding is the weapon they'd use again. But anyway,' Manon said, sensing too much of this talk could spoil the evening, 'I will keep you posted if anything changes. She knows now she can come to me if it gets too much for her – I am pretty sure I made that clear. I thought I might have a word too with her new pal Sally.'

'That makes sense, provided she doesn't tell Li Min you've approached her.'

The evening passed all too quickly for Manon; she and Charles felt entirely comfortable with each other. They had coffee, and Manon turned down a brandy to accompany it. She pointed to the living-room wall, which was decorated with a plethora of small framed prints and watercolours, haphazardly arranged – a gallery in miniature. 'I like your pictures,' she said. 'And the mini-gallery effect.'

'Thank you.' He hesitated, then said haltingly, 'Actually, it's my wife's doing, though she never lived here. In London she had the staircase wall chock-a-block with pictures. I thought I'd try to replicate it.'

'You've done it very well.'

He didn't reply, suddenly looking terribly sad. Manon was taken aback by the sea change in his mood; had what she said been so clumsy? She determined not to let it spoil the evening or end it precipitately.

Fortunately, Charles seemed to sense her discomfort. 'I'm sorry,' he said. 'You think you've got over things, and then they pop up and give you a smack. Then a second smack for presuming you were getting over it. Forgive me.'

'It must be awful being at the mercy of memories.'

His eyes widened slightly. 'Yes, that's an excellent way of putting it. You're sailing along and everything's dandy, then out of the blue something reminds you of—'

'Her. Or for some people "him".'

'It's nice of you to be so understanding. You'd be surprised how obtuse some people can be.'

'I'm not sure I'd be very surprised at all!' And she was glad when he laughed at this. 'Listen,' she said, 'I've had a very nice evening and a very good dinner but I better be off now. I've a lot on tomorrow, thanks to our friend Li Min.'

'Of course.' He was peering out of the window. 'But it looks dreadful out there. Let me run you back in the car.'

'Oh, no. It's not a long walk. And certainly not worth the petrol or the carbon emissions we're meant to justify.'

'All right. Then I'll walk you back.' Before Manon could protest, he added, 'I could use the exercise.'

The mist had lifted outside, but there had been some drizzle – the tyres on the cars on Banbury Road hissed against the wet tarmac. Manon and Abbot walked in silence much of the way, which at first seemed odd after all the talk between them in his flat, but after a while seemed perfectly natural. They were easy with each other, Manon thought, any nervousness about this 'date' long gone.

When they reached her corner on Woodstock Road, she said, 'You don't have to go any further.'

'Of course I do. I need to see you safely home – after all that's happened.'

It was said so cheerfully that Manon couldn't object. She hoped he wouldn't want to be asked in; the evening had been so pleasant she didn't want to risk spoiling it.

The street was silent. The only noise was the sound of their footsteps and the cars on Woodstock Road behind them. They walked on in silence, then Manon heard a slight swooshing noise, further up the street. Abbot heard it too. They both stopped instinctively to listen.

It sounded like running water and inwardly Manon groaned – a leak? Or another gift from her burglar?

They moved on slowly and the noise grew louder. 'What on earth—' Manon started to say, but Abbot quietened her with a pat on the arm and a whispered 'Hush'. Ahead of them on the right, out in the front garden of the house next to hers, she saw a stream of water rise and fall in an arc that caught the light of the moon.

Drawing close, Manon saw an old woman, white-haired and wearing a housecoat, standing in the middle of her small front patch of lawn, lifting the hose slightly to send it up and down onto the rose bushes at her garden's front edge. She must have seen them, for suddenly the stream of water stopped.

'Good evening,' she said improbably – it was close to eleven o'clock after all. The woman went on: 'You must be my new neighbour.'

'Yes. I'm Judith Davidson. And this is my friend Charles.'

'I've seen you about but we've never spoken. I'm Becky Carlson. It was I who called the police.'

'Ah, you saw the intruder in my back garden?'

'I did indeed. To be honest, at first I thought it was you. Your landlady had told me she had a new tenant. I hadn't met you so I assumed the woman was you.'

Manon started to nod and then realised what had been said. 'You saw a *woman* in the garden?'

'That's right. Didn't the police tell you that?'

Manon thought hard. Had the pair of police officers actually said it was a man who'd broken into her kitchen? Or had she just assumed it? She couldn't remember for sure, but whoever this woman was she'd had no business being in the back garden, even if she was not the burglar.

Becky was talking again. 'She was older than you but I just assumed she was the new tenant, as you and I hadn't met.'

Charles asked, 'Did you get a good look at her?'

'I suppose so,' said Becky rather uncertainly 'Long hair and *not* very nice.' Manon forced herself not to laugh. 'Older than you, my dear, and if you don't mind my saying, much less attractive. She wasn't dressed for gardening, if that's any help.'

'What do you mean?'

'She was dressed like a middle-aged PA. I should know because I used to be one myself.'

They said goodnight to the neighbour, then Abbot stopped when they reached the gate to the front garden of Manon's house. 'Thank you for dinner,' she said. 'I had a lovely time.'

She wondered if she'd said something wrong as Abbot stayed silent. He looked preoccupied. 'Sorry,' he said suddenly. 'I had a great time too. But I was just thinking about what Becky said.' He gestured towards the neighbour's house. 'And I wonder if the woman she saw was Nina Pierpont.'

36

THE NEXT MORNING ABBOT drove directly to the Elm, only stopping to tell his assistant he had an emergency dentist's appointment.

When he arrived, Amy was behind the desk in the office again. Abbot's disappointment must have shown, for she said, 'Are you looking for Ms Pierpont?'

'Yes. Is she still ill?'

'No, not at all. You've just missed her. She's going to be working at St Felix's for a few days. Someone there's come down with 'flu and they've told Nina to cover for them.'

'Who authorised that?' he demanded.

Amy sensed his anger and looked down at her desk. 'I believe it was Professor Cole, sir.' She pointed down the corridor. 'You've only just missed Nina. She went out the back way.'

He walked down the corridor in the direction she had just indicated and came to a glass door overlooking a courtyard. From here he could look out over the fields behind the Elm and was able to see the figure of Nina Pierpont, walking quickly up the field, just short of the barn. For a moment he thought of following her, but then decided to leave things as they were. For what could he say if she challenged him, accused him of following her? Slowly, he retraced his steps and found Amy still sitting at the desk. 'I've just seen Ms Pierpont walking towards the barn. Have you any idea why she is going there?'

'No, sir,' replied Amy. She stared down at her computer but he could see the red flush rising in her cheeks and creeping around the back of her neck. She looked the picture of guilt and discomfiture.

He walked back to his car feeling irritated that he, who was supposedly in charge here, seemed to be shut out of things that were known to others. He started the car and was going to set off towards Oxford but immediately noticed the old Land Rover parked by the five-bar gate in front of the barn. Gillroy had been unenthusiastic about him examining the place unaccompanied, but screw him, Abbot thought angrily. This building belonged to the Institute, he was the Institute Director; no one was going to keep him out. And if there was an awkward encounter with Nina Pierpont, so be it. He got out of his car, pushed open the gate and walked up the rough track to the barn. He found the going heavy in his street shoes, the grass growing freely on the track, wet and full of clumps – no one had levelled it for years, it seemed. He was out of puff by the time he reached the open door of the barn.

Inside he saw no one. Nothing had changed: the same tools were leaning up against one of the walls. He noticed that on the opposite side there was a door standing half-open. But going to it and looking out, away from the Elm, down the hill towards what looked like a transverse dyke, he saw no sign of anyone.

So where was Nina Pierpont? She had definitely been heading this way. He turned back and quickly explored the barn. Nothing. A ladder led up to a loft approximately half the size of the barn floor beneath, but apart from its bare boards there was little else to see except for, improbably, a wheelbarrow, which must have been hell to get up the ladder.

Baffled, he climbed down to ground-level. He didn't know what he was looking for, but sensed something was being withheld from him. He reluctantly conceded defeat; he'd found nothing suspicious here, which was in itself suspicious – for where was Nina Pierpont now?

As he emerged from the barn, he almost ran into Gillroy, who started at the sight of him. He was holding a fat brown envelope, which he hastily stuffed into one of his jacket pockets at the sight of Abbot.

'I was after Ms Pierpont,' Abbot said, 'I saw her walking in this direction. Have you seen her?'

'She doesn't come here. She works at the Elm,' he said, jerking his finger in that direction.

'If you see her, please tell her I need to talk to her.'

'I won't forget,' said Gillroy with a scornful laugh, walking away.

Abbot turned to go back to his car, and as he did so caught sight of the figure of Pierpont rounding the back of the Elm towards the rear car park. She must have seen him arriving and taken pre-emptive action so as not to have to talk to him – which, paradoxically, told him all he needed to know.

37

Louise Donovan's plane landed half an hour early, reaping the benefit of a strong Gulf Stream tailwind. It made Louise's madcap idea, formed after a drink before dinner as the jet turned away from the Canadian coast towards Heathrow, seem more sensible since it gave her even more time than her schedule initially provided.

She was en route to a conference in Saarbrücken, but had been unable to get an earlier connecting flight from London. Faced with spending twenty-four hours in a hotel at Heathrow, she had suddenly recalled that Oxford was just an hour away on the fast coach from the airport. And her friend Manon was there.

She had enjoyed Manon's visit to her in Harvard and wondered if she had ever made contact in Oxford with the Chinese girl Louise had wanted her to meet. Li Min? Yes, that was her name. Well, perhaps she would soon find out, thought Louise, as she collected her bag from the conveyor and strode through Customs.

Not that she expected to find out much else about her friend's activities. She had always sensed that Manon lived behind a façade, one she had erected from the get-go. Her work was something in the Defense Department concerned with oil and gas reserves, though what fuel sources had to do with defence Louise neither knew nor cared to enquire.

When Manon had come to work at the US Embassy in London, it had soon become apparent to her friend that she was in fact working for the CIA's London office. After Louise had become entangled with an MP whose background turned out to be highly dubious, Manon and her colleagues had been able to ascertain his true origins and to rescue her from a dangerous relationship. Louise had never pressed her friend for all the details – but in the ensuing débâcle it had become pretty clear that she had become involved in a highly sensitive security services operation.

But what Manon was up to now she was back over here was a mystery. St Felix's seemed to be perfectly normal by Oxford standards – very old from the photos on its website, built of honey-coloured stone, another in the university's long list of mid-sized colleges of medium renown. Respectable if not outstanding. The only remarkable thing about it was that it had an Institute, fairly recently founded, which seemed to specialise in postgraduate studies for foreign students. So Louise was puzzled, though right now she simply hoped her friend was still there and would be glad to see her.

Twenty minutes later, when the bus was joining the M40, Louise suddenly wondered if what she was doing made any sense at all. She'd had a postcard from Manon – a picture of a distant view of the city from an outlying hill, full of spires and towers – but otherwise her friend had not been in touch. Manon's cell phone number hadn't worked; she must have got a new phone. Ordinarily Louise would have emailed or rung the college she knew Manon was attached to, but that had not been a possibility when she had hatched her impromptu plan at an altitude of 35,000 feet.

If Manon couldn't put her up, she would find a hotel; it would be cheaper than London anyway. Louise hoped her friend was in residence, though if not had a backup plan to do the whole tourist thing, have a quiet dinner and then go to bed. Her flight the next day wasn't until the late afternoon, so she would have ample time to do a little more sightseeing and get back to the airport.

Her bag was light and from Google Maps she saw that St Felix's was only a few minutes' walk away from the bus terminus on Oxford's Gloucester Green. The neighbouring plaza was packed and busy on a market day: with grocers and butchers, a fishmonger, and a row of stalls, mainly Asian, selling exotic street food from Malaysia, Singapore, the Philippines, Korea and half a dozen other countries in the Far East.

Leaving the crush, Louise walked up George Street. Her phone showed the location of St Felix's. When she mentioned Manon's name to the porter there, he didn't recognise it, but suggested that the Institute was probably the place she was looking for. He explained it was at the back of college and she walked through the quad until she saw the new building.

Inside there was a woman sitting behind the reception desk. She eyed Louise and her bag. 'Can I help you?' she asked without much helpfulness in her tone.

'I hope so,' said Louise. 'I'm here to see Manon Tyler. Is she in today?'

'That's not a name I'm familiar with. Just a minute.'

The woman opened a drawer and took out a list.

'She's American,' said Louise helpfully.

'American?' queried the receptionist. 'Are you looking for a student or a staff member? The only American member of staff I know of here is the researcher, Ms Davidson. Are you sure you have the right place?'

Louise replied hesitantly, 'No, I'm not. The porter sent me down here. The only address I have is St Felix's College.'

Louise wondered what she had got herself into; she suspected she was digging a hole for herself – and maybe for Manon. Fortunately, the imminent stand-off she sensed coming was pre-empted by a man who had been lingering nearby. In his forties and fit, thought Louise. He said to the receptionist, 'I'll take over, Ms Pierpont. Hi,' he said with a smile to Louise, who unaccountably found herself blushing. 'Come with me. I reckon we can find the right Manon Tyler for you.'

As they walked away, he said quietly to her, 'There's only one of them here.'

38

Deng always gave Li Min little notice of their meetings, but this summons was particularly abrupt. She was on her way into town on the shuttle bus, Sally sitting next to her, when WhatsApp sounded its clarion high-pitched *bing*. The message read: *Come to the cemetery where we met before in twenty minutes.*

She could just about make it, thought Li Min as the bus moved slowly along Botley Road. But how did Deng know that? Did he think she could just magically materialise on St Cross Road whenever he wanted her to? She supposed that unless she were being watched all the time by foreign intelligence, an impromptu summons reduced the chance of their meeting being observed. Though, ironically, the only intelligence service likely to be watching Li Min belonged to her own country.

She saw Deng waiting for her on the bench in the rear corner of the graveyard. It was suddenly colder after several weeks of spring warmth, and she had bought a light coat in John Lewis the day before. Deng was himself bundled up – he wore an overcoat with reason, since the day was unseasonably crisp, the wind biting. It reminded Li Min of her time in Cambridge Massachusetts, where on the Common near Harvard Square the buds would suddenly appear on the trees, like tiny buttons, and the now-higher sun would cast a rich light across the greening grass.

Deng had had a haircut, which made him look young, raw-boned and angry. He seemed tense, though comfortable enough with their meeting place; usually he was extra-alert, watching to see if she were followed, looking around in all directions, acting as if even the bench they sat on might be bugged. But not today – he seemed to be focused entirely on what he had to tell her.

'I have instructions for your work,' he said, not even bothering to say 'hello' as Li Min sat down on the bench beside him. They were shielded from view by a large holly tree.

'My work is going well,' she said defensively. 'And I filmed the two people as you told me to.' She could not bring herself to mention Sally's name, hated the fact that she was dragging her friend into an intrigue she did not yet understand.

'Excellent,' said Deng; the compliment sounded mechanical. 'Now it needs to be put to use. I have a script for you to follow, based on the specifications I have given you before. It will require some ingenuity to achieve it, but from what you have told me, you have the basis.'

He reached inside his coat and handed her several A4 pages.

Li Min scanned the pages, at first quickly, then more slowly as she took in what they contained. They were in the form of a film script. No names had been used: Male One and Female One were the only designations, and the only two characters in the first few pages. Li Min was well versed in the brief history of deepfakes and kept her distance as much as possible from anything defamatory or incriminating or just downright sleazy. And sleaze, she realised now, was what she had expected to find in whatever film scenario they were ordering her to construct. But there was nothing sexual going on in the mini-drama scripted on these pages. It was far worse than that.

'What is the purpose of this?' she demanded as the nature of what she was supposed to create became clear.

'That is not something you should worry about or query. Your sole responsibility is to follow orders.' He sighed irritably. 'Time and again, you ask why you are being instructed to do something. I ask you formally to stop that, unless you no longer wish to pursue your studies here – or anywhere else for that matter.'

'I ask a question and you threaten me.' She was as always alarmed by Deng's threats, but now she was also angry.

'No,' he said impatiently. 'I merely remind you of your duty to pay proper respect to the authorities of your country and act in accordance with their very modest requests. In return, you are allowed to live and study here, to pursue your work without interference, even to socialise with suspect characters from alien countries.'

He meant Sally, Li Min thought, still furious. Every time they met, he approached her, carrot in hand – then, *whoosh*, a stick emerged.

'I am not talking about me,' she said firmly. 'Sally would never do this.' She pointed to the script.

'It is not a question of what *she* would or would not do. It is a matter of what people believe she would do. And that is where you will be instrumental.

'Tell me, does this Western girl suspect how you will be using the film you have shot of her?'

'No. As far as she knows, she could be anyone – I needed stock footage as they call it. Meaning it didn't matter if it were her or someone else being filmed. I just needed a living, breathing body.'

Deng smirked and looked at her with bogus admiration. 'After you succeed at this, you could have a fine future in the movie business.'

39

Arthur Cole was in a state, to use his mother's expression – he had been a nervous child. Since the meeting at the Chinese Embassy, his stomach seemed to contain a knot the size of a football.

He looked at his favourite Ming vase, the most precious item in his beloved collection. Normally the mere sight of it would soothe him, but not today. Instead, images of disaster came to him – of the vase cracked and missing a large piece at its base; then an even more hideous vision of its porcelain completely crushed into a mound of dust.

What was wrong with him? Why could he not pull himself together? he thought with a sigh as he purposely looked away from the vase. He knew the answer, he supposed; he just didn't like acknowledging it. He had been a fool to think his informal alliance with the Chinese, the chance to build his collection, would come without a price. But now it was time for him to pay.

If only they had picked another way in which he could be of service. Had he not always shown willingness to fulfil their requests, to grease the wheels that led to their substantial presence in the heart of one of the world's leading institutions of higher learning? Cole had always been happy to intervene on their behalf, confident that he was helping to foster a better understanding between the West and the true China, the one of his youth, the China he loved.

But those Embassy requests had always been positive, or at the worst harmless: Cole would be asked to host a dinner for visiting Beijing dignitaries in the college's private dining room; Cole would be the university sponsor for a series of annual lectures on China, and would arrange to have them delivered in the Sheldonian Theatre, a Christopher Wren building of international fame. Or, less positively perhaps, but still hardly a hanging offence, he would persuade a faculty member to allow a Chinese student to come to study at the Institute when perhaps his or her credentials were not up to scratch. A picture of Mr Chew flickered briefly in his mind before he banished it. Cole was good at this kind of thing: the exercise of – what did they call it these days? – soft power. That was it. He could lobby fiercely or subtly as the situation required; he knew after so long here which buttons to push to open a door; which door to avoid lest he double-lock it. But the one thing he had never even remotely imagined doing was now being demanded of him. Arthur Cole was neither violent nor a man of action. Yet the people in the Embassy were asking him to be both.

The intolerable Mr Deng – what an odious creature! – was now his primary contact, usurping that role from Yìchén, the young man Arthur Cole had liked to think of as a friend. Deng was not only uncouth, he was also relentless, constantly demanding updates from Cole on the progress on what he insisted on calling 'The Project'. Project? Cole shook his head just thinking about it. When did a project involve harming someone physically – because surely that was what they were asking for, since how else did one get rid of this American woman who called herself a librarian?

As for progress, there had been none. Deng had demanded a report, but so far Arthur Cole had simply ducked giving a response. When Deng phoned him here in his rooms, Cole claimed he was in the middle of a tutorial and would have to ring him back. But he didn't, and when the phone rang again he didn't answer it. It was an ostrich-like position, but Arthur Cole liked ostriches. Or at least had nothing against them.

There was a knock on the door, which surprised him enough that he jerked in his chair. He was not expecting anyone. Who could it be? Deng, come up from London to beard him on his home turf? He was strongly tempted to stay silent until the visitor went away, but then there was another knock, and the familiar sound of a shrill female voice. 'Professor Cole? Are you there, Professor Cole?'

'Coming,' he said wearily. Once he had heard that voice twenty times a day. Nina Pierpont had been his assistant throughout most of his five-year term as Director of the Institute, and had been perfectly competent. Neither of them had warmed to the other, however, and it was to his great relief that she had moved to the newly reconstructed Elm as its manager, and thereafter was largely out of his working life. Yet here she was again. Why?

'Nina,' he said, opening the door. To his surprise, Pierpont came in without being asked, where once she would have hovered until he invited her. This seemed to be a newer, more confident woman, unrecognisable from the person he had hired.

She sat down in the chair usually occupied by a student, an upright wooden one that discouraged doziness. 'That man is too much,' she said sharply. 'The way he spoke to me.' She shook her head.

'Who are we talking about?' Cole said mildly, though he had a good idea.

'Charles Abbot, of course. Who else?'

This was not the first time she had complained about the man. Cole should be flattered, he supposed, since it was clear her loyalty remained with him. But instead he was irritated; he had far greater things to worry about right now than bruises inflicted on Pierpont's *amour propre*.

'But never mind,' she said. 'That's not why I'm here.'

'Right. What can I do for you?'

'I've been asked by Mr Deng at the Embassy to help out.'

'You know Deng?' It had never occurred to him that Deng might be in touch with colleagues of his, much less with his former assistant. She was hardly a senior or significant figure, just an administrator of a minor sort. Cole had originally hired her out of desperation, having interviewed half a dozen others first. He'd offered the assistant's job to three of those candidates in turn, but for some reason each had turned him down. Only this drab, dour woman had been willing to work for him, but he had never in their five years together even considered letting her in on the closeness of his relations with the Chinese.

So he was taken aback to learn she was acquainted with Deng; he would not have thought the MSS agent even knew who she was. Why had he or Yìchén not consulted Cole first? It was annoying, and also made him uneasy.

'I do now. Yìchén put him on to me.'

'And how do you know Yìchén?' he asked peremptorily. Yìchén had only arrived on the scene after Pierpont had moved to her job at the Elm.

'Don't you mean, how does Yìchén know me?' she asked, seeming to enjoy Cole's manifest unease. 'I met him through Mr Lau, who is Yìchén's superior now,' she said smugly. 'I have some specific orders from Yìchén, as I gather you do too. Better still, there's a plan that's come direct from the Embassy.'

'There is?'

'Yes,' she said, sounding very sure of herself. Cole wondered why she was being deputed and not him. 'What's the matter?' she said. 'Is your nose out of joint that the Chinese consulted me about this? Me, your lowly former assistant.'

'Not at all,' he said defensively. 'I specifically recommended you to Lau as someone with her ear close to the ground.' This was not true; even if the Chinese had explicitly asked him to find someone else to assist, he would never have recommended the likes of Nina Pierpont. But he felt forced to lie now, if only to let her think she had his support – when as soon as she left, he would be on the phone to Yìchén raising holy hell.

'That sounds like wishful thinking to me,' said Pierpont. 'I think your memory's probably playing tricks on you. You would have let me know if you had recommended me, but there was never a snowball's chance in hell of that!' She stared at him, steely-eyed, and he found himself looking away. 'I know what you think of me. Grumpy and dim. You patronised me for years – don't bother to deny it. That would be one insult too many, even for stupid old me.'

There was anger as well as satisfaction in her tirade. Cole had never seen either emotion from her before in his dealings with this woman. He could see she was enjoying making these revelations, like Superman delighting in throwing off the suit from his day job and revealing his true superhero colours.

She continued: 'Mr Lau first made contact with me over three years ago while I was still your assistant. He must have noticed me, bringing the biscuits in with your coffee.' She laughed bitterly. 'At first there wasn't anything in particular he wanted me to do. I think I was an insurance policy in case you had second thoughts about helping the Chinese. Don't look so shocked: you aren't the only one they don't entirely trust. It wouldn't surprise me at all if they had somebody keeping an eye on me as well.'

He was about to protest when she waved at him dismissively. 'Let's not squabble about who they trusted the most. What matters is that Lau eventually wanted me to report back on the Chinese students at the Elm. They already had some people working for them there. I'm sure you can guess who one of them is – it's pretty hard to overlook Mr Chew. Not that he's really a student. Anyway, turning to the matter at hand,' she said like a veteran barrister, 'the point is simple: Lau and Yichén asked you to take care of something for them. We both know what that is. And whichever way you look at it, you've flunked it.

'I did warn them once that they should never expect you to do anything that might jeopardise your position in college. That you had too many of what you would probably call scruples. Other less charitable souls might see you as being too much of a coward. Whatever, they've grown impatient with the delay so they've called me in to take care of the matter. Which, with your help, I fully intend to do.

'Don't sulk,' she told him sharply, and his chin lifted angrily at the rebuke. With a malicious smile at the mix of outrage and amazement in his expression, she went on, 'Please listen carefully. I need you to send an email. Don't worry – you'll still get to act the gentleman, as always.' This was said snidely, as if she was resigned to playing the villain's role. Or, more accurately, the role of semi-invisible drudge. 'Arthur,' she said, and he stared at her, startled by her use of his Christian name; he could not think of any previous occasion on which she had done so. 'That's all you're going to have to do – send an email.' She held up a piece a paper with a couple of lines of handwriting on it. 'Here is what I want you to say.'

40

Li Min had run the finished rough through a filter that imparted a consistent if grainy feel to the visuals, and the audio had a barely detectable background hum throughout, like a fan whirring nearby.

The video began, apparently filmed by a hidden camera. From the angle, it seemed the camera must be tucked into a bookshelf. It was fixed but had a wide lens; in the middle of its frame Sally Washington was reading at her desk in her room at the Elm.

With the sound of a knock on the door, the audio kicked in and Sally said, 'Come in.' Seconds later a young man was visible in the right side of the frame. From his profile it was clear he was Chinese, dressed neatly in black wool trousers and wearing a blue roll-neck sweater.

'Have a seat,' said Sally, pointing to a chair that was on the very edge of the screen, but the boy ignored her and remained standing.

He said in Mandarin, 'I have brought what I promised.'

'I don't speak Chinese, Lee. I told you that already.'

'I keep forgetting. Because your mother is Chinese, I assumed…'

'Lazy thinking,' the girl said caustically. This was not the Sally Washington Li Min knew, but then with a start she realised it was the Sally she herself had made according to the Chinese script; sharp, sarcastic, knowing. A million miles from the fun-seeking, California-loving young woman Li Min now considered her best friend. The stark contrast seemed terribly unfair to the real-life model, but Li Min told herself that it was a clue, however buried, that this was a deepfake.

'Anyhow,' the girl on the screen declared, 'let's get down to business. You've brought the cash?'

'Yes.' The Chinese boy reached into the front pocket of his trousers, and his hand emerged with an envelope in it. A normal letter-size envelope but one that was bulging with whatever it contained. Still standing, he handed it to Sally, but when she started to open the central drawer of her desk, he said curtly, 'Count it before you put it away.'

Sally shrugged but put the envelope on the desktop and carefully unsealed its flap. She gave a short laugh as she reached in and brought out a handful of banknotes. Flicking through them, she said, 'Christ, it's all in ten-pound notes.'

'You should be pleased,' said the boy, now acting more assertively. 'Easier to spend this way. You don't want to leave a trail of fifty-pound notes all over Oxford.'

Sally said nothing but began to count a note at a time, putting each one down in a growing stack. At 250 she ran out. She looked up at the boy. 'If I missed one, that's too bad. I'm not going to count them again.'

'No, it's right. Two hundred and fifty of them. And the same again when you send in your first report. That will make a total of five thousand pounds. All yours provided your report has something of value in it. You are going home for Christmas, aren't you?'

'How else am I going to find something of value to you?' she demanded.

'Understood. We will pay you every month for as long as our relationship remains fruitful.'

'Great,' said Sally with patent insincerity. Then she asked, suddenly sounding weary, 'So I guess I'm now a full-blown spy, aren't I? I mean, taking money for the information you want from my father.'

'I'd see it as a service rendered to my government. Without harming yours.'

'Oh, sure,' Sally said, the sarcasm returning to her voice. 'Try telling that to the FBI. Or the CIA.' She paused then added more softly, 'Or to my father.'

The boy seemed unwilling to argue the point. Changing the subject, he said, 'A man from our Embassy in London, Deng, will be here to meet you in the next few days. He will text you in advance. He can best describe what they want you to discover when you are at home over the holidays.' Sally's eyes widened slightly at the prospect of another person in the know, and the boy said a little weakly, 'I am just the middleman.'

'Courier more like. But I know: don't shoot the messenger. They're always blameless. Like you,' she added tartly. She said with a resigned note in her voice, 'Is there anything else?' The boy shook his head and Sally said, 'I'd offer you a drink but… I don't want to.'

The boy bowed his head briefly, as if wounded. 'Goodbye,' he said after a moment, and went out of the door. Sally Washington turned and fingered the stack of notes on her desk. Then she yawned and the deepfake ended, the screen turning to black.

Li Min closed the lid of her laptop. She was never going to win an Oscar for this short film, but normally she would have been more than satisfied with her work. Especially with its technical side, since the fake combined the essentials of the script she had been given with a slightly amateur aspect – like the slight grain to its background – that gave it extra plausibility. No one would think such a flat and untheatrical rendition of a meeting would be anything but real. There was not a single whole sentence in the deepfake that Sally Washington had uttered in real life, but no one watching it would be able to tell. Even Li Min could not be sure what she had filmed and recorded of the Chinese boy, Lee, and what was AI-generated. That was the true test – the equivalent of the famous Turing test – of a deepfake. In a couple of years it would be a commonplace feat, Li Min knew, but for now it was extraordinary.

Yet there was no satisfaction for Li Min, only a growing wave of anxiety that threatened to edge into outright despair. The deepfake showed Sally taking money from a Chinese boy. There could be only two reasons for that: sex or secrets. There was nothing sexual about their interaction whatsoever; instead there was explicit language indicating that she was being paid to procure information for the PRC. Sally herself had said as much: *I'm now a full-blown spy.*

A sceptic might say, very well, but what use is she to the Chinese? She's an American party girl playing at higher education. What is she going to be privy to in Oxford that would persuade the Chinese to recruit her? What secrets is she going to come across in her studies of International Relations?

But that was to misunderstand the target in this seduction scenario. It wasn't Sally the Chinese expected to know things of value. She simply didn't, and despite the implications of what she and the Chinese boy discussed in the fake, there wasn't anything of value she could find out on her own. For all the mentions of her father, Sally wasn't going to get anything out of him. He was far too experienced and professional to bring confidential documents home or to talk about his work to anyone outside the Defense Department – not even his closest kin would get a look-in there.

So at first the deepfake Li Min had built, and the role Deng and Co. wanted Sally to play, seemed ill-conceived and most unlikely to deliver the goods; Li Min could not see the rationale of what she had been ordered to do.

But then, as she had lain in bed the night before, sleepless and agitated and puzzled, the answer came to her. She had been mistaking the mini-drama of the film with what the Embassy people really wanted to happen. Sally was never going to give secret information to the Chinese. She was simply supposed to *look* like she was doing that, credibly enough that if the deepfake were ever seen by a judge and jury – Li Min pictured her friend extradited back to Washington D.C. – the case would seem open and shut. God knows how many years in prison the girl would be sentenced to, but a conviction was a safe bet, and incarceration for years an inevitability.

Sally's father would know that as soon as he saw the deepfake. He sounded the model of a doting family man. How would he feel, knowing his daughter was going to do hard time in federal prison because, ultimately, of his refusal to cooperate with the Chinese? Would he stand by and let that happen – watch like a neutral observer as members of a jury were swayed by the damning, inculpating film? He might believe it was fake – Sally would *know* it was fake after all – but how could he persuade the FBI of that?

If the agents of China were careful in their approach, circling slowly and softly, letting the blackmail be implied rather than issued as a threat, would not Mr Washington at least consider cooperating, for the sake of his daughter? He would be reassured by the Chinese that it was only minor secrets he would be required to hand over – at first anyway. The poor man, Li Min thought with a sigh; to face such a terrible choice. Commit treason or let his daughter take the fall, with paternal prison visits to Allenwood or some other federal penitentiary (Li Min had googled 'American prisons'), where the rest of his daughter's youth would be spent.

But if he had the world's worst choice to make, Li Min had a choice too, and one that would obviate the need for Mr Washington to do anything. Or know anything, since if he never saw the deepfake he would be none the wiser. Mr Lau or Mr Yìchén or creepy Deng would hardly desist from their blackmail plot simply because Li Min wanted them to. 'Dream on, girl' – that was what Sally had said to her when Li Min confessed her secret passion for Timothée Chalamet. She suppressed a giggle, then sobered when she realised what she might well have to do. She would do it for Sally, she realised, and somehow that made her more determined than if she were only doing it for herself.

41

Much as she liked Louise, her unannounced arrival was the very last thing Manon needed just then. Abbot had seemed almost amused by the confusion caused when Louise presented herself to the receptionist in the Institute. Manon might have been equally entertained had he not let slip that it was the dreaded Nina Pierpont who had been manning the desk at the time. That dragon was the last person Manon wanted to know about her true identity. Well, perhaps not the last; Arthur Cole would still take precedence in the stakes of potential enemies at St Felix's.

But she was nonetheless glad to see her friend and happy to put her up in the flat. Tired as she was, she was pleased that Louise seemed to be content with having supper at home, and they sat down together with bowls of stir-fry and a bottle of Beaujolais.

There were obvious limits to what Manon could tell Louise about her life in Oxford, or more specifically her work, but it was taken for granted that she had no more become a librarian than Louise, a keen but entirely amateur skier, was going to compete in the next Winter Olympics. But although Louise avoided asking for any details, she felt able to ask after Li Min. 'Have you met her?' she asked.

'I have. We've got together a couple of times. I suppose you could say we are friends now, or at least friends in the making.

If I'd known you were coming, I would have tried to get hold of her – we could all have had coffee together.'

'Oh, good. I'm sure you're a big help to her. She seemed awfully upset about being ordered over here. Did you ever learn why her government was so keen for her to come here?'

Trust Louise to zero in almost uncannily. Manon hesitated, and Louise, noticing, said, 'Sorry, I didn't mean to put you on the spot.'

'It's OK. Whatever the reason, I think it's fair to say our friend Li Min is having some doubts about her transfer.' And she related a sanitised version of their recent meeting in the cocktail bar.

Louise nodded and said, 'I almost called you about her last week.'

'Oh, why?'

'I ran into one of her fellow students, someone who was at the party I went to that night. She told me that just the day before, a group of Chinese officials had come to the AI lab and demanded to see any work Li Min might have left behind – stored on the central file server for that group. They tried to claim that because they had been paying for her tuition, her work was their property. They were very insistent, but the professor was not impressed and sent them packing. They had some nerve, don't you think?'

'Individual rights are not the strong suit of the People's Republic,' said Manon, though she was startled by this news. If the PRC had sent representatives to Harvard to try and blag their way into Li Min's old work files, it could only mean one thing: they didn't trust her.

The next morning, she walked with Louise down to the bus station and put her on the coach to Heathrow, promising to keep in touch and to visit her again at Harvard when Manon was next in the States. Not that she knew when that would be, or even how long she would be in Oxford. She was meeting Li Min the next week, but if the girl remained under the thumb of the PRC, then who knows for how long Saunders would want her to stay in Oxford, hoping the Chinese girl would finally turn. She sensed Li Min was wavering, but recognised too how scared she must be. Her masters were ruthless.

Professionally, Manon was intent on doing everything she could to persuade Li Min to come aboard; it would be a coup if she succeeded in this, and from what she had guessed it would prevent the Chinese from doing something awful with whatever project Li Min managed to finish at their behest. Personally, she realised she liked Oxford, though was it the town and university or – forcing herself to be honest – Charles Abbot that drew her to this place? She could not deny the attraction she felt towards the man, or fail to notice how her heart beat faster whenever she was in his company.

He seemed drawn to her as well, often sitting with her at lunch in the Senior Common Room, finding at least one reason each day to drop by her office on the floor beneath his own, sometimes with an excuse ('just seeing how you're getting on with the papers'), sometimes without offering any reason at all.

How often in her training had she and her fellow trainees been warned against personal involvement with people met in the course of an operation? All the time. Crossing that line dividing professionalism from personal life was viewed as a cardinal sin; it was made clear it would not be tolerated and was grounds for instant dismissal from the agency.

Steady on, she told herself. She'd done nothing wrong. Whatever she felt about Charles Abbot, their relationship was, if not strictly professional, then in no sense a romantic one.

Back at St Felix's she made her way to the Institute and her office. There she took her laptop out from the locked drawer in her desk and booted up the machine. She checked her college address for emails first. There were quite a lot of them. Abbot had put her on the General Circulation list of college announcements, saying it would help familiarise her with the place, and there were usually half a dozen of these each day. The Christmas fund for kitchen staff; the arrival of a new porter; the announcement of a string quartet concert at the beginning of Hilary Term after New Year's. That sort of thing. But now she saw with a quickening of her pulse a personal email from Arthur Cole.

What did he want? she thought with irritation. He had cut her dead at lunch earlier in the week, as if the guided tour of his ceramics exhibition and the reserve in the cellars had never taken place a few weeks ago, or if it had, then she had somehow failed to react in the expected way.

But his message was friendly, almost suspiciously so:

Dear Miss Davidson,

I hope you enjoyed your visit to the collection. It occurs to me that there was one item in particular you did not see but might like to – it has an extraordinary history that quite coincidentally involves St Felix's.

I would be happy to show it to you and if it is of interest I suggest you pop round to my rooms. I could do five o'clock today if that suited you; if not, do suggest some other times.

Yours ever
Arthur C.

This was puzzling. Why was he being so nice? And why did he use the words 'pop round', which didn't seem his style? What could this 'particular' item be, and why had he not shown it to her when they had met before? How she wished she were more comfortable with her cover story. She had done her best and was continuing to read the press with a selective slant towards any story about China, but she sensed Arthur Cole was sceptical about her. It was not that he doubted she was a China scholar, since she had never pretended more than a passing interest in the country. But it seemed he was not impressed by her credentials as a librarian. This was galling, but better that he merely considered her a little slow – and over-promoted – than that he suspected she had a covert motive for being here.

Part of her was tempted to ignore the email or at least delay replying, for she was concerned about Li Min, and worried that time was moving on with nothing to show for her efforts. But she needed to feel Arthur Cole was content with – or at least not passionately opposed to – her presence in the college, since the last thing she needed was a dust-up with him. And the last thing Charles needed either, since it would certainly involve him.

Charles was typing on his laptop when she tapped on his door. 'Lunchtime?' she asked mildly.

'Ah, great,' he said, leaving his keyboard. Behind him, through the large modern picture window, she could see the tower of St Michael's Church on the north end of Cornmarket. 'Do you mind lunching al fresco?' Charles suggested.

'Of course not.'

'The Common Room has better food – but we can talk more privately outside,' said Abbot, turning towards her. 'You have a choice: tuna mayonnaise and sweetcorn, or tuna and sweetcorn with mayonnaise.' He grinned. 'Or I can run out to Pret and get something else.'

'Tuna it is.'

They went outside and sat at a little round table with the sandwiches and a large bottle of sparkling water. Manon told him about her invitation from Arthur Cole, and Abbot's eyes widened. 'Why is he being so friendly?'

'That's what I'd like to know. I somehow don't think it's my reputation as a Sinologist.' When Abbot laughed, she added, 'He made that clear again when he showed me his exhibition and all the surplus pots he keeps in that mouldy basement.'

'It's funny – there are always complaints here about a lack of storage space. You'd think they would have grabbed the old wine cellar as soon as it was free. They could dry it out easily enough.' Abbot's expression turned serious. 'I just hope Nina Pierpont hasn't put two and two together about you. She used to be Cole's assistant – before my time. But my understanding – from McCaffrey, who is always a fount of information about people – is that Cole was relieved when she moved to the Elm as the manager.' He looked thoughtful for a moment. 'Put it this way: he didn't fight very hard to keep her.'

'Well, I've replied to him and will go see him. But for now I'm trying to stay focused on Li Min. We're supposed to meet up next week.'

42

It was going to be sooner than that. Returning to her office after lunch, Manon found an email from the Chinese girl.

Hi Manon, I have phoned through the Porters' Lodge and you are not in but I hope you get this. Please could we meet today, if possible? At the same place as our first meeting at three o'clock if possible. I hope you might give me advice. Yours with best wishes, LM

It was almost two o'clock; she realised she and Abbot had been chatting for over an hour. She replied, *Yes. See you there.* Consulting the directory, she found Li Min's mobile number listed and dialled it, but it went straight to voicemail. She left a message saying much the same thing as her text, taking care not to mention where they would be meeting. She herself would have picked a different venue. The bar was too central and too close to St Felix's for her liking; it was also where they'd met before, and even if they'd shaken off any surveillance before their talk, Mr Chew had found them soon enough in the Covered Market.

So forty-five minutes later she was careful about going to the Varsity Club, walking some way east on the High then reversing her steps; stopping in several clothing stores where she looked from the interior out of the front windows to see if anyone was hanging about – no one was. When she entered the bar, this time it was almost empty at three o'clock on a weekday afternoon, and she took over a corner table where there was no one sitting within earshot.

She sat for ten minutes, waiting to order until Li Min arrived. The girl was late and after another five minutes Manon began to wonder if she had lost her nerve or something bad had happened to delay her. Despite all her best efforts to stay calm, she was growing distinctly edgy until a voice called 'Judith!' and she turned to find Li Min advancing. Manon stood up and rather to her surprise received a hug from the girl. They both sat down as the waitress came over.

'Coffee for me, please,' said Manon. This was not a time for Margaritas. She was glad when Li Min followed her example, though she ordered tea.

'I'm so glad you got my message,' the young woman said when the waitress had gone. 'I was worried you might be away or weren't checking your phone. I'm sorry I'm late but when I took the shuttle in, Mr Chew was on it.'

'Was that coincidence?' Manon was alarmed to think Chew might be following her.

'I don't think so. We're all convinced he's been put here by the Party to keep an eye on us.'

'You're right to think that.'

Li Min nodded. 'He's pretty scary. Anyway, he hardly ever goes into college, so when I saw him on the Broad I thought he must be following me. I ducked into the Old Bodleian and took the tunnel to the Radcliffe Camera – I doubt he's ever set foot in the place. I am hoping he's still waiting for me to come out of the Old Bod.'

'I got your message.' Manon paused then added, 'It sounded important.'

The sentence hung in the air between them and Li Min lowered her head for a moment. Then, a little hesitantly, she lifted her chin and looked Manon in the eye. 'I thought you might give me some advice.'

Manon smiled, a friendly grin. 'I'll do my best. Why don't you tell me what you want advice about?' When the younger woman still hesitated, Manon said, 'Li Min, you can tell me as much or as little as you like. I want to help, so obviously the more I know the better. But I'm not going to push you. Just tell me one thing: is it about your work?'

Li Min nodded, and the waitress arrived with their drinks. It was a useful interruption because it seemed to give time for the Chinese girl's resolve to stiffen. When the waitress had left, she said, 'You know, when I described my lab work you seemed quite sceptical about its implications.'

'I'd say "worried" rather than sceptical.'

'Well, in either case, you were right. I feel like I have been so naïve! Just like the students I've met who have fallen in love with the technology they work on and never think about its impact. Cal Tech was full of them. Some go on to make fortunes with new start-ups, but I'd say almost all of them are doing it for love rather than making money. Love of what software can do, or what they can get it to do, regardless of the wider picture.' She took an absent-minded sip of her tea.

'Do you think that's true of you?'

'I would not have said so before, but yes, I'm no better than them. As I told you, my work is about manipulating video and audio feeds so that the final result – a streaming file – looks completely real. It's designed to fool people, and all I could think of was the benefits it could have.'

'You mentioned some of them before. I wasn't worried about any of those.'

'I know,' said Li Min. 'But you saw that you could show people doing *bad* things as well.'

'I can't imagine you'd misuse the technology that way,' Manon said.

'No, but where I was stupid was forgetting all about the fact that other people could – and would. I was too caught up in my own work to notice what other people might be doing in theirs.'

Manon looked at her coffee cup, saying lightly, 'And does that involve you somehow?'

She waited, still looking at the cup. This was the key moment, and she knew she couldn't press – it had to come from Li Min, as if unsolicited by Manon. She could steer the conversation, but invisibly, and now she told herself she had to keep her mouth shut, wait and hope for a result. It looked to be touch and go but then Li Min seemed to make a decision. She began to talk.

At first, she spoke in a technocratic theoretical language that Manon could not fully understand. So she let it wash over her, happy for the principles of audio-visual replication and something called LLMs to go by, unappreciated by her. But talking about them seemed to give Li Min confidence as she inched closer to the actuality of what she had built, and what it could be used for.

'Throughout my time at Harvard I had to meet with someone from the Embassy in Washington. A man called Deng. He wanted me to supply details of the research work the other students were doing. I admit I did do that, though to be honest, I don't think much of it was of any real value to the AI group in Beijing. For one thing, it was usually too narrow in focus. But Deng insisted on monthly reports with as much material as I could take out of the lab.' She looked at Manon, her expression downcast.

'No one could blame you for that,' said Manon firmly. 'You had no choice.'

'No, I didn't really, not if I wanted to stay at Harvard. And at least it wasn't my work Deng was interested in, back in Boston. But then even that changed.' She paused, gathering her thoughts. 'You know, I am sure people wondered why I moved from Massachusetts to Oxford. There were not really any obvious professional advantages to be gained.'

'OK, so why did you move?'

'Didn't your friend Louise tell you? I told her.'

'She seemed to think you didn't have much choice; that you were told to come here by your government and that if you refused they would no longer fund your studies.'

'Correct.'

'Which leads me to ask why they wanted you here?'

Li Min looked out of the window towards the spire of the University church. 'Deng himself moved when I did. He now works from the London Embassy. He came to see me in Oxford and told me to make friends with Sally Washington.'

'Which you've done. But you can't possibly regret that – you like Sally.'

'I would not regret it if that were all. But Deng wants me to use her in a deepfake they have ordered me to make. The terrible thing is that, by coincidence, I was already using Sally for stock footage. Otherwise she might have said no – the Embassy people could not have blamed me for that.'

'This deepfake – do you know what it would be used for?'

'Deng would not tell me that, and I only learned what was to be in it when he gave me a script last week. But I am confident they want to use it for blackmail.'

'Blackmail Sally? How? Does it show her in a bad light?' Manon wondered if Sally had been lured into bed by someone and secretly filmed. That kind of blackmail seemed to be rife on the Internet. But then why go to the trouble of commissioning a deepfake when a simple video would suffice?

'Yes, it does – if you're not a patriotic Chinese. It shows her taking money.'

'From the Chinese?'

'Of course – it is meant to show that she is agreeing to work for my government, and in return is being paid.'

'And that's what you have been building?' Manon could not have said she was surprised by the scheme, but the fact it was now possible to carry out such a plan was shocking nonetheless.

'That's what I have now built.'

'Has your government got it?' Manon tried to reduce the tension in her voice as she asked this crucial question.

'Not yet. They don't know I am finished, though they expect to get it soon. No later than tomorrow, or they will – how do you say it? – cut up rough.'

'Yes,' said Manon, giving a quick smile. 'But how do you think they will use the deepfake?'

Li Min took her time replying. 'I can't know for sure, and I am the last person they will tell. But I guess they can use it to blackmail Sally or her family. Put it this way: if I give the finished film to them, it will not be used to *help* my friend.'

'But if you don't give it to them, they won't be pleased with you,' said Manon, keeping her language euphemistic. Li Min seemed fearful enough without Manon compounding it.

'You can say that again,' the girl replied. She looked more calmly at Manon now, as if sensing that giving in to her nerves would merely make her quandary worse. 'I can't betray my friend like this, but I am frightened what Deng and his friends will do if I do not comply. Not just to me, but to Sally.' She said glumly, 'I don't know what to do. If I don't give the streaming file to Deng, I will lose everything I've worked for.'

This was the least of her worries, thought Manon, but decided not to say so. Li Min seemed to sense this anyway.

She said, 'It's possible that they might… want to punish me in other ways.'

'Hurt you?'

Li Min nodded. 'Or members of my family.' She seemed close to tears.

Manon decided not to hold back any longer. She was flying by the seat of her pants, since both Saunders and she had assumed they'd have at least a little time to plan their moves, if and when Li Min signalled that she wanted to come over. Instead, Manon reckoned they had at most a night and part of the following morning. Deng would wait that long from the sounds of it, but not much longer.

Nothing she was about to say had been authorised, but it would be fatal now to ask Li Min to hold fire while Manon cleared things with her superiors. She said, suddenly assertive, 'Listen to me. You've probably guessed by now that I have some… connections… with the American government. I'm going to contact them right away and explain your situation. They already know who you are, and what you work on.

'I can't give you full details yet but what I can tell you is this: we can keep you safe. We will protect you in case the Embassy sends anyone or tells anyone to punish you. That's our highest priority. Then we can make sure you have enough money to live on. We'll sort out your fees too, but that can wait until next term.' Unless she wanted to go back to Harvard, but Manon dismissed the thought; choices like that could wait. She continued: 'Do you understand? These are no idle promises. I give you my word, we will protect you and help you. As for the file, do not – whatever you do – send it to Deng. Once you've done that, you will no longer have any leverage over the Embassy, and who knows what they'll decide to do.' The fear had to be that they would want Li Min out of the frame for good. Her removal would get rid of the one person who could denounce with absolute certainty the deepfake for what it was.

Li Min took a deep breath. 'I understand. But what do I do now?'

'Well, first of all you finish your tea.' Manon was pleased to hear Li Min laugh, though slightly shrilly. 'When we're done here, I want you to take the bus back to the Elm. Go to dinner as usual; sit with Sally if that's what you normally do. But after dinner, make some excuse and go back to your room. You need to be on your own. Tell Sally you have an urgent deadline, if that's easiest, or that you have to talk to someone on the phone – your parents maybe? Whatever works.

'But I want you to stay in your room for the rest of the evening – and keep your door locked. Don't open it for anyone you're not absolutely sure of, and with your friends – even Sally – say that you're sorry but you're busy and will have to see them tomorrow. Text me when you go to bed, and tomorrow morning please text me first thing to say you're OK. Don't worry if it's very early, I'm an early riser. I'll have made some calls once I'm back in college today, so by morning I'll have got the ball rolling.'

'What's that?' asked Li Min, baffled by the idiomatic language.

'Sorry. Arrangements will have been made to get you out of here. I'll tell you later today if you should take the shuttle bus into college or wait at the Elm until someone comes to collect you.'

Li Min looked mildly alarmed at the speed with which this was proceeding, so Manon tried to reassure her. 'Don't worry, you'll be able to go back to your own work – the work *you* want to do, not that the PRC wants you to. This is just until we know you'll be safe. That shouldn't be long. And you will be well protected until then.'

Manon was counting on MI5 providing a safe house where Li Min could stay, and also some armed protection. It would probably be in London, but it didn't really matter where. Failing an available safe house, they would have to use a hotel, though they would still need MI5 to provide some muscle to guard the girl.

'Deng will wonder what has become of me,' said Li Min, still sounding anxious. But Manon was glad of this in a way, since it meant Li Min was now concerned about her own safety. 'I know, but you need to buy some time. Through until tomorrow morning if you can. What I suggest is that you should delay for as long as you can this evening – tell him you are putting the finishing touches on the fake and that it's not quite done. Hopefully he'll buy that.'

'For this evening perhaps,' Li Min said. 'But then he'll lose patience. He will come looking for me tomorrow or send someone else. Even someone already in the Elm.'

She shuddered and Manon realised who she was talking about. 'Mr Chew?'

Li Min nodded. She was looking scared again, Manon realised, so she said quickly, 'OK, if you think he's about to blow up, then send him a file. How do you communicate?'

'It's an MSS protocol for documents. Heavily encrypted. It's really just WhatsApp being ripped off.'

'OK, then use it to send him a file, ignore any reply and try and get some sleep.'

'Send him the file? I thought you said—'

'You aren't going to send him the *real* file. The real "fake". Whatever you do, don't send him that.' Manon was thinking furiously while Li Min waited, looking still on edge. 'I know. Here's what I think you should send him.' And fortunately, when she heard the idea, Li Min laughed again but without the shrill note of before.

When the waitress came and asked if they wanted more tea or coffee, Li Min took the lead and shook her head. 'No, thank you,' she said. 'We're done here.'

43

Saunders felt caught on the hop. Manon had phoned to say that she was seeing Li Min urgently, but he had not expected the situation to unravel at such speed. Li Min had completed the deepfake far sooner than anyone had expected. The Chinese must have been putting a good deal of pressure on her to finish her work, and it would be difficult for her to stall them any longer. It was quite clear that Deng was going to insist on getting the goods the next day. If he didn't, that would likely be the last day that anyone here would see Li Min.

What was needed now was local assistance to ensure that she was kept safe and out of the hands of the Chinese until she could be whisked away. Saunders rang Wilson at MI5, only to be told by his efficient private secretary that Wilson was in Australia and would not be back until the following week. 'But I was told that if you rang, I was to put you straight on to his Deputy David Kenton. I know he's at his desk at the moment, please hold.'

Kenton turned out to be cool and businesslike. He listened quietly to what Saunders said and replied, 'Yes. We can provide a safe house and a couple of minders. Do you expect to need armed protection? When will you be able to let us know when and from where the subject needs to be collected, and are they male or female?'

Saunders heaved a sigh of relief at the quiet competence of Kenton, and they went on to discuss names, numbers and such details as there were at this stage.

Fortunately, Saunders had his ducks lined up in Washington D.C. The Secretary of Defense had been informed that an effort might be made to blackmail Donald Washington, his expert in sub-aquatic missiles. When Washington himself had been told that the plot involved his daughter Sally in some way, he had naturally been very concerned and wanted to fly over to the UK at once. This might have jeopardised the entire operation being run by Saunders and Manon, and Donald Washington was eventually persuaded to stay put in D.C. after receiving assurances that both American and British Intelligence were charged with ensuring no harm came to his daughter, and that the CIA already had an agent on the ground near her.

44

Manon had walked with Li Min and seen her off on the shuttle bus to the Elm, then returned to her office where she had called Saunders right away on his secure line. After that there was nothing to do but wait for his call back, telling her what support had been lined up, and decide what to do with Li Min the next day.

Then she remembered the invitation from Arthur Cole. Looking at her watch, she realised she could just about make it in time. It was five to five and she could in fact get to his rooms bang on time if she left now. She looked thoughtfully at her phone, then with alarm as she saw her battery was nearly dead. She had just about run out of charge. She didn't like leaving it behind, but reckoned she wouldn't be more than half an hour with Cole, so she plugged the phone into a charger and left it on her desk, taking care to lock her office door as she left.

On the dot of five then, Manon stood outside Cole's rooms, dreading another encounter with the man, yet curious about what was so exciting that he had to show it to her. Why her in particular? That made her more curious still.

She knocked and heard footsteps coming to the door. When it opened, Manon was astonished to see Nina Pierpont standing there, looking slightly flushed, as if she too had rushed over for this meeting. 'Is Professor Cole here?' Manon asked.

'Miss Davidson,' Pierpont said gratuitously. 'Professor Cole is indisposed, I'm afraid. He's gone home – not feeling well at all.'

What a relief, thought Manon. She could go back to her desk and wait for Saunders to ring. She said, 'I'm so sorry to hear that. I'm happy to come back when he's feeling better.'

'He asked me to stand in for him.' Seeing the uncertainty on Manon's face, Pierpont said firmly, 'He was most insistent.'

'Really? The thing is, I'm kind of busy today, so if you don't mind, I'll take a rain check and set another time with him when he's back.'

Pierpont's disappointment was plain to see, if unexpected. She said, 'It's just that the object he wanted you to see won't be here after today. It's only on loan.'

Something about this sounded odd to Manon. 'Can you tell me what it is?' she asked.

'Potentially, it's a gift to the Institute. Something very rare and of considerable value. I'd better leave it at that until you've had a look at it. It won't take long, I promise.'

Her voice, usually harsh and thin, had softened now. It was clear to Manon that Pierpont had indeed been tasked by Arthur Cole, and had steeled herself to do his bidding. The woman even seemed to have dressed up for the occasion, as she wore a suit that looked expensive if drab. Doubtless, too, she had boned up on the entire history of whatever wretched *objet* she was about to produce. Probably another goddamned pot, thought Manon, wondering how Saunders was getting on with the British.

Pierpont's expression now was openly imploring, and Manon's resolve to go away weakened. It shouldn't take long, she told herself; a quick inspection with an ostentatious show of interest, declaration of admiration, and presto, she would be home free and able to get back to her office. 'OK,' she said, 'but please can we do this quickly? Is it here?' she added, tipping her head towards the room. Probably one of the jumble of pieces Cole kept on a side table.

She was about to step forward and enter but Pierpont didn't move. 'No,' she said, 'but come with me.' She moved out onto the landing, closing the door behind her. 'We'll be there in a second.'

Once again Manon was led across the main quad and onto the site of the old Senior Common Room. Halfway there, Pierpont suddenly said, 'There was a woman here the other day asking for a friend of hers. She said the friend was working here as an archivist. I thought it must be you she wanted but she asked for a different name – Manon something.'

'I wonder who that could be.'

'What, this woman or the archivist?'

Manon forced herself to give a little laugh. 'Both, I guess.'

'She had red hair... expensive clothes.'

'Beats me,' said Manon. 'I hope she found her friend.'

'I wouldn't worry about that. Charles Abbot showed up and seemed to know who she was looking for.'

They had arrived at the old Senior Common Room and Manon stayed silent. But this was all a little unnerving. What did Pierpont suspect? If she knew for sure who Manon really was, she wasn't likely to be telling her about Louise's appearance at reception. But she must wonder or she wouldn't have brought it up at all.

They went in, then took the stairs down to the cellar. Here Pierpont fished out a fistful of keys on a ring from her jacket pocket. She unlocked the door in the corridor, then the door to the wine cellar, and finally the door to the large room full of packing cases that Cole had told Manon contained the rest of the collection. She looked questioningly at Pierpont.

'It's down there at the end,' she said, pointing. The room seemed darker than it had been when Manon was last here. She took a couple of steps forward, and then, sensing that the other woman was no longer behind her and hearing the door slam, turned back. As she did so she was grabbed in a vice-like grip. Struggling, she felt a sharp prick in her arm. She went limp and knew nothing more.

Ten minutes later, Mr Chew switched off the lights, rubbing his hands together, satisfied with his work. He turned the key which Pierpont had left in the lock outside and took the bunch with him, locking each door behind him as he left the building. Then he strolled nonchalantly to Professor Cole's room and returned the keys to the drawer in the desk.

Some hours later Manon regained consciousness to find her legs fastened together by tightly tied ropes and her arms similarly secured behind her back. She could feel tape of some kind covering her mouth. She was propped up against a wall, completely helpless.

45

Deng had been no happier than Li Min to be transferred to the UK. But he had not felt at liberty even to hint this to his colleagues and superiors. 'At liberty' – it had taken him some time to understand this concept, which he considered a characteristic fantasy of the West. Obligations were real; so was duty. Liberty, on the other hand, seemed like so much hot air. Certainly, he had never known it.

Growing up in a poor Szechuan village, he had struggled at school but managed to join the army, earning a regular salary and eating ample food each day – a considerable accomplishment. Life inside the military was regimented, yes, but he found that comforting since civilian life had always seemed to him to be an anxious and chaotic battle to survive.

Once enlisted he had not relaxed or grown complacent. He had been diligent and dutiful, so much so that he had come to the attention of his regiment's Intelligence officer, who had recommended the young soldier to his superiors as a suitable recruit. More very intensive training had followed, and it had turned out that Deng, for all the sparseness of his education, was smart. His gift for languages was rapidly discovered, and soon he was recruited by the Ministry of State Security.

Deng had never been very good at waiting: his last written assessment had cited impatience as his one failing, and it was impatience he was showing this afternoon. For several hours he had skimmed the Chinese papers and magazines the Embassy subscribed to, resisting the impulse to text Le Min. She should have been finished by now according to her own estimation when they'd last met.

He was in the Embassy building on Portland Place in London, since there he could be sure of secure and confidential communications with Li Min in Oxford. Otherwise, he had a bare and uncomfortable room in a flat owned by the Embassy several streets away at the top of an Edwardian house, the lower parts of which were occupied by junior doctors. The cooking facilities were inadequate and the hot water often failed. So he was more than happy to spend his spare time in the Embassy, where there was always food available from the kitchens.

On the top floor next to the Comms room was a small office meant for Comms room staff working twelve-hour shifts. It seemed to be little used. Along with a desk and chair, the room had a sofa, which proved useful for catnaps when Deng worked late into the night – and recently, virtually every day.

Now, unable to wait any longer, he texted Li Min.
You should be done now.
A reply came in some fifteen minutes later.
Almost. I have made a mistake. Some people do.
When can you send the finished file?
She replied, *You will have it shortly.*
This wouldn't do, he thought, but if he pressed her too hard she might simply ignore his further texts. If he drove to the Elm where she lived, he would probably find that in the interim she had finished and he had made a pointless trip.

He was yawning by midnight but reluctant to give up. *Where are we?* he texted.

Almost there was her brief reply.

At two he was still in the room, and at three he was there in body if not in mind, for he was on the sofa, sound asleep, dreaming about his parents.

He woke to the sound of traffic on Portland Place. Rubbing sleep from his eyes, he went straight to the laptop on his desk. It was 6.30 in the morning. To his delight he saw the new file and downloaded it. Then he sat back, feeling excited as he began to watch the deepfake.

It began with a blonde girl reading at a desk. He recognised her from the mugshots Mr Chew had sent him of Sally Washington, whose father would be the target of this operation.

On screen there was a knock on the door and a Chinese boy entered the frame. Lee, who had been suborned by Mr Chew to help out Li Min – without being told what it was for. He would have to be cautioned, Deng thought, told to speak to no one about his role in this, or indeed about what he thought Li Min was doing. That should not be a problem: according to his file and a report from his teachers back in China, Lee was willing to serve the state in any capacity and was thoroughly reliable.

He listened as Lee spoke to the American girl. 'What's up, Sally?' he asked in fluent English. The accent was pure American and Deng remembered that Lee had spent six years at MIT in Massachusetts and was only here in the UK for a year; he held some postgraduate research fellowship according to the file.

'Not a lot,' the girl answered.

Deng was slightly puzzled. According to the script he'd provided, the two of them should have got down to business from the beginning. Yet here Lee was not talking like the recruiter of a source. Then he said, 'I've got something for you.' That is more like it, thought Deng.

'Don't tell me. Three million dollars,' said Sally, laughing.

What was going on? Deng asked himself

'Nothing like that,' said Lee. He took an envelope from his pocket and Deng relaxed.

Lee handed the envelope to Sally as the script dictated, and she duly opened it, which followed the stage directions Deng had given Li Min. But to his great surprise, when Sally opened it she found only a single sheet of paper inside. There was no stack of banknotes.

'Oh,' said Sally happily, 'an invitation!'

Lee said, 'We Chinese students will be celebrating the New Year. We wanted to invite our friends from the West to attend. I hope you will feel able to come.'

'I won't only *feel* able, I *will* be able. It goes in my diary right now,' she said, reaching inside her desk drawer. Deng watched incredulously as she wrote down the date of the celebration. This was all unforeseen deviation from the script he had received from his own superiors at MSS headquarters in Xiyuan.

Deng was baffled. When would Lee tell the girl what the Chinese wanted her to do? Perhaps they had decided to skip the actual exchange of money, though without the transaction the evidence would rely entirely on the words spoken between them. These had better be crystal clear. So far there had been absolutely nothing to suggest Sally was willing to work for the PRC.

'Thank you,' she said as she put her diary back and pushed the drawer shut. 'I'm flattered you thought of me.'

'Not at all. You have been our good friend.' Was this the preamble to asking her to prove her friendship by being willing to spy on China's behalf? Deng's hopes rose but only briefly, for Lee suddenly gave a little bow of his head and then announced, 'I must be leaving now. Thank you for accepting.'

'Nothing would keep me from it,' said Sally cheerfully.

'Goodbye then.'

'Goodbye.'

And he left the room while Sally resumed reading at her desk, and after a few seconds the video faded and the deep-fake ended. Just like that.

Deng's incredulity was being replaced by a growing sense of outrage. What was Li Min playing at?

This time he didn't text her but made a video call.

She didn't take the call. Deng was furious now, and only partially appeased when he tried again and this time Li Min answered. He could see she was in her room at the Elm. She looked as though she'd had a sleepless night; her eyes were bleary and had bags under them. She must have spent hours putting this stuff together, he thought crossly. What had she been thinking?

'I received the file but…' He hardly knew how to describe it, such was his anger that she had disobeyed orders so flagrantly.

'But what?' asked Li Min impatiently.

'It's completely wrong.' He struggled to keep his anger under control; it would do no good for him to give way to it. 'There is no money exchanged as in the script; there is no mention of what she is doing to earn the money; no reference to her working for the Ministry of State Security.'

'I don't understand,' said Li Min, obviously perplexed.

'You've sent me a film of your friend, the American girl, and the Chinese boy Lee, as instructed. But he gives her some invitation to a party and she says thank you very much. And that's it. You haven't followed the script at all.'

'Oh, no,' said Li Min, suddenly looking distraught. 'I've sent you the wrong one. I made that film at Sally's request. She's in a drama group and she needed to make a short film for it. It's not actually AI-generated; there's nothing fake about the two of them.'

'I don't care what it is! It's of absolutely no use to us. What happened to the real deepfake?'

Li Min hesitated. 'I have it on the server at the lab, but it's protected from remote access. I was working there almost all night. I've only just come back to the Elm.'

More delay then. Frustrated, Deng said, 'I need it now.'

'I'll send it to you from the lab. I'll take the shuttle in.' She made a show of looking at her watch. 'There's one in five minutes I can catch if we stop talking now.'

'Go. Then send it right away.'

'I can't send it from the lab. It could be traced back.'

'Then return to the Elm and send it from there.' He had reached the limit of his tolerance. What a mistake it had been to assume this woman would understand the importance of what she had been asked to do. Did she not realise the dire consequences for everyone if she failed to cooperate? Deng would return to China in semi-disgrace, but if he had any say about it, Li Min would go back in a box.

Deng didn't like London, but if the stupid girl did as she was told, he would soon travel to the US to help with the approach to Donald Washington. With his mission successfully completed, in due course he would return to Beijing. Home at last… until his next foreign assignment, he supposed.

But a different fate lay in store for Li Min. She would have done what they asked, but she would not be told to what use her work had been applied, and there would be no reward for her. She knew enough, in fact, to become a liability. And the longer she stayed in the West the greater the chance she would want to stay for good, and that someday – possibly to help her acquire permanent residence, or even citizenship – she might reveal that her work on deepfakes in the West had not always been benign.

The chances of her doing that might be small, but he sensed from her recent attitude that she would do anything to stay here, and it was not worth taking the risk of her blabbing, which would be disastrous. No, when Li Min went back to China to visit – she had not seen her parents in two years – she would find herself forced to adapt once again to her mother country's ways. Because she would never be allowed to leave China again.

But for now, he needed her to supply that deepfake. There could be no further excuses. And just in case, he would take additional steps to make sure she handed it over quickly. He was not prepared to take Li Min's word for anything.

46

Li Min followed Manon's instructions carefully, except for having dinner with Sally and the group. Instead, she had bought a sandwich and an apple at M&S in town, which she ate for supper in her room, making sure the door was double-locked. She had opened it once when Sally knocked, concerned that she hadn't come to supper, but Li Min was prepared for this. In a cheerful but preoccupied voice, she said that she had an overnight assignment she must finish.

Other than that, no one disturbed her. Judith Davidson had asked her to text before bedtime and she did, just briefly, saying she was fine. To her surprise, her text went unacknowledged, and there were no communications from Judith when she woke early the following morning. Judith had told her they would meet at St Felix's when Li Min arrived in town, and that she should be ready to leave Oxford. So she had spent some of the evening packing, though she would not be taking anything much but her handbag and laptop case with her. Judith had said they would either come to collect her belongings later or someone else would send them on, once Li Min had left Oxford. But why wasn't she replying now?

She went to catch the shuttle bus, and was sitting in it texting Judith again, waiting for the half-full vehicle to leave for town, when suddenly the driver opened the front door and Mr Chew climbed up the steps and came down the aisle.

Fortunately, another student, a boy from Mumbai whom she recognised from the dining hall, was already sitting beside her, so Chew could not sit next to her. Instead he sat down in the seat directly behind. As the bus set off, Li Min suddenly heard Chew's voice, close to her ear, talking in Chinese, knowing the boy next to her would not understand what he said.

'I'm surprised to see you on your own. Where is your white girlfriend?'

Li Min struggled to decide how best to answer. On the face of things, Mr Chew had no officially sanctioned authority over her, but although she knew full well by now that he was an undercover state security officer, not a student, she had to avoid having a public row with him, particularly when her priority was to find Judith Davidson. So all she said was, 'She's ill.'

'Oh,' said Mr Chew in mock-surprise, 'how sad. Do you think you can manage it on your own?'

'Manage what?' she demanded, annoyed enough by him to override the anxiety he induced in her.

'You have something to fetch for Mr Deng, I understand. I suggest you attend to that at once.'

'I have a meeting in college first. It would arouse suspicion if I were absent,' she said, grasping for the first lie she could think of.

'You realise any further delay will have severe consequences for you?'

'Thanks for reminding me,' she said tartly. She wished this man would leave her alone. She needed to find Judith.

'And not just you,' he continued unperturbed.

Something in his voice chilled her. 'What is that supposed to mean?'

'You are not the only one who will pay the price for failure to produce what is expected.'

What did he mean? Who else would pay a price? Judith? Did Chew know about her somehow? Who else could it be?

'The white girl – Washington – will be considered a severe liability. She knows too much now about this fakery of yours.'

'Deepfake,' said Li Min, without the usual sharpness to her tone. A sense of dread was growing within her and she found it hard to speak boldly. 'It's called deepfake.'

'I don't care what it's called. I am not here to receive lessons on AI. I am here to remind you of your obligations and see that you fulfil them. Otherwise…' He let the sentence hang unfinished. Then he went on, 'And for the white girl too there will be no happy ending.' He waved a hand at Li Min. 'Go to your meeting, but keep it short. You need to be at the lab very soon.'

They reached the outskirts of Oxford and then the drop-off point near St Felix's, where Li Min got off without looking behind her, though she was certain Mr Chew would still be monitoring her movements. She went into St Felix's, narrowly avoiding bumping into the head porter who was giving directions to some visitors. She turned round and saw Chew standing outside on the pavement.

She was upset by her encounter with him but enough in control to phone Judith. There was still no answer, and she tried to calm down and work out what to do. She did not feel safe here, not with Chew just outside the Lodge and still no sign of Judith. Where could the American woman have gone? Had something happened to her? Chew would hurt anyone if ordered to, she sensed, but he had been at the Elm that morning so hopefully had not been anywhere near Judith. But even if there had been some emergency – she thought wildly of a parent dying, or a friend killed in an accident – surely the American agent would still have answered her texts or at least told her she would be out of touch for a time.

Judith had been insistent that Li Min would be leaving Oxford very soon. Should she now do that on her own? Walk to the station and take the first train out of here? She would have to lose Mr Chew but thought she could do that.

That way she would be safe, for a while at least, which was a reassuring prospect. But she saw the drawbacks. Where would she sleep? If she had to go to a hotel, how long could she afford to stay there? And where would she go next?

There was another even more potent downside. Her fleeing would not protect Sally at all. If anything, it would leave her more exposed, and Sally had no reason to suspect that she was in trouble. Li Min could not do that to her friend. But neither could she give Deng the actual deepfake she had created. That would in its own way do just as much damage to Sally.

They would be coming for her soon enough, Deng and Chew and probably some other thugs called in by him. There would be more than enough of them to subdue and terrorise and possibly murder one unprotected student. But better her than Sally, Li Min decided, and it was then she knew she had to get back to the Elm, find her friend before she left for St Felix's and warn her of the danger she was in before Deng and his men had the opportunity to strike. Li Min would normally have rung her but she was filled with distrust now – Deng might well be monitoring her calls. It was too big a risk to take. She had made up her mind to return to the Elm, helped by the realisation that she was not doing this for herself. Better to face the music than to run and hide – and leave her friend unprepared for the punishment Deng was about to inflict on her.

47

Saunders was famously calm when all around him grew tense and anxious. But he was now extremely worried. The eight o'clock check-in agreed with Manon the evening before had not taken place. She hadn't called, and thinking she might have got confused over who was initiating the communication, he had tried to reach her. No one had answered. This seemed odd for in his experience she was very reliable, and Fleishman over in Langley, who knew her very well, had always said she was a safe pair of hands.

He kept trying through the rest of the evening, and even – he was insomniac – through the night. He alerted Kenton at MI5 as well, who promised his colleagues would help look for the missing agent. Saunders had tried CIA email, CIA video calls, encrypted texts and audio-only phone. Nothing – just the anonymous message: 'Please leave a message after the beep.'

When this silence continued in the morning he had quickly showered and changed and gone to his office in the Embassy in Nine Elms, where his worry mounted as he learned that none of his colleagues had heard anything from her either. His immediate concern was for Manon's safety. He feared that her cover had been blown and that some action had been taken against her, initiated either by Deng at the Embassy or his sidekick Chew at the Institute. But there was also Li Min to consider; what would she think now that Manon had seemingly disappeared?

He decided to phone Abbot, but learned only that the Institute Director hadn't seen or heard from Manon.

'No big deal,' said Saunders, not wanting a partner in his anxiety, but from the tension in Abbot's voice could tell he was alarmed as well.

'We usually see each other every morning – I drop by her office to say hello or she drops by mine. But she wasn't there when I went by. I supposed she had a meeting elsewhere,' Abbot said. He paused then said tensely, 'Tell me what I should do.'

'Just call me if you hear from her. And stay put. I'll be down with you as soon as traffic allows.' For Saunders' sense of helplessness was magnified by not being there on the ground where it seemed this case would be played out.

Next he rang Kenton at MI5 to put him in the picture. Kenton broke into his explanation. 'I'll come with you,' he said, 'and you can tell me the whole story in the car. I'll join you across the river and put colleagues here on the alert. We may need surveillance and I'll let the transcribers know in case they pick up anything relevant. But don't forget that we're probably dealing here with the Embassy of a foreign country, and a particularly sensitive one too. We don't want a huge diplomatic incident.' And with that he put the phone down before Saunders could respond.

Soon after Kenton arrived, they were on their way to Oxford. Saunders was behind the wheel of a four-wheel-drive with British number plates that had no link to either the American Embassy or British Intelligence.

Kenton was a big man with a tense manner. He said, 'We're ready to set surveillance on Deng, but so far he hasn't left the Embassy. Which reminds me: a Westerner we've only just now managed to identify visited it last week. A man named Arthur Cole of St Felix's College – he was the previous Director of the Institute that seems to be at the centre of whatever is going on.'

Saunders said, 'The first thing we should do is call on Abbot. He hasn't heard from Manon but he may have some idea where she's gone. At least I hope so.'

48

Deng decided to give Li Min until 10 that morning. He continued to text her but she no longer replied. He decided not to wait any longer but called Mr Lau and got authorisation for a car to take him to Oxford. Before he left, he called Chew.

'Where is the girl?' he asked without any preamble.

'She has come back to the Elm. She's in her room and I am down the hall. My door is open so I will hear her if she comes out again.'

'Have you spoken to her?'

'Not since she took the bus into Oxford. When she came back, she was surrounded by students and I did not want to risk a confrontation.'

A good thing too, if she had finally retrieved the deepfake, thought Deng. 'When did she get back?'

'Half an hour ago. She did go to the lab – I was following her. But she didn't stay long.'

She would not have had to if she were merely copying a file. Which she had subsequently had plenty of time to send on to Deng. She was playing with him, creating a slew of problems and issues that all led to one result – no deepfake. Enough was enough, he decided. 'I am leaving now and coming down there,' he announced. 'Stay where you are – unless she leaves her room. If she does, stick to her like glue. Is that understood?

I no longer trust Li Min at all. But I can't extract anything from this wretched girl unless we are face to face. Then she'll talk. I will make sure of that.'

Saunders and Kenton found Abbot in his office, staring blankly at the documents on his desk, his attention obviously elsewhere. He got up and joined them at the table in the room. Saunders said, 'I think everyone here is up to speed. We learned yesterday that Li Min has finished the deepfake that the Chinese wanted. Manon persuaded her not to give it to them, but to fob them off with something harmless. So far, so good. But today things seem to have fallen apart. We haven't achieved any of our objectives, to put it mildly. We have lost Manon, we are out of touch with Li Min, and we don't know what's happened to the deepfake itself. I think we have to assume Li Min has not handed it over to her Chinese controllers, which makes it critical that we find her and find her fast. We need to know in what form the deepfake exists and who has it.'

Kenton added, 'We spent yesterday making preparations for Li Min's exfiltration. We have a safe house ready and we've alerted the police that we may need some protection so we can look after her at short notice, if that's how it turns out.'

'From what Li Min told Manon just yesterday,' said Saunders, 'the deepfake doesn't show Sally Washington taking drugs or sleeping with some boy; it's far more damning than that. It shows her taking money from the Chinese and vocally indicating that it's payment for spying for China.'

'What if we're wrong and she has already given this deepfake thing to them?' said Abbot.

'Then our interest in Li Min would, necessarily, be greatly reduced.'

'That still leaves Manon,' Abbot said, who was drumming the fingers of one hand on the tabletop.

'Of course it does, and within these four walls I am happy to tell you that she is our other top priority – finding where she's gone and why, and making sure she hasn't been harmed. Now, do we know anything about her schedule yesterday – and today?'

'Not really,' said Abbot. 'Her work here didn't involve anyone else directly. She would check in with me, but that was as much to make sure we kept an ear to the ground as anything to do with the papers she was meant to be cataloguing.' He pointed at the laptop on his desk. 'If she kept an appointments diary it isn't on our system.'

'Manon called me from here during the afternoon yesterday to tell me that Li Min needed to be exfiltrated today,' said Saunders. 'But I haven't had any contact with her since and she has gone off air.'

Suddenly Abbot remembered something. 'She told me yesterday that Arthur Cole wanted to see her – to show her something. He didn't tell her what it was. She said she was going to call on him but didn't say when.'

'Then we'd better go see him ourselves before we do anything else,' said Saunders. 'He may have been the last person who saw her.'

'I can take you to his room,' said Abbot. 'I can't guarantee he'll be there, but let's go and see.'

49

Arthur Cole looked shattered. His eyes were red-rimmed and his face was drawn. The knock sounded like a knell to his troubled mind. He walked to the door, wondering what he would find, and opened it to an intimidating pair of men fronted by Abbot, the self-opinionated prig he had always disliked. The other two looked official. Cole let them in and went to sit behind his desk. His hands were shaking and his voice was weak and tremulous.

He had always feared that his relationship with China would be misunderstood. It was a country that had once seemed to him the acme of civilisation, centuries old and secure in its humanity and traditions of thinking; the home of an art tradition that was serene and yet striking. He had assumed that this wonderful country would remain the same forever.

But recently a new crop of Chinese officials had arrived in London. They were discourteous and had become more and more demanding. Now they were issuing orders to him as though he were a hired hand rather than a committed sympathiser. But their most recent demand was the final straw. They had told him to get rid of Miss Davidson. What could they have meant by that? He didn't know, didn't want to know and wasn't prepared to play any part in it.

Ms Pierpont, who astonishingly also seemed to be in touch with the Chinese officials, had begun to treat him as though she was his superior, conveying instructions from the Embassy to him. On this occasion he had accepted her offer to take the problem off his hands. He had known it was weak of him, but he was at the end of his tether with these crude, aggressive people. He had given her the key to the cellar when she asked for it, and he had then gone home and stayed there until this morning. God knows what she had done, in his absence. Now here were these official-looking characters led by a tense-faced Charles Abbot, trying to find out what had happened to Miss Davidson. What on earth could he say to them? He had no idea what the Pierpont woman had done, but he could guess that if Davidson was missing it was likely to be for some very unpleasant reason. What could he say? What should he do?

He looked at the three figures standing in front of him and decided that he had only one option: that was to tell the truth as far as he knew it. Well, up to a point maybe, as he realised that he was already an accomplice to an abduction, and was beginning to fear that he might soon be accomplice to a murder. There was no need to disclose any of that.

So he described how his relationship with the Chinese Embassy had changed in nature, especially once Mr Lau had passed him on to Yìchén; now they were trying to treat him as a lackey, and that was something he had not been prepared to accept. When he had received the order to dispose of Miss Davidson, it had been the last straw. Whatever had happened to her subsequently had been none of his doing. True, he had invited Miss Davidson to come and see a new acquisition, but that was the extent of his involvement. He had departed from the college at five, leaving the key to his room with Nina Pierpont, and that was the last he knew of the matter.

The effort of explaining all this had exhausted him, but when he looked up from his desk at the faces of his visitors, all he could read there was contempt and obvious disbelief. He said, 'I know I should have told someone. But this world is not one I understand. I am not a man of action, I am a scholar.' And he put his head in his hands and started to sob.

Then the questions began again, cold and insistent. Where could Pierpont have taken her? Cole shook his head to show he had no idea. Then where was this new acquisition he'd wanted to show her?

'I don't know,' Cole insisted. The ensuing silence seemed to unnerve him, for he suddenly said, 'There is no new acquisition.'

His interrogators all looked appalled. 'Then why did you say—' the man called Saunders started, and stopped as he belatedly understood. He said sternly, 'You invented it to lure Judith here, didn't you? Didn't you?' he demanded, almost shouting now.

Cole nodded slowly. He said, sounding pathetic, 'I was told I had to.' His face had drained of colour; he looked dreadful.

Abbot said, 'Where would Pierpont take her? She must have picked a place in readiness.'

'I don't know,' Cole said feebly.

'Think, man,' said Abbot. 'You must have some idea.'

After a long silence, he said, 'Honestly, I don't.'

'You'd better hope we don't find out you've been lying,' Abbot said to him, shaking his head in disgust.

'Let's go,' said Kenton.

When they left, Cole remained seated at his desk, his head in his hands.

Outside in the quad, Kenton turned to the others. 'Why should the Chinese have taken action against Manon? And why now?'

Saunders said, 'They must have broken her cover. They might have seen her meeting Li Min and assumed she was an American spook. We know that their plan for Li Min has reached a critical stage. They must have decided that they needed to get Manon out of the way so she couldn't screw it up. As we've just heard, Old King Cole refused to have anything to do with it, so the job was handed over to this Pierpont woman, who must be on the Chinese books too.'

Kenton broke in. 'Do you think we should find Pierpont and ask her what the hell she's done?'

Saunders seemed to be considering this when Abbot, who had been quiet until now, spoke up. 'Hang on,' he said. 'I have an idea.'

The other two looked at him curiously, waiting for an explanation. But Abbot only said, 'Give me five minutes.' Then he strode away, walking rapidly across the quad. As Kenton and Saunders watched his progress, they realised he was marching straight back to Arthur Cole's room.

50

When she came to, Manon's first reaction had been relief that she was still alive and breathing. She had tried to move a hand but both were tied together behind her back. Her next thought was to yell for help, but when she attempted it she couldn't open her mouth. It had been taped shut.

Gradually she was coming to her senses. Now she realised she was lying next to the door of the inner store room. Outside it lay the anteroom with its heavy steel door to the deserted corridor beyond. Even if they hadn't taped her mouth, she could probably scream the place down without being heard. How long did they plan to keep her here? she wondered. And who were 'they' anyway? The Pierpont woman and whoever had grabbed her from behind. Someone very strong.

Why had they done this to her? Even if they suspected she was no librarian but a CIA officer, why would they abduct her? They must know there would be hell to pay if they were caught.

Then she saw why – it was obvious. To get her out of the way, so they could work on Li Min. Threaten her, seize the deepfake – and then what? Manon shuddered to think. By the time they let her go it would be too late. The deepfake would be in the hands of the Chinese Embassy security people.

She wondered if Cole were part of the plan to keep her here, and she asked herself how long that would be. Maybe forever, she thought glumly, since it struck her that he was the only person who came here at all, checking on the overflow pieces of his collection. Upstairs was scheduled for renovation, but not until the following autumn; there was literally no reason for anyone to explore down here.

How long had she been here anyway? There was so little light in this subterranean cell that it was impossible to tell if it was day or night. She didn't wear a watch and had left her phone in her office on charge before going to Cole's room, though Manon could not in any case have reached her trouser pocket to see it, not when she was trussed like a chicken ready for the oven. As she peered around, shivering in the damp darkness, she started to despair.

All she could hope for was the improbable arrival of Saunders or Charles Abbot, coming to her rescue. But why would they even think to look for her here? She had mentioned Cole's oddly friendly invitation to Charles; they had even discussed the motivation behind it. But she had not told him the time of her appointment; he might not even know she was missing. No, more likely the next person she saw would be the sinister Nina Pierpont or even the dreadful Mr Chew – had it been he who had attacked her and tied her up? By the time they let her go it would all be too late. It might even be too late already. And what if they didn't come – it might be weeks before anyone else did. Manon might be a skeleton before she was found…

Then an even darker thought took hold. What made her think that if Pierpont or Chew or even musty old Arthur Cole came down, they would let her go?

Of course they wouldn't. They'd all be arrested as soon as she told Saunders or the police what they had done to her.

They could never risk that. If they came at all, they would come to kill her.

At first she thought she was imagining the noise. A faint reverberation, possibly the sound of footsteps, but then – yes, definitely – the clang of a heavy metal door swinging slowly open. Then a key in the lock of the inner door, being worked a bit before it turned. She readied herself. Who would come first? Pierpont? Chew? She hoped whatever they did to her it would be quick and painless. That seemed the best she could hope for.

And then there was a voice, and a switch was flicked, and the room was flooded with light, so bright she could not see at first who was in the doorway. Then she heard the voice again and then another, and was astonished to find the voices seemed familiar.

One voice rang out above the other. 'She's here!' cried Charles, rushing forward and lifting her up by wrapping his arms under her shoulders. 'Has anyone got a knife to get these ropes off?' he asked urgently. Two other figures had entered the room behind him: Saunders and the MI5 man. Kenton took a Swiss Army knife from his pocket, opened the blade and started hacking at the rope around her ankles. 'I'm sorry, but this might hurt,' said Charles as he pulled the tape sharply from her mouth. 'Thank God you're alive.'

'What the hell were you doing to get yourself stuck down here?' said Saunders, sounding unsympathetic but actually shaking with the relief of finding her safe.

Manon gasped, 'It was Pierpont. She brought me down here, and it must have been that man Chew who knocked me out with some sort of jab.' Her voice was rasping from disuse. 'How did you know where to find me?' she asked.

Both Saunders and Kenton looked at Charles. 'Arthur Cole,' he said.

'When we all first talked to him, he claimed not to know where you were. It was a regular Pontius Pilate performance. But it didn't ring true. So I went back and saw him again. I told him that if so much as a hair on your head was harmed, he would be facing a prison sentence. And even if he managed to stay out of gaol, I would ensure he lost his fellowship and was expelled from St Felix's–' Charles smiled wryly '–That seemed to upset him even more than the prospect of prison.

'It also occurred to me that if he allegedly had something "special" to show you and it wasn't in his rooms, then it might be that they'd take you somewhere you'd been before – if only to allay your suspicions. He finally admitted that was the case but then wouldn't give me the keys – he claimed he had lost them. Fortunately, they had spares in the Porters' Lodge.'

Manon sighed. 'My meeting with Cole was to have been at five p.m., but when I arrived he wasn't there; Pierpont was. And that's when I came down here with her. She told me that Cole had gone home ill and had asked her to stand in for him and show me his new acquisition. That's about the last thing I can remember. Then I came round and found myself in the dark, all tied up.'

Charles said, 'I think there's still a vestige of conscience in Cole. He seems very shaken.'

'But what's happened to Li Min?' Manon asked. Charles was rubbing her ankles to help restore the circulation as she waited for Kenton to free her hands.

'We don't know yet,' said Saunders. 'Now that we've found you, we can focus on finding her.'

Kenton added, 'We've arranged the safe house and are all ready to receive her.'

Saunders said, 'But obviously you've missed your rendezvous with her. It's crisis time, for them as well as us. I'm only afraid she'll be in the hands of Deng by now.'

Getting to her feet slowly, breathing in deeply, Manon said, 'Please can we get out of this dungeon and find out what's going on? The Chinese must know by now that Li Min has been in touch with me. They must suspect that I know their plan, but they won't know whether I had time to pass it on before they got to me.'

As they reached the open air upstairs, Manon supporting herself on Charles' arm, Saunders said, 'We don't know whether they have got Li Min or not, but we have to stop them taking her out of the country if we possibly can. The same applies to the deepfake. We don't know where it is.'

Kenton added, 'I think the best thing to do now is to get to the Elm as quickly as we can and try and find her.'

Saunders said, 'I agree. But, Manon, you're really in no shape to do any rushing about right now.'

Manon shook her head. 'I'll be a bit wobbly on my feet at first, but if I can get some water and sit down for a bit, I figure I'll be OK.'

Kenton, who had just switched on his phone, said, 'I've got some messages from the surveillance team who are following Deng.'

They all stood, huddled together in the quad, while Kenton listened to them. 'It's not very good news,' he said at last, putting his phone in his jacket pocket. 'Apparently Deng left the Embassy at ten-thirty driving a dark blue Toyota Prius with British number plates and no diplomatic identification.

He went west on Marylebone Road, which turns into the A40. Our surveillance team were with him at that point, but it seems they lost him on the motorway.'

'It's easily done,' said Saunders sympathetically. 'Did they get any sense of where he was headed?'

'They reckoned he would go to Oxford, which made sense, and in fact he was heading that way. But just before junction seven he pulled over into a layby. He was shielded by a couple of lorries and the guys didn't spot him there until it was too late for them to stop. They waited for him to catch up but he didn't come past. They now think he must have turned off at seven, bound for Thame, about fifteen miles from here.'

'When did all this happen?' asked Saunders.

Kenton looked at his watch. 'About an hour ago, while we were hearing Cole's confession.'

Charles said, 'It might be worth ringing the Elm before we go, just to see if Li Min has gone back there.'

'Shall I have a go?' said Saunders. 'It might sound more official coming from a person they don't know.' He dialled the Elm and spoke to someone, then waited for what seemed a long time to Manon. Finally, Saunders finished his call and said, 'The woman who answered says Li Min's not there. I asked her to go check the room, but I don't think she did. Isn't the manager there the woman who put you in the wine cellar?'

'Pierpont,' said Manon. 'We can't believe a word she says. I think we should get down to the Elm right now and see what's happening.'

At this point Saunders said firmly, 'There are two important jobs needing to be done. First, we must locate Li Min and try and prevent her falling into the hands of Deng and the Chinese. So Kenton and I will go down to the Elm and see if she is there, and if not, what clues we can pick up as to where she has gone. Equally importantly, we must find Sally Washington. We have been keeping her father informed as we've learned more about what's been going on, and he has asked us to take her under our protection when the right moment comes. That in my view is now.'

He turned back to Manon and said, 'You are the only person who can do that job without risking a bad reaction from Sally. As you know, according to operational rules, after your abduction and the drugs you were given in the cellar, you should do nothing until you have been checked out by the medics. But I'm disobeying orders on this occasion. I can't afford to lose you. I need you here. You are the one with the best chance of persuading Sally to do as we ask without making a fuss and causing delay. I suspect she won't want to go to a safe house, or to go back home either. You need to get her to accept the situation. Charles, would you be good enough to help by finding out whether either Sally or Li Min is in college at the moment? And Kenton and I will go down to the Elm and see whether we can find them there.'

Kenton intervened to say, 'We already have two policemen outside in the Broad looking for Li Min, and I will give them Sally Washington's description too.'

Charles said, 'I'll gladly do what I can to help. The porters have already been alerted to ring me if they see Li Min, and I can add Sally to their brief. And the housekeepers at the safe house are already in my office awaiting their instructions. We'll all keep in touch, and join up again when we can.'

Saunders said, 'Manon, you will need to explain to Sally what is going on and find out what her part in it has been.

We must learn from her urgently how much she knows about what Li Min has been doing and why she seems to be so important to the Chinese Embassy. This needs doing quickly and without scaring the girl. As soon as you learn anything useful, let us know.'

Manon's initial air of disappointment had gone. She said, 'That sounds like a good plan.'

51

AT ABOUT HALF-PAST TWELVE, Deng parked his Toyota Prius by the dilapidated barn, behind Gillroy's old Land Rover. This meant the car was not visible from the road leading to the Elm. Rather more important, arriving on foot would be more discreet than leaving his car parked by the front door.

He found Nina Pierpont back in her office. When she saw Deng standing in the doorway, she stiffened and did not rise to greet him. He stepped into the office and closed the door behind him.

'Is Li Min still here?' he asked, thinking the girl had better be, since he'd heard nothing from Pierpont on his drive down.

'She is,' the woman said tersely, and Deng realised Pierpont was worried. She must have found her relationship with the Chinese more than she had bargained for. At first she would have appreciated the retainer, a matter of a few hundred pounds each month – trivial, though probably not to her – with little or nothing asked in return. But she was paying the price now.

Deng said, 'This American woman – Davidson. What has happened to her?'

'She's taken care of for now. She is locked in a disused part of the college where no one ever goes. She is tied up and gagged; no one will be able to hear her.'

'Good.' Though God knows what to do with her once he had the deepfake, he thought. He could not see any way they could let her go.

Pierpont must have pondered this as well, for she asked, 'What is going to happen to her? We can't keep her there forever.'

'I don't see why not,' he said, then realised from Pierpont's reaction that this alarmed rather than consoled her. He shook his head. 'Obviously we will have to deal with her, but only once I finish my other business. Assuming I get the information I need from Li Min, nothing will be done to harm Davidson.'

Pierpont looked relieved, and Deng realised that though made of sterner stuff than Arthur Cole, she too seemed to feel concern for others. He didn't care about anyone but himself and would be out of the country before anything needed to be done about Davidson.

'Mr Chew is waiting for you upstairs,' she said now, as if offering information of value.

'I know,' said Deng. 'Listen, if anyone arrives looking for Li Min, I want you to keep them talking, and text me right away. On no account let them come upstairs until you hear from me. Is that understood?'

She nodded as he stared at her. He said, 'Has Chew got the key to Li Min's room?'

'If you mean the master key then yes, I lent it to him. But I must have it back in case it's needed.'

She would get it back when he was good and ready to give it back, Deng thought.

He left the office to go upstairs. In the south wing, he walked quietly along the corridor. When he passed the room

Chew had told him was Li Min's, he stopped briefly and listened, but there was no sound from within.

Deng found Chew standing just inside his own room down the corridor, only thirty feet or so from Li Min's door. 'She hasn't come out at all,' Chew said before Deng could even say hello. 'She's got the door bolted so I can't open it with the master key. Do you want me to break it down?'

'Absolutely not,' said Deng, appalled. He forgot sometimes that Chew's instincts were always violent, that the man preferred taking by force what anyone else would prefer to take by persuasion. 'I want you to stay where you are until I bring her here. You have the kit you need ready to go?'

'I do.'

'OK. I hope to be back shortly – accompanied this time.'

Deng retraced his steps and stopped by Li Min's room. He knocked, tapping his knuckles quietly against the wooden door. No sound came from inside, but Deng was not surprised. He put his mouth close to the door and half-whispered, 'Li Min, it's Deng. I hope you have the file from the lab with you. Do not be afraid; I am sure Mr Lau will understand any delay because, you see, your friend Sally has had an accident. She asked for you before she became unconscious. She's at the hospital – the John Radcliffe, I believe it is called. I said I would come to tell you and drive you there. You must hurry; the accident was…' and here he let his voice falter '… serious.'

This time he heard movement inside. She was getting up, he thought, and waited for her to unlock the door. But instead, as he heard her approaching, she said, 'I do not believe you. I saw her last night and she was fine.' There was a pause, and Deng racked his brains furiously for what he should say next. But Li Min went on: 'And she was fine two hours ago when

I spoke to her on my phone. She was going to take the bus into college.'

Deng was so used to obedience from the agents reporting to him that he felt unnerved by her response. He could not have said he had really expected Li Min to believe him; what he had assumed was that she would *obey* him. But here she was, openly defiant, not just doubting his word but voicing her doubt, and acting on it – or rather *not* acting, since her door remained firmly closed. What the hell should he do? Deng wondered frantically, feeling at a loss how to proceed now that he realised his usual method of persuasion wasn't working.

Deng was not an imaginative person. His professional strengths were his efficiency at his job, an unflinching obedience his superiors could rely on, a useful if chilling lack of sympathy for the agents he ran and, when necessary, a considerable capacity for ruthlessness. There was nothing in any of these traits that required imagination.

But now, quite atypically, he had an inspiration, which he grabbed at like a man overboard unexpectedly thrown a lifebelt.

'I know all this,' he said. 'She took the bus and went in to college. But when she got off the bus she was attacked.'

'*What?*' The alarm in Li Min's voice overrode any disbelief. 'What do you mean, "attacked"?'

'It is my fault,' said Deng, lowering his voice to sound contrite. 'I should have seen it coming. I thought he could be trusted to control himself. I admit, I asked him to follow her, but I said nothing about hurting her. That is the last thing I ever wanted. You must believe me.'

'Who are you talking about?' Through the door, Li Min sounded completely confused. 'What have you done?'

'You must believe me when I say I had no choice. Mr Lau said Sally had to be watched. There was only one person I could ask to do that – as I say, I thought he could be trusted. I was wrong.'

'Oh, God!' said Li Min. Her voice came from closer to the door. Any minute now, hoped Deng, she would open it, throwing caution to the wind in her consternation. She said, sounding furious, 'You asked that bastard Chew, didn't you? What has he done to Sally? Why has he hurt her?'

'Your friend realised Chew was following her, so she confronted him. Then she ran. He chased her and when he caught up, she got hurt.'

'*Lao tian ye*!' she shouted in the Mandarin of her childhood. *Oh my God*. 'Is she all right? Is she alive?'

'Yes, of course.' He added, faking indignation, 'Chew wasn't trying to hurt her. He says it was an accident – that she tripped and he tried to break her fall, but when he grabbed her, he accidentally broke her arm. And then she fell anyway and hit her head.'

'Her head?' Li Min sounded distraught.

'Yes.'

'Who is looking after her?'

'She is at the hospital, like I said. She is conscious now. I called just before I came here.' He paused then said, 'The nurse on the phone asked me who you were.'

'Me? Why me?'

'Because your friend was asking for you.'

And he let this sink in. Providing more detail might lead to further questions – and doubt. He forced himself to wait.

'I don't know how to get there,' she said, suddenly sounding uncertain.

'I do,' said Deng confidently. 'I have a car here, and I'll take you. But we need to hurry.'

The silence as Li Min considered this was becoming worryingly prolonged, but at last she broke it. 'I am not going anywhere with that man Chew.'

'Of course not. You are going with me; only me. So come now. She will be in the hospital overnight, apparently, so she will want some things from her room.'

And to his great relief, the next sound he heard was the locks turning, and then the door opened a crack and then a little more, until he saw the eyes of Li Min staring at him. Deng stood back, fighting his instinct to push the door open and rush in, and then Li Min opened the door wide and quickly stuck her head out, looking down the corridor both ways. Satisfied now that Deng was on his own, she came out to join him. She had put on a coat.

'Come with me,' he said, and they moved away along the corridor, Deng hoping devoutly that Chew would hear them coming and not stick his head out from his room and be seen. Deng readied himself for that possibility nonetheless, by letting Li Min walk slightly ahead of him on his right side – the same side as Chew's room.

They were just short of his door when suddenly Li Min slowed. 'This is not the way to Sally's room,' she said. Suspicion had re-entered her voice, but when Deng kept walking, she automatically moved forward too. Her head was turned towards him, waiting for his response, her eyes on Deng as she drew level with Chew's open door.

Deng suddenly gripped her tightly by the shoulder with one hand and seized her waist with the other, then bundled her through the open doorway and into Chew's room. As Li

Min shouted in surprise, the door closed behind them and the massive figure of Chew appeared. Deng let go, and Chew threw one arm around her at chest-height, pinioning both arms to her sides, and with his free hand pushed a soaked cotton cloth over her face, clamping it hard against her nose and mouth.

Li Min tried to struggle, kicking out with one leg, trying fruitlessly to free her arms. But then the Sevoflurane mix on the cloth took hold, filling the room with its strong chemical odour and subduing Li Min almost immediately. She was still conscious, Deng could see from her blinking eyes, but Chew kept the cloth firmly in place until her eyelids closed and she fell unconscious.

'OK?' asked Chew, removing the cloth.

Deng nodded. He was relieved to see that Li Min was breathing – not always guaranteed when using knockout drugs. There had been a boy in Hong Kong, a student activist, who had died within a minute of receiving too large a dose. There had been no scandal, the local police being too timid to investigate, but to this day Deng regretted missing the chance to interrogate him.

'I'll get the suitcase,' Chew said, lifting the limp figure of Li Min and putting her down on his bed. Then he went and retrieved a large suitcase from the room's single wardrobe. Unzipping it, he put the open suitcase on the floor, first taking off her coat and shoes, and then carefully placed the girl's small supine figure inside, fitting her in by bending both her knees and tucking her arms against her sides. He went into the bathroom, picked up a hypodermic syringe from where it lay on the washbasin, returned to the room and jabbed it into her arm. 'That should keep her quiet for a few hours,' he said, and zipped the suitcase shut.

Deng said, 'Open the zip a little. Can you manage the case on your own?'

'Of course,' said Chew, and confirmed this by lifting it with one hand and dangling it in mid-air. It might have been holding feathers from the ease with which he handled it. He looked at Deng, who said sharply, 'Where is your transport?'

'It should be in the back car park by now, if you gave Gillroy the right instructions.'

Deng didn't like this tone. He said sharply, 'You'd better text him. Now! And open that zip a little more. Just an inch or two.'

'Why?' asked Chew, which annoyed Deng even more. It was not for Chew to question a simple order. He said, 'The girl has to breathe. We don't want a corpse on our hands.' Not yet at any rate, he thought. He added, 'Be in touch once you get to London.'

'Where will you be?'

What was going on? First Li Min talked back to him; now even this thug was out of line. 'I must check the girl's room.' He had not told Chew anything about the deepfake and wasn't about to start now. 'I need the master key.'

He held out his hand and for a moment Chew just looked at it. Eventually he handed over the key and texted Gillroy, who told him that he would be round in about twenty minutes. Chew looked at the suitcase, cursed Deng and wished he had left the drug-soaked handkerchief inside it. Then he sat down to wait for Gillroy.

Meanwhile, Deng walked back to Li Min's door and, looking around to make sure he was not being watched, unlocked it and entered the room.

There was no sign of her laptop. Could Li Min have hidden it somewhere else? It didn't seem likely; she would want to keep it close, and not take the risk of someone finding it. Especially if it held the deepfake file. But she might have hidden it within her room, and he started to look in the usual places first: flipping the mattress of her thin single bed onto the floor; checking the wardrobe where he carefully patted every inch of the hanging clothes. Nothing. Then he kicked himself when he found the laptop sitting in the desk's central drawer.

He was tempted to boot up the machine and look for the deepfake but prudence prevailed. Li Min might well have erected a barrier of passwords and encryption that he was not qualified to penetrate, or worse, a booby trap that would destroy the file if someone unauthorised tried to open it. Better to leave it to the experts; one had arrived from Beijing the day before, precisely for that purpose.

He needed to make tracks before he was spotted. The Davidson woman was out of commission, but people would be looking for her, especially if she was really working for American Intelligence. In that case the link between Davidson and Li Min would be known to Davidson's superiors, and they would have forensics all over this room later today.

Deng looked at the bedding and mattress tumbled over the floor, wondering if he should tidy up. No, he decided, there wasn't enough time. And besides, he was secretly proud of the fact that the mess he'd made would show the MSS had got here first. Finding the laptop case in the wardrobe, he put the computer in it and slung it over one shoulder. He was itching to know whether Li Min had delivered the goods after all, but either way she would not be seeing this room again.

Downstairs he found Pierpont in her office. She seemed agitated. 'I've had a call about Li Min,' she said. 'Wanting to know if she was here.'

'Who was asking?'

'Some American man.'

'What did you tell him?'

'I said I hadn't seen her. He asked me to check her room, and I pretended to, but I said she wasn't there.'

'And I wasn't here either. Understand?' Deng returned the master key, chucking it onto the desktop; otherwise the Western security people would be sure to ask who had it.

She nodded, reluctantly. Don't worry, thought Deng, we won't be using you again.

Then he left the building and walked up the track to the barn without a backward glance.

52

T̲HE AUDI TURNED OFF the main road towards the Elm. Kenton was in the passenger seat and Saunders driving. As they approached the building they saw the shuttle bus. Saunders pulled the car over and they watched the stream of students boarding. A girl in a yellow parka, with a tousled mop of streaky blonde hair, was being helped on board by a couple of young men.

'That girl doesn't look well,' said Saunders. As he watched, he added, 'I think it's Sally Washington... In fact, I'm pretty sure it is. Kenton, ring Manon and tell her and Charles to meet the bus.'

As he made the call, a Land Rover swung out of the gate of the field to their left with a man in workwear at the wheel. It continued on towards the car park at the back of the main building. At the same time a Toyota Prius, which had been concealed behind the Land Rover, started down the hill from the barn at the top.

Saunders said: 'That Toyota is Deng's car! Let's find out what he's been doing. And who was that in the Land Rover?'

'I gathered from Charles that the Institute has an odd-job man he doesn't really trust,' Kenton said. 'Name of Gillroy. That must have been him.'

Saunders grunted. He backed swiftly down the road and manoeuvred the Audi into the open gateway, blocking it and forcing the Toyota to stop abruptly.

Trapped in his car, Deng's face was a picture of fury. He pushed both fists angrily against the steering wheel until the Toyota's horn sounded in a long harsh blast.

Saunders and Kenton got out, leaving the Audi blocking the exit. As they moved to the driver's side of the Prius, Deng emerged, swearing in angry snatches of Chinese. 'You are trespassing,' he said, half-shouting. 'This is private property. Kindly return to your automobile and depart.'

Kenton said, 'This land is owned by St Felix's College and we have the authority to tell you to leave. We don't need to explain our presence here; you do.'

Deng changed tack. 'Actually, I was merely parking here. The lot at the Institute is very muddy. I wished to keep my vehicle clean.' He seemed to be aware of how lame this sounded.

'What business did you have at the Elm?' asked Kenton.

'Attending to the welfare of Chinese students. I visit often.'

'In what capacity? Who do you represent?'

'The Chinese government, of course. I work at our Embassy in London.'

'I see no diplomatic plates on your car,' said Kenton. 'I'm sure you won't mind opening your boot.'

'Boot? Ah, do you mean the trunk?'

Saunders said: 'Call it what you like – we want you to open it.'

'Sadly, I cannot do that,' said Deng, looking almost theatrically dismayed. 'The car was involved in an accident in London the other day, and the "boot" was damaged. It will not open.'

'It looks fine to me,' said Saunders. 'Let me have the key.'

'Sadly, the key is at the Embassy, awaiting the lock's repair.'

'Really?' said Saunders. 'It's usually the same key as you put in the ignition. Let me try that one. I promise to be very careful.'

Deng must have run out of ingenious excuses. 'No,' he said simply.

Saunders said, no longer so polite, 'You haven't a choice. We need to inspect the boot, and one way or another we are going to do it.'

Kenton had by this time walked to the back of the Audi where he found a toolkit, which he laid on the ground behind the Toyota. The next thing Deng heard was the sound of hammering.

Deng's voice rose and grew louder. 'If you damage my vehicle there will be serious consequences for you all. I am here as an agent of the Chinese Embassy. You have no right to detain me or to damage my possessions. Including this car. I forbid it!'

'Forbid away,' said Saunders caustically. 'I'll have a go,' he said to Kenton, who handed him the tools. 'Believe it or not, I've done this a couple of times before.'

They all gathered close to the boot, suddenly tense as Saunders went to work. Deng stood apart from them, though when he brought out his phone, Kenton walked over and took it out of his hand.

'You'll get it back,' he told the seething Deng. 'Once we've got the boot open.'

There was a small sharp bang as the lock gave way and the lid swung open.

The boot was empty. Li Min wasn't there, dead or alive.

'Bloody hell,' Kenton said.

Saunders managed to close the boot again, though the lock was loose and the lid's edge had been badly dented.

Deng said, 'I see you are disappointed. Perhaps one day you will let me know what you thought you would find. For now, I can only say you have needlessly damaged my property and you will hear more about that.'

'Send us the bill for the repair and we'll pay it right away,' said Kenton.

'That is not all we will be sending,' said Deng, happy to work himself up again. 'We will file an official complaint as soon as I return to London.'

'Please do,' said Saunders wearily.

'I take it I am free to go,' Deng said. It was not really a question.

Saunders looked at Kenton and the Englishman nodded. Both of them realised they had no grounds to detain Deng further. Saunders said, 'Yes, you may go,' and Kenton went and moved the Audi.

After they had watched Deng leave, Saunders turned to Kenton and said: 'Interesting. He never asked who we were. Anyway, let's get to the Elm and find out about Li Min.'

They parked the car in front and went in. Nina Pierpont was at the desk in her office and looked up at them, her expression a mixture of surprise and alarm.

'Is Li Min here now?' asked Kenton.

Pierpont paused, studying them, apparently trying to make up her mind what to say. At last she said, 'She's gone on the bus to Oxford.'

'I'm from the Foreign Office,' said Kenton, 'and I have instructions to speak to Li Min personally, so I must be sure that she's not in her room. I assume you have a spare key. Will you let me have it, please?'

He spoke firmly and with authority. It was clear that Nina Pierpont was in two minds. Finally, she decided not to argue, handed over the master key without comment and told the men where to go.

Upstairs in Li Min's room, they surveyed the mess that Deng had left behind him.

'Wherever she's gone, it doesn't look as though she's expected back,' said Saunders. 'I wonder if they found what they were looking for. Anyway, I don't see any point in staying here. She's obviously gone.'

Further down the corridor, one of the doors stood ajar. Saunders pushed it and went in. On the floor was a woman's coat and a pair of slip-on shoes. Saunders picked up the coat and shook it. 'This belongs to a very small woman,' he said. 'And Li Min is barely five feet tall.'

Saunders went into the bathroom. When he emerged, using his handkerchief, he held up a syringe that had been lying in the washbasin.

Kenton said, 'I think we should leave this room as it is. We may need the police to look around, depending on what happens next.'

Saunders said, 'It looks to me as though this girl is being taken out of the country by force. We don't know how they intend to do it, but we should get down to the Chinese Embassy as quickly as possible and try to prevent it. They have a head start, but whoever has her, we know it isn't Deng.'

Back downstairs in Pierpont's office, they handed over the master key. 'By the way,' Kenton asked, 'whose room is number eighteen?'

Pierpont hesitated. Reluctantly she said, 'I believe it belongs to Mr Chew.'

Kenton shook his head. 'We'll want to talk with you again,' he said sternly, 'just not right now. The police will be with us then, and I must tell you it will be under caution. Please don't even think of leaving town before we return.'

Then they left without further comment. As they emerged from the front door and checked their phones, Saunders said, 'I'll ring Charles now to let him know what we've found and ask how they're getting on with Sally. Do you mind driving while I call him? We need to get to London pronto. I'll tell him to follow with Manon as soon as they're finished with Sally.'

53

Charles was waiting at the bus stop in Oxford when the shuttlebus from the Elm arrived. He watched as the students piled off but there was no sign of Sally. Strange, he thought, and climbed onto the bus to see where she had gone. He found her curled up on the back seat fast asleep.

'Sally,' he said, shaking her by the shoulder. 'Wake up! You've arrived in Oxford and I want to talk to you.' She recognised him but looked confused, wondering why the Director of the Institute was shaking her awake.

'What's happening?' she asked.

'It's all right,' said Charles. 'There's nothing to worry about but I have a message for you from your father, so please get up and come with me.'

Sally stood up shakily. Supported by Charles, she climbed down from the bus and walked with him the short distance to his office in the Institute.

Once they were there, he said, 'I would like to introduce you to my colleague Manon Tyler.'

Manon, who had been sitting waiting for them, now stood up.

'Manon, this is Sally Washington – Sally, this is Manon. I think it's best I leave you two to talk undisturbed. I'll be next door if you need me.' Charles went out of the room, gently closing the door behind him.

Sally Washington's appearance was absolutely dreadful. Her nose looked red as if she had a cold, her cheeks were pallid and both eyes deeply shadowed.

Manon asked gently, 'Are you OK? You don't look very well. Here, sit down.'

The girl's shoulders sagged as she flopped down into a chair. 'There was a party last night at the Elm.' She gave a small sad smile. 'I got a little carried away with the punchbowl.'

Manon felt relieved. The girl had been poisoned all right, but by alcohol and through her own volition. Chew had not got to her.

'There's coffee in the pot, would you like me to pour you some?'

When Sally nodded, Manon poured two steaming cups of coffee, and placed one in front of Sally on the table.

'Am I in trouble?' the girl asked. She sounded apprehensive.

'Not as far as I'm concerned,' said Manon. 'Sounds like you partied hard and I wouldn't advise a repeat, but you haven't broken any laws.'

She smiled at Sally, who nodded dully. Then her expression changed to puzzlement. 'Aren't you the librarian? Li Min's new friend?'

'That's right.'

'I thought your name was Judith. But Mr Abbot called you something else.'

'My name is Manon Tyler, but Li Min knows me as Judith Davidson.'

'Why use an alias?'

'Because I couldn't use my real name without people wondering what I was doing here.' Sally was still looking doubtful, so Manon added, 'Don't worry – I'm not a scammer. I work for the US government, like your father does.'

'Do you know Dad?' asked Sally eagerly.

'I don't, but he has been in touch with my boss at the Embassy in London. I work in Intelligence and came here to investigate some activities of the Chinese that have come to our attention. Illegal activities,' she added in case there was any question.

'Like what?' asked Sally, and Manon could see she was sceptical.

'The Chinese government is subsidising students to attend Western universities. In return they are expected to report back on any cutting-edge work going on in these institutions.'

'Well,' said Sally, cranky from her hangover, 'maybe so. But what's that got to do with me? Is it because my mother's Chinese?'

'No. It's because you are a friend of Li Min's and our understanding is that she used you to film a scene with a Chinese man in order to make a deepfake.'

Sally shook her head. 'No, that's not right. It was for her degree work – her thesis.'

'That's what she told you, but it isn't true.'

'Why should I believe you when you aren't even using your real name?'

Manon had expected resistance – better to prepare for the worst – and clearly Sally's hangover was reinforcing this. She said quietly, 'You are quite right to question my credentials. I can assure you that I am an officer of American Intelligence, but if you need proof of that, then I suggest you ring your father.' She took her phone and pushed it across the table.

'Dad knows about this?'

'He does and he's worried sick. He wants you to come home at once. Obviously that's up to you, but I would take his advice. Please go ahead and call him.' Manon made a show of looking at her phone. 'He should be in his office now.'

Sally thought about this for a moment. 'No, that's OK. But I still don't understand what this has to do with me? When Li Min filmed me, I wasn't doing anything awful – just sitting at my desk and then talking to Lee. He's one of the students living at the Elm.'

'The film shows you agreeing to spy for the Chinese.'

'What?'

'Relax. I know you didn't do that. It's a deepfake. You know what that is?'

'Of course,' said Sally, and Manon realised that though less than ten years apart in age, they were of distinctly separate generations.

Sally said, 'Wait a minute. Are you saying Li Min made a deepfake using film of me and Lee?'

'I'm afraid I am.'

'She never told me,' Sally said indignantly. 'How could she do that? We're friends – at least, we're supposed to be.'

'It gets worse. We think the Chinese were going to use the deepfake to try and blackmail your father. He was the ultimate target.'

'But how could filming me be used to blackmail my father?'

'It seems the film shows you accepting money from the Chinese student. And in it you say something sardonic, like, "Now I know what spies feel like." I suppose the idea was that you would be exposed as a spy unless your father cooperated with the Chinese.'

'How do you know all this?' Sally demanded, clearly still hoping none of it was true.

'From Li Min and from deduction – and some prior knowledge of how the Chinese operate.'

'Why would Li Min tell you anything about it? You are not Chinese.'

'Li Min decided she couldn't go through with it. That's the good news.'

'I wish she'd told me herself before she filmed me.'

'I know. But you have to understand the pressure she was under. Her fees and her living expenses – they are all paid for by her government. She didn't want to come to Oxford in the first place.'

'Really? Then why did she?'

'Because she was ordered to. If she'd refused, she'd be back in China now, probably working in a factory.'

'I didn't know any of that,' said Sally. 'But why is she disobeying them now and not before?'

'Because it involved someone else, someone she cares about. She decided she couldn't betray a friend. That's you,' Manon added, just in case there was any doubt.

Sally was silent for a minute, digesting this. She said, 'I guess I should thank her rather than be mad at her.'

Manon decided not to reply to this. There was no point making Sally feel guilty. She said instead, 'Tell me something. Did Li Min give you any idea of how she was making the film? Or say what it would be used for?'

Sally shook her head. 'No. She used to tell me about her work in the lab, but to be honest I would just tune out. It was all way over my head. I'm not very technical.'

'Me neither,' said Manon, and grinned. Then, serious again, she said, 'We have a problem. Li Min was supposed to meet with me and then leave Oxford for a while – to make sure she was safe – but for various reasons the meeting didn't take place.'

'So where is she now?'

'That's the problem: we don't know. The Chinese were expecting the deepfake by now and I'm just praying they don't know where she is either. If that's the case, it's crucial we find her before they do.'

'Would they hurt her?'

'I hope not,' Manon said, and shrugged. 'But it's impossible to predict. The only way we'll know for sure is if we get to her first. But she's not the only one they might be looking for.'

'What does that mean?'

Manon sighed. 'I'm not trying to alarm you, but the Chinese may decide to wipe out any trace of the work Li Min has been doing – they don't want a scandal in this country. But that means they have to make sure no one talks – and not just Li Min. There's young Lee for one…'

'And there's me,' said Sally dumbly, looking slightly shocked.

'Like I say, I don't want to scare you, but I'd be less than honest if I pretended there wasn't the possibility of the Chinese abducting you.'

'Really?'

'Believe me, it's not far-fetched. And your father agrees one hundred per cent. That's why I want you to go to a property we have the use of – a safe house as they're called. There you'll be looked after and, more importantly, protected. Will you agree to do that?'

For a moment Manon had a terrible feeling Sally might say no. She was a free spirit after all and clearly capable of showing a stubborn streak. Manon said, 'You can call your dad to discuss it if you want.'

Sally thought about this, then shook her head. 'No. I'm a big girl and can make my own decisions. When do we leave?'

54

On the way to London Kenton was driving carefully, observing all the speed limits. When they passed High Wycombe, Saunders' phone buzzed. He was on the call for several minutes, mainly listening rather than talking. When he put the phone down, he said, 'Good news this time. That was Manon. Sally has agreed to cooperate, and even as I speak she's on her way with your men to the safe house. Manon said it took some persuading, and the girl was pretty upset to find out what has been going on. It seems clear she had no idea Li Min was using her for anything but an anodyne film that would show off her friend's AI prowess. But now she understands Li Min didn't have any choice; she also understands why we want her out of Oxford for the time being.'

'It sounds like Manon did a great job.'

'Don't tell her that,' said Saunders jokingly, 'or she'll want to transfer to the State Department and become a diplomat. But I've told her to come down with Abbot ASAP. If Li Min does show up here, she might be wavering – the Chinese would have worked on her, I guarantee. Manon is the only one of us who knows her, so if there's a confrontation, I want her to plead our case with Li Min.'

Just then a dark blue Golf came up close behind them, flashed its lights and then overtook them.

'That's part of our surveillance team,' said Kenton. 'They were in a village near the Elm. I told them to keep their distance unless they heard from us. I didn't want them spotted by Pierpont or Deng. And I wanted Deng to think he'd lost them through all that nonsense at junction seven. But now I want them following him, though they'll pull back a bit once the other team shows up. There won't be any car Deng's seen before within eyesight. If he tries the same trick again, or if he veers off or takes an exit, they'll let us know.'

But there were no tricks or deviations from Deng and, as the surveillance team in the Golf reported, within ninety minutes he had negotiated the traffic outside Oxford and then that in West London, where he turned onto Marylebone Road and drove down Portland Place to the Chinese Embassy. Here the road split to either side of the trees planted in a central reservation. According to the Golf, which was just arriving, Deng parked in one of the slots jutting from the median. With scarcely a glance around, he got out and hustled into the Embassy, carrying a laptop bag.

By then Saunders' Audi had arrived at the junction with the North Circular Road and a quarter-hour later, when they reached Portland Place, they passed Deng's car without a glance. Further down the street, two plain-clothes policemen were standing in a couple of empty parking spaces, there to keep away anyone trying to park. They waved Kenton into one of them and he pulled over then turned the engine off. Sighing, he said, 'Not sure what our next move is.'

Saunders said, 'I'm assuming that if Li Min is still alive, and they want to keep her that way, then sooner or later the

Chinese will try and get her into the Embassy. We can't touch her there.'

They sat waiting impatiently for over half an hour, and then a dark green BMW pulled in beside them. Abbot was at the wheel and nodded to them as Manon got out of the passenger seat. She came round and Saunders put down his window.

'Sally's reached the safe house now,' Manon said. She looked across Saunders at Kenton in the passenger seat. 'Your driver must have gone like the wind.'

'Is she OK?' asked Saunders.

'Nothing that a couple of aspirin and some black coffee won't cure.' And Manon explained the reason Sally had looked so ill.

'It must have been some party,' said Saunders.

Kenton laughed and then said: 'If she's at the safe house, then we don't need to worry about her at the moment, though she must be anxious about Li Min.'

'I bet she is,' said Manon, who shared that anxiety but was glad that at least one of the girls was now safe. 'What do you think they'll do with Li Min?'

Saunders thought for a moment. 'Take her back to China, I guess. They'll try to smuggle her out of here and put her on a private jet for Beijing. She won't go willingly, but they can deal with that. It could be that Deng knows where she is, but couldn't do anything about it once we showed up. We do know she's not with him.'

'So someone else is holding her?' said Manon. 'Maybe they've taken her straight to the airport.'

'Maybe. If so, we can't do anything about it. But it's more likely they would bring her here first. Even the Chinese won't have a private jet permanently on call.'

Kenton said, 'So all we can do for the moment is wait.'

'How are you feeling now, Manon?' Saunders asked.

'Much better,' she said firmly, though she was still a little woozy. 'But I could use some air. If you don't mind, I'd like to stretch my legs a bit.'

Kenton said, 'Why don't you have a look at the Embassy's back door in Weymouth Street, to see if there's anything going on there? You'll spot our guys in a blue Golf and a grey Vauxhall, keeping an eye on the situation.' He turned and looked at Saunders. 'Though there is a limit to what they or any of us can do, bearing in mind that we don't want a big diplomatic incident.'

'Understood,' said Saunders. 'Off you go, Manon, but don't go too far, and message us if anything is happening.'

She crossed the road to the west side of Portland Place, turned into Weymouth Street and walked slowly along the south-side pavement. It was a busy one-way street of brick and stucco houses with parking on both sides. On the other side of the road, the Embassy building ran for forty yards or so. There were two side doors into the building; the smaller had peeling black paint, badly faded, and looked as though it was hardly ever used. Perfect for sneaking someone in, Manon thought.

Further along, she was glad to see a grey Vauxhall saloon and a blue Golf tucked into an adjacent mews. So the rear of the Embassy was being covered. But with Deng now inside, who could be holding Li Min? And would they really try to bring her here?

Manon had walked a few hundred yards and almost reached Harley Street, famed for its many medical practitioners and specialists, before she turned back towards

Portland Place. The street was lined with parked vehicles, few empty spaces visible to either side. She watched as an ancient Land Rover turned the corner and passed her going towards Portland Place, then slowed down, the driver clearly looking for a space.

Funny seeing a Land Rover of that vintage in the city. It was not the standard urban SUV of the very rich, the unnecessary accoutrement for people with more money than sense. This was the real thing, a testament to the longevity of Land Rovers as working vehicles.

It struck a chord in Manon and then she knew why. Gillroy at the Elm drove a Land Rover just like this one, though the driver of this vehicle – she could tell even when viewing them from the back – was taller than the maintenance man and had black hair. Gillroy didn't have much hair at all.

The driver had found a place and pulled in. He sat there staring at his phone as Manon drew level with him on the other side of the street.

And then she felt her blood run cold.

It was Chew. Manon looked away quickly, hoping his focus would stay on his phone.

What was he doing here in Gillroy's Land Rover, last seen with the maintenance man driving it some seventy miles away on a hill west of Oxford?

She quickly took out her own phone and, without stopping, texted Saunders. *Come quick Weymouth Street Chew here!* She sent the text and, thank God, it was delivered right away. She cast a quick glance back and saw Chew getting out of the Land Rover. There was no mistaking him; he was enormously tall.

He walked to the vehicle's rear and, for the first time, glanced along the street. Manon quickly turned round to face Portland Place and kept walking. When she sneaked another look back, she saw that he was opening the rear door of the Land Rover. He seemed entirely relaxed as he reached inside and slowly pulled out a big suitcase.

She glanced quickly back and saw the parked Vauxhall with two men in the front seats. If she went back to alert them, Chew might see her up close or, worse still, might go through the little side door into the Embassy, out of their reach.

Having taken the suitcase out, Chew closed the Land Rover's rear door. Then he stepped onto the pavement, carrying the case in his right hand. It must have something heavy inside, for strong as Chew was, he seemed to be walking slowly, deliberately.

There was no sign of Saunders and Kenton, and the Vauxhall's occupants were not paying any particular attention. Manon had to do something fast; in a minute or so he would have reached safety.

Without further thought, she crossed the street, approaching Chew on the pavement. When she was only a few feet away, she stopped in front of him and did a theatrical double take. 'Hey,' she called out to him. 'I really like your suitcase. Where did you get one that's so big?'

She could see he wanted to ignore her, but now she was directly in his path. 'Seriously,' she said, 'I've been looking for a bag like that forever. Where did you find it?'

'A store,' he said at last. 'In China,' he added, now staring at her. Did he recognise her? They had never met face to face, but he had seen her in the dark wine cellar and might have seen her mugshot on the college network.

They were only thirty yards or so from the Embassy door. When would Saunders come? And why didn't the occupants of the Vauxhall see her talking to Chew?

'Excuse me,' he said gruffly, and still holding the suitcase in one hand, made to move past Manon.

'Are you Chinese then? I mean, did you buy the case in China?'

'Yes, like I said,' he replied, and with Manon still blocking his path, added, 'Excuse me. I want to get by.'

Manon didn't move, and Chew decided he'd had enough. He put the case down and stood with his arms hanging loosely at his sides. There was something threatening in the calmness of his stance, the confidence he had in his dauntingly powerful physique.

'You are in my way,' he said. 'I need to go. Please move.'

'Have we met before?' she asked, and this time Chew reacted. He took a step towards her.

'Why do you say that?' he demanded. 'Who are you?'

She had to keep him here, even if it meant revealing more than she wanted to. 'Don't you remember? In Oxford... we met in Oxford. At the Institute.'

Chew's eyes widened as he stared at her again. 'Perhaps,' he said, and she sensed he recognised her now.

'Your name,' she said, hoping to God the cavalry was on its way. 'It's Chew, yes? They call you Mr Chew.'

'I know you,' he said, his voice suddenly a threatening, frightening growl. 'Get out of my way, Miss Librarian. Get out of my way,' he repeated.

He had picked up the suitcase now and for a moment she was scared he was going to sling it at her – he looked strong enough.

'I can't let you by, Mr Chew, not until you tell me why you are here.'

That did it. He took two steps and this time extended his free arm and pushed her hard, his palm against her sternum. Manon stumbled and fell; she landed on her back with a great thump, her elbows hitting the pavement and just preventing her head from doing the same. Chew started to walk towards the little back door, and just then the grey Vauxhall moved, roaring past and pulling up with a screech of brakes ten feet ahead of him in the middle of Weymouth Street.

Two men got out – neither of them much more than half the size of Chew. But they looked fit and unintimidated. They were in plain clothes of jeans, trainers and gilets. The younger-looking of the two stepped forward to confront Chew.

'Stand where you are,' he commanded. His partner had got out on the driver's side and was also approaching, but from the middle of the street. Neither man seemed to be armed – there was no sign of any weapons – and Manon wondered how they would keep Chew from reaching the back door of the Embassy. She struggled to get up but only managed a kneeling position since her arms kept giving way when she tried to lever herself to her feet. The pain from her elbows was agonising.

Chew put the suitcase down on the pavement in front of him. Casually, as if he had expected to do this, he reached behind him and brought out a hardwood truncheon he must have had tucked into the back of his shirt and trousers. He wielded it in one hand, spreading his legs a few inches and clenching the fist of his other hand. 'Let me through or you will both be hurt,' he announced to the two men.

'Leave the case and you can go,' shouted a new voice, and Manon saw Saunders hurrying to join them, along with Kenton.

'The case stays with me,' said Chew. 'It's mine. Now let me through!' And with a remarkable show of agility, he picked up the suitcase and ran for the little wooden door, gripping the truncheon in his other hand. To Manon's dismay, the short-haired younger officer seemed to be moving out of the way. Saunders and Kenton were too far away to help, and the other officer was still stranded in the middle of the street.

'Don't let him get away!' Manon shouted.

There was a small popping noise and the truncheon fell from Chew's hand. His entire frame seemed to twitch, then twitch again convulsively; and this time it was Chew who fell, onto his knees and then his back, where he writhed on the pavement as if stung by swarming bees.

The younger officer came into Manon's eyeline now as she ignored the pain in her elbows and somehow clambered to her feet. His attention was not on her, however, but focused on Chew. 'Stay on the ground or I'll tase you again!' he shouted, but Chew looked in no condition to stand up, the agony he felt only slowly subsiding.

Saunders was with Manon now, steadying her and asking urgently if she was OK. 'Yes... the suitcase,' she managed to say.

The other officer had already retrieved it, and as Saunders went and held it steady, he unzipped it. It stuck twice as he moved the zip, but then it flapped open and something large rolled out, slowly unfolding, almost like a gigantic flower.

Manon saw limbs straightening out: two arms, and then two legs, and finally the face of Li Min.

Like Manon in the cellar, her mouth had been taped but Li Min ripped it off now, and there was no other restraint – the suitcase had been prison enough it seemed. She rubbed her eyes and shook her head hard, and then with Kenton's help, got to her bare feet. Manon went over to her while Saunders zipped the suitcase shut. 'They took away my shoes,' Li Min whispered. 'I want them back. They're Louboutins,' she said indignantly. Manon smiled.

Chew still lay on the pavement, though after a few moments he managed to sit up. The officers had taken away his truncheon. When he staggered to his feet and headed for the wooden door, they looked at Kenton, who nodded. They let him go.

Traffic had backed up on Weymouth Street, and an irate driver gave a blast of his horn. Kenton helped Li Min into the back of the grey Vauxhall.

He turned to Manon and said, 'In the car with her. Quickly, please, so we can get the traffic moving again.' To the driver he said, 'Take them to the American Embassy and we'll meet you there.'

As the Vauxhall drove away and the traffic started to move again, the Golf came out of the mews down the road, joined the stream of traffic and stopped beside Kenton and Saunders, two wheels up on the pavement; the empty suitcase was put into the back and driven off.

Kenton and Saunders crossed Weymouth Street, walked back to Portland Place and spoke to Abbot in his car. He had seen nothing of the goings-on in Weymouth Street, was relieved to hear that Li Ming and Manon were safe, and on hearing that Saunders was now heading for the American Embassy, decided to go back to Oxford.

'You've been great,' said Saunders, 'and I'd like to buy you a drink when things have calmed down.'

'Fine,' said Abbott with a smile. 'I'll hold you to that.'

Kenton had crossed the road and climbed into the parked Audi, where he rang his press relations people and told them to quash any story related to goings-on at the Chinese Embassy. He would give them the line to take when he got back. Finally, he arranged for the Land Rover to be driven away.

Saunders got in and started the car. They drove off, heading for the American Embassy. Meantime Weymouth Street returned to its bustling self.

55

In the Vauxhall as they were being driven to the US Embassy, Manon was still anxious.

'Li Min,' she said, 'what's happened to your laptop with the deepfake on it? I'm worried that if Deng's got it, they could still do a lot of harm, especially to Sally.'

'Oh, I expect he has got it – I left it in my room,' said Li Min cheerfully. 'But it won't do him much good, because it hasn't got the deepfake on it.'

'Thank God,' said Manon, feeling a rush of relief. 'Where is it, then?'

'I've got it stored on the server at the lab.' And Li Min explained that even if the Chinese tech experts managed to get into the lab's network, itself improbable, they would not be able to open the file. 'It's got special encryption they'll never crack,' she said, grinning. 'And you'll like the password, Judith.'

'Why's that?'

'It's just a jumble of numbers and symbols, but it ends "ping-Deng-pong".'

Manon smiled, and then she said, 'Li Min, before we go any further, I think I should tell you that my real name is Manon. Judith was the name I adopted so that the Chinese wouldn't get to know who I actually am. I think you already know what my real work is.'

Li Min said with a smile, 'I was starting to have a pretty good idea. But what I don't know, Manon –' she hesitated over the name '– is whether it is British Intelligence or American that you work for?'

'It's the CIA, and Mr Saunders whom you just saw is my boss.'

When they reached the US Embassy they were waved in by the security guard. Up in Saunders' office they were told appointments had been made for them at the medical centre to ensure that neither of them had suffered any long-term effects from the drugs they'd been given or from their respective confinements – Manon in the wine cellar and Li Min in the suitcase. As it turned out, Manon had not suffered any broken bones but her elbows where they'd hit the pavement would be painful for several weeks.

Otherwise, after all the drama, nothing very exciting happened. Manon was beginning to understand that however dramatic the climax and conclusion of a case, what follows inevitably seems anticlimactic. Saunders suggested that she should go with Li Min to the safe house in Wandsworth where they would find Sally, who had already been there for several hours. He said he would like Li Min to visit his office after her medical appointment the next day, to talk about her future.

In the event, the UK government signified its disapproval of Chinese activities by giving Deng and Mr Chew until the weekend to leave the country. More senior Embassy officials, specifically Yìchén, the Cultural Attaché, and his boss Mr Lau, were cautioned in a frigid meeting in Whitehall but otherwise left to go about their business, nefarious as it had proved to be. The Chinese were told that Li Min had been granted asylum in the United Kingdom while her future was considered. In the meantime, she had destroyed the deepfake she had created, as well as the film footage and audio of Sally and Lee she had used as building blocks for it. A large pending gift to the Institute was quietly withdrawn by the Chinese government before it could be rejected by the Fellows of St Felix's, but coincidentally the same sum was offered to another college a few weeks later from a new Scandinavian foundation, not Norwegian this time but Swedish.

A couple of days later Manon returned to Oxford to tidy up her papers and say goodbye to Charles. Saunders had given her leave but wanted her back soon; he had other urgent cases he wanted her to work on. As she approached the college, she noticed that the flag on the chapel was flying at half-mast, and wondered why.

'Who's died?' she asked Charles as she went into his office.

'It's rather sad,' he said. 'Arthur Cole. Apparently, he committed suicide on the evening of the day we spoke with him and found you in the wine cellar. Hanged himself from a beam in his room, I understand. He had a romantic vision of the glories of ancient Chinese civilisation and was broken-hearted about the crude way its modern diplomats behave. As I told you, they'd asked him to get rid of you – a job that was then delegated to Nina Pierpont. He has left his collection of Chinese ceramics to the Institute, but I'm afraid we'll have to put most of it in storage or else give it away – we simply don't have the space to display it all.'

He sighed and went on. 'By the way, I've got rid of Pierpont, though no thanks to the police, who just let her off with a caution, even though she was working for the Chinese. As was that maintenance man at the Elm, Gillroy, though that would have been harder to prove. I believe he's got a new job as caretaker at a sixth-form college. I doubt the Chinese have much interest in any service he can perform for them there, so Gillroy's moonlighting is at an end,' he said, smiling. 'In any case, our government in its infinite wisdom made it clear they don't want either of them prosecuted, since that would make the whole affair public.'

After this initial meeting Charles was busy. He went to London where, unbeknown to Manon, he was thoroughly debriefed by Kenton and Saunders, and on the next day he was occupied with a succession of St Felix's dons who were concerned by the rumours they'd heard of a Chinese attempt to kidnap one of their students.

It was only on her final day that Manon found him alone in his office. 'I wanted to see you before I left,' she said, noticing that he was looking out of the window rather than at her.

'That's good of you,' Charles said quietly. 'I suppose you'll soon be busy back in London.'

'I expect so,' she acknowledged. 'It's an irritating feature of the job: they like to keep us occupied.'

'Well, if it ever brings you back into this neighbourhood, I hope you'll let us know.' She was glad to hear him say this and hoped he would say more, but he didn't.

Finally, she said, feeling slightly desperate, 'London's only an hour away, you know.'

He smiled but still didn't say anything. Maybe she had misjudged the situation all this time; maybe he just wasn't interested. She said, 'Well, I guess it's goodbye then. Thank you for all your help.'

For a horrible moment she thought he wasn't going to reply. Then he said, out of the blue, 'Do you usually work Saturdays?'

'Not if I can help it. And if I do it's at home.'

'I'm going to be in London next Saturday, seeing a potential benefactor in the morning. He said he can only spare me an hour. So I was thinking...' Charles paused, seeming uncertain again.

'I'm free all day,' said Manon firmly, as if putting down a marker. She smiled at him encouragingly. 'Your move, I believe.'

A NOTE ON THE AUTHOR

Dame Stella Rimington joined the Security Service (MI5) in 1968. During her career she worked in all the main fields of the Service: counter-subversion, counter-espionage and counter-terrorism. She was appointed Director General in 1992, the first woman to hold the post. Now the author of the bestselling Liz Carlyle series of espionage thrillers as well as two books in the Manon Tyler series, she lives in London and Norfolk.

A NOTE ON THE TYPE

The text of this book is set in Adobe Caslon, named after the English punch-cutter and type-founder William Caslon I (1692–1766). Caslon's rather old-fashioned types were modelled on seventeenth-century Dutch designs, but found wide acceptance throughout the English-speaking world for much of the eighteenth century until replaced by newer types towards the end of the century. Used in 1776 to print the Declaration of Independence, they were revived in the nineteenth century and have been popular ever since, particularly amongst fine printers. There are several digital versions, of which Carol Twombly's Adobe Caslon is one.